Unprotected WITNESS

by
Guy Slaughter

A Write Way Publishing Book

I
THE FINDING

It was chilly in the car.

He longed for a cup of coffee, strong and black and hot, knowing it could abort his mission by sending him in search of a john. He wished for something to read, knowing he mustn't betray his presence by turning on the dome light to look at a paper, a book or a magazine. He yearned for a cigarette, knowing even one could resurrect the craving for nicotine he'd been two years burying.

He started the car engine. The illuminated digits on the dashboard clock showed 9:30. He flipped on the heater and reveled in the comforting blast of warm air. Then he cut off the motor again lest it attract the attention of a passerby. A man seen sitting alone in a darkened car across the street from a residential apartment building could arouse suspicion, trigger a telephone call, bring a cop to ask questions, spook the quarry. True, there were fewer possible noticers now that sidewalk and street traffic had dwindled, but an occasional car still wheeled past and an occasional pedestrian still clumped by.

The futility of yet another vigil likely to prove as fruitless as all those before it deepened his depression. Should his time perhaps be spent pursuing other means of tracking down his prey? Was it stupid to be sitting alone in a cold car watching apartment-building doors in a strange city a twelve-hour drive from home? How long could he keep Fifi Malloy waiting for something tangible to show her bosses before she lost her patience and wrote his project off as a bad investment?

The flash of approaching headlights interrupted his reverie.

The car slowed, the brake light on its rear fender showing red. The vehicle swung curb-ward on the far side of the street to park beyond the apartment building. The headlights went out. The dome light flared as the driver-side door opened. A man emerged into the pool of yellow light dripping from the overhead street lamp. His build looked right—tall, slope-shouldered, long-necked.

Sam Jeffreys felt the rush of adrenaline that always accompanied an apparent breakthrough in a story chase. The man's clothing was right. His nattily creased black fedora and navy-blue topcoat were Cornelius Nicora's habitual cold-season costume for as long as Jeffreys had known him.

The shadowy figure slammed and locked the car door, only his back showing. He started toward the apartment entrance, and Jeffreys saw with elation that his walk was right. The long, shoulder-dipping, body-swaying strides he'd recognize anywhere told him the search was over, the quarry about to be treed.

"Now," Jeffreys coached himself, watching the man glide through the apartment entrance and disappear inside its foyer. "Give him time to get in, then follow, confront, reassure, and sell."

He climbed out of the car, scarcely able to contain his jubilation. Stretching to ease his cramped muscles, he headed across the street. Inside the apartment building's foyer, he barely glanced at the row of mailboxes he'd studied so carefully two hours before. He thumbed the push button labeled 408—*Charles Nelson*—the name that led him here. He waited for what he now was confident would be a familiar voice from the speaker behind the brass grillwork in the wall.

"Hello," the voice said. The rush of adrenaline became a flood. It was Cornie's.

"Hi, Cornie," he said into the grill. "It's Sam Jeffreys."

There was a pause. Then, "Sam who?" Cornie's voice said. It sounded strained. "I ... you must have the wrong party."

"C'mon, Cornie," Jeffreys said. "We both know better. Let me in. I've got a proposition for you."

"Who's with you?"

"Nobody. I'm alone."

"Okay," the voice said. It sounded resigned, Jeffreys thought. "Come up, but you better be alone."

The inner door buzzed. Jeffreys grasped the knob and pulled it open. Inside, he saw a security-guard station. Its desk and telephone were unattended. Beyond it was an elevator cage, its door standing open. He stepped into it, punched the 4 button, whooshed upward, stepped out when it stopped. He saw 406 in brass numbers on a door across the hall, 408 near the far end. He walked to it, knocked.

"It's unlocked," Cornie's voice came through it.

Jeffreys shoved it open. It was Cornie, facing him from six feet inside the room. He was wearing the habitual dark suit, white shirt, blue necktie. The wavy black hair was immaculately cut and combed straight back. He held a revolver at belt level. It was pointed at Jeffreys' belly. The hammer was cocked.

"Whoa," Jeffreys said, raising his hands. "Aim that thing the other way."

Nicora looked beyond him into the hallway, the revolver unwavering. "You alone?"

"I told you I was."

"Shut the door and lock it."

Jeffreys did, lowering his hands and turning his back on the gun. When the bolt slid into its socket, he swiveled to face Nicora. The gun was still trained on his navel. The hammer was still back. He raised his hands again.

"How'd you find me?" Nicora demanded.

"It wasn't easy."

"They said it wasn't possible."

"They were almost right. I've been forever tracking you down."

"Why?"

"Because I need you."

"For what?"

"To help me write the story of your life."

"Forget it," Nicora said. He waved the gun as though in dismissal. "Anything else?"

"No," Jeffreys said. "Just that. But I can't forget it. I'm committed."

"What's that mean?"

"It means I *have* to write your story."

"Why?"

"Because I've got a contract."

"Me too," Nicora said. "With a hit man. For all I know, you're him."

"That's silly," Jeffreys said. "I need you alive to help me write the book."

Nicora's eyes narrowed, though the gun didn't waver. "Book? Not a newspaper story?"

"I don't work for the paper anymore," Jeffreys said. "I took early retirement after you went into the witness protection program. I've been looking for you ever since."

"How'd you find me?" he demanded again.

"Put the gun down and I'll tell you."

Nicora lowered the gun muzzle, released the hammer. "Well?"

Jeffreys dropped his arms and held out his hand. "First things first. It's been a long time, Cornie."

Nicora shifted the revolver to his left hand. His handshake was without warmth. He waved Jeffreys to the couch. "How'd you find me?"

"Through Angie," Jeffreys said, looking around. There were draperies on the windows opposite the door. Archways perforated the right and left walls in the middle of the room. One would lead to a bedroom and a bath, he decided. There'd probably be a kitchen through the other. He took off his hat and trench coat, tossed them onto the couch and sat down. "Is there a cup of coffee in the house?"

"Angie told you where I am?" Nicora said. He scowled his disbelief. He still held the gun, now uncocked and pointing at the floor.

"Not knowingly."

"What's that mean?"

"I checked out the addresses she sent mail to. I figured you and Marge would contact her when you got settled into wherever the feds relocated you. I figured if you told anybody where you were, it'd be your daughter. And then I figured she'd write you."

"You found me by chasing Angie's mail?"

"Right. Lots of mail. I visited a whole slew of other addresses before I got here. They all turned out to be wrong numbers, of course, like friends, other relatives, in-laws, her husband's friends, his folks. One lead took me clear to New Orleans before it petered out. What about that coffee?"

"How'd you get hold of Angie's mail?"

"I didn't. I just copied the names and addresses off the envelopes she sent out. I ... had this friend in the post office."

"A snitch," Nicora nodded. "With a price tag. I know how it works." He perched on the couch arm alongside Jeffreys and laid the gun in his lap. "No coffee," he said. "There's such a shitty little kitchen here I only eat out."

"No problem," Jeffreys said, listening for the sounds of

somebody else in the apartment, breathing, moving, rustling. There were none. "Marge isn't here?"

"Nuh uh," Nicora said. "She came into the program with me when they moved us to New Orleans. But she was scared shitless that everybody on the street was gunning for us, so she decided she wanted out. We told the feds. They stashed her someplace else when they switched me here and gave me a new name. I don't know where she is or even who she is. We figure she's safer this way."

"Probably right," Jeffreys said, marveling at the ends to which the government went to protect flipped crooks and the families of flipped crooks so their testimony could be used to help prosecute unflipped crooks. He salivated over the juicy reading such revelations would make.

"Only now you found me," Nicora was saying. "That means others can, too. And Marge. I wish I never let them bastards talk me into joining this goddam program."

"You'd rather be sitting in a federal slammer marking off the years on a perpetual calendar?"

Nicora shrugged. "The seven months I did seemed like forever, but at least I wasn't looking over my shoulder all the time."

"Now you are?"

"Bet your ass, I am."

"Bad dreams?"

"Damn right."

"I'm no psychiatrist, but I think you'll feel better after you talk it out."

"Talk what out?"

"Everything," Jeffreys said. "Your fears, your dreads, your memories, your nightmares. Your story. The whole enchilada."

"So you can write your goddam book?" Cornie said. He sounded unimpressed.

"Our goddam book," Jeffreys said. "It's your life, and we'd be writing it."

"What part of my life we talking about?"

"All of it. Your growing up a wop kid in a Polack neighborhood. Your war-hero exploits. Your political climb. Your career in politics. Your indictment. Your trial and conviction and time in prison. Your new life as a protected witness."

"How? How would we write it?"

"You'd tell me about it, I'd put it into manuscript form."

"Just the two of us?"

"Right. Plus my editor."

"Who's he?"

"She. The lady editor who works for my publisher."

"Nuh uh. Forget it. I'm not trusting any she-male to keep my ass covered."

"Whoa," Jeffreys said. "She'll be in her office in New York working the copy I—we—send her. She won't even know where you are."

Nicora shook his head. "Why would I want to get involved in a deal like that?"

"For money," Jeffreys said. "For history. It's a fascinating story, a reflection of our times."

"I hated history," Nicora said, but Jeffreys had seen his eyes flicker at the mention of money. "What's in it for me?"

"Half of whatever it brings," Jeffreys said. "The book carries the Cornie Nicora by-line, with as-told-to-me attribution. I've already sold the outline. We split whatever else it earns."

"You sold the outline?"

"Right. That's why I've got to deliver the book."

"What'd you get for it? What kind of money we talking about?"

Jeffreys shrugged. "The advance was all mine. What we'll split, I don't honestly know. Maybe big bucks, if I get it right. Hopefully hardcover, then paperback, then a movie sale if I write it well enough. Add magazine excerpts, serialization, even. You've got a hell of a story."

"You'd expect me to tell you everything I know? Name names?"

"Damn right. Everything. Names and dates and dollars. Who first bought you, when and where and for how much. Who kicked back how much when you were the mayor peddling city contracts and city jobs. Who paid and who shared and who you paid when you were county commissioner. What you got from whom for what when you were sheriff, including who in the mob paid you how much for protecting taverns with syndicate-owned electronic slots and for busting non-mob joints. All of it, I want, Genesis to Revelations."

"I already told most of it to the feds."

"So now you'll be telling it to me. And to the rest of the world. All in deep detail. Like how much kickback money there was in the incinerator project that cost East Chicago taxpayers twenty-two million."

"Seven mill," Nicora said, "carved up in a lot of pieces." He looked at Jeffreys quizzically. "They told me you got a hunk of it."

"They told you wrong," Jeffreys grinned. "One of your people propositioned me, and I played along for a while. Fellow named Harry Woods. A real crude character, addicted to loud suits and no neckties. He was lobbying the legislature, pushing an enabling bill to let cities build and run municipal incinerators with property-tax dollars and federal-state subsidies. Got it passed, too."

"He had help. Including some wheels in the governor's office. That the kind of crap you're interested in?"

"And more," Jeffreys said.

"You'd want to see my yearbooks?"

Jeffreys shrugged. Cornie's high school pictures might make good dust-cover art. Even classmates' blurbs evaluating him as most-likely to steal or least-likely to survive could be of some interest.

"Sure," he said. "More than that, though, what I really want is you describing how it was to walk in the shoes of the kid-next-door war hero who's making sausage in his parents' grocery store one day, the most influential politician in his end of the state the next, and then jailed for corruption."

"You want to make me out a real sleazy son of a bitch."

Jeffreys shrugged. "That's where the money is. Reporting sleaze. We'll want every reader to feel superior to this rich and successful politician who's really a thief and a crook. We want ordinary, moderately sinful citizens who cheat on their income taxes and covet their neighbors' wives to buy the book so they can consider themselves virtuous compared to this rotten public official with both hands in the till. But we also want them to weep a little at hearing the judge impose a twenty-year sentence, to recoil at the thought of being hauled off to prison in manacles and leg irons. And we want them to know how it feels to snitch on former cronies, Mafiosi, killers, to be on the mob's hit list, to pretend you're somebody else, to wonder who's there whenever your doorbell rings."

"You sure you want all that shit? I give you names and dates and dollars, it could make you a target, too."

"Not if nobody knows I know it until it's published," Jeffreys said, reciting the investigative reporter's catechism. "Once it's in print, everybody knows what I know, and there's no point in taking me down."

"What about this goddam witness protection program? You want to know how that works, too?"

"Damn right," Jeffreys said. "I want to know how it feels to leave your family and friends and start a new life in a new place under a new name. To close out your bank accounts and empty your safety deposit boxes and carry all your worldly possessions around in a shoe box or as diamonds stuck in a body cavity. How it is to be always looking over your shoulder for a guy with a gun or a knife or an ice pick."

"It's hell," Nicora said. "You sure you want to know about it?"

"I'm sure," Jeffreys said. "It's how we'll humanize you. You aren't very sympathetic as a corrupt public official selling taxpayers out to crooks and scoundrels. After we establish that, we'll paint you as a husband and a father forced to leave family and friends to avoid two hundred years in prison or instant execution by the crooks and scoundrels your testimony topples."

"What you want is for me to tell the world I'm a rotten son of a bitch turned cry-baby and looking pathetic."

"That, too," Jeffreys acknowledged. "And if we do it right, maybe you'll be played in the movies by Warren Beatty or Jack Nicholson or Robert Redford."

Nicora's eyes flickered again. He said, "I get half the take?"

"Down the middle."

"When would we start?"

"Now," Jeffreys said. "I'll move in here so you can begin talking to my tape recorder right away and for as long as it takes. Have we got a deal?"

Cornelius Nicora, Jeffreys remembered from the years he watched him in action as a reporter covering a crooked politician not yet unmasked, always made up his mind in a hurry.

"Deal. Except I've got a job eight to five Mondays through Fridays. It's the front that covers my ass. We work around that, right?"

"Right," Jeffreys said, trying to hide his elation. "Handshake, or formal contract?"

"Handshake. Contract's a dirty word."

"*Touché*," Jeffreys grinned. "So we've got a verbal agreement. The terms are clear: You talk, I write, we go halvies." He extended his hand.

Nicora shook it coldly. "You get the couch. There's only the one bed."

"No problem. I've been sleeping in the car a lot lately."

"You pay half the rent."

"No problem," Jeffreys said again, reminding himself of the old saw about a leopard's inability to change its spots. Cornie, despite the millions he stole over the years, was still a tightwad. "Be happy to pay my share."

"Okay," Nicora said. "We're in business."

Feeling almost giddy, Jeffreys picked his hat off the couch, stuck it on his head, stood up, shrugged into his coat. "I'll get my stuff out of the car. You want to punch the door buzzer again when I ring from downstairs?"

"No need," Nicora said. He disappeared through the left-hand archway and reappeared in a minute carrying two keys. He handed them to Jeffreys. "Spares. The brass one's for the security door in the lobby. The silver one fits this door."

Jeffreys snapped them onto his key chain and left, closing the door carefully behind him, hearing its latch snick into place.

He rode the elevator downstairs in a cloud of euphoria, trotted past the deserted security guard station, hastened outside and across the street, retrieved his bag from the car trunk, recrossed the street, let himself back in through the locked foyer door, stepped into the elevator, and punched the 4 button.

He heard the shots just as the cage doors were sighing shut. There were three of them from somewhere above, measured, muted, distant, distinct.

The elevator whooshed upward. The doors sighed open. Jeffreys dove through them. He pounded down the short hall, suitcase in hand, to Cornie's apartment at its end. The door stood open. He strode inside, stepped on something, stopped. It was a gun.

Cornelius Nicora lay on the rug in front of the sofa, facing away from the doorway. He was on his left side, bent at the waist, knees drawn up. Blood welled from the back of his head.

Jeffreys picked up the gun. He recognized it as the one Cornie'd held pointed at his navel. It was warm and smelled of cordite. He heard footsteps behind him. He turned to see a frowzy-haired woman in a housecoat staring in at him from the hall. There were rollers in her hair. Beyond her, a grey-haired man in a bathrobe peered from a partially opened door across the hallway.

Jeffreys walked to the body, fighting acceptance of the unacceptable. He'd been planning the book for more than two years. He'd written its outline in his head a hundred times, put a dozen versions on paper before sending one off, rewritten that version repeatedly before Fifi Malloy said go. So how could it now be lying unseen there on the floor with Cornie, as dead as the corpse itself? And why did he feel such grievous loss at its quiet death, yet no sorrow at all over the bloody killing of the human being whose life story it would have chronicled?

A voice mumbled something unintelligible from across the hall where the grey-haired man in the bathrobe had been. The door to 407 still stood partially open, but the old guy had disappeared.

Jeffreys heard a heavy footstep, breathing. He turned to face a monstrous man in a too-tight security guard uniform. His features were hidden behind a walrus mustache and a heavy beard. He smelled of eucalyptus and menthol, Jeffreys noted absently, like those super-strong cough lozenges. The flap of his empty holster was sticking up at an angle from the unfastened Sam Browne belt that looked too short to close around his belly. There was a .357 revolver in his hand, its hammer back. It was pointed at Jeffreys' face.

"Drop the gun," the man said.

Jeffreys looked down at the little .32 he still was holding.

"I called the cops," the old guy in the bathrobe shouted

from across the hall. "They're comin'."

Jeffreys let the gun fall to the floor. Looking into the muzzle of the weapon menacing him, he set down the suitcase he was still carrying, and slowly raised his hands.

"Ah, boy," he said. "I bet you people think I shot him."

II
THE JAILING

The Bloomburgh police were professional, efficient, and fair, Jeffreys told himself, sitting on a hard jail cot and nursing a cup of coffee in the one-man holding cell.

Two uniformed cops had been the first to show. They were knocking on the foyer door when Jeffreys and the guard stepped off the elevator. The guard waved Jeffreys into the chair behind the security desk. He strode to the door, flung it open, and dropped the kick-leg to hold it that way.

Jeffreys decided the two quick-arrival newcomers were probably cruising the neighborhood when their dispatcher got on the radio and ordered them to the shooting scene.

One took custody of Jeffreys. He cuffed him with his hands behind him and read him his rights from a card plucked from a tunic pocket.

The other talked to the security guard in low tones for a moment, then walked to the elevator and disappeared inside it. The security guard went outside, taking his cough-drop smell with him, presumably to usher in later arrivals.

The custodial cop didn't question Jeffreys. He just stood silently in front of him alongside the security guard's desk, apparently awaiting reinforcements.

The next arrivals wore the white uniforms of paramedics.

"Dispatcher says the patient's dead," one of them said to the cop at Jeffrey's side. The rising intonation of his statement made it a question.

"Beats me," the cop said. "I ain't been up there."

"The dispatcher's right," Jeffreys said. "The patient's got three slugs in his head."

The paramedic nodded, followed his partner to the elevator.

A fat, florid-faced man in a light-colored overcoat and a baseball cap came in. He carried a camera and a clipboard. A deputy coroner, Jeffreys guessed.

"Where's it at?" the newcomer asked the cop.

"Fourth floor. Ambulance guys and my pardner are already up there."

The newcomer nodded his acknowledgment and strode to the elevator.

Another siren moaned down outside from soprano through mezzo into alto, went mute, and two more men came through the foyer. One wore a trench coat and a snap-brim fedora. The other, bare-headed, was in a thigh-length car coat. Detectives, Jeffreys decided.

"Lab guys here yet?" the trench coat asked the uniform cop, eyeing Jeffreys.

"Nope. Paramedics're upstairs with my pardner and Wesley from the coroner's office. That's all."

The detective grunted. His hatless companion jerked his chin at Jeffreys, said, "Who's this?"

"The security guy says he found him at the scene with a gun in his hand. I already read him his rights."

"Hang onto him while we take a look," car coat said.

The two strode into the elevator cage as another siren sounded outside, neared, faded, and died.

Two uniformed policemen came in. Both wore zipper jackets over their tunics. They were carrying cameras, lights, leather equipment cases, cardboard boxes. Crime-lab technicians,

Jeffreys decided. They stopped at the security desk, grinned at the guard, nodded absently at Jeffreys without apparent curiosity or rancor.

"Hi, Bruno," one said. "You still on midnights?"

"Four to twelve," Jeffreys' guard said. "Workin' over. I always catch these goddam shift-break deals since they cut out time-'n-a-half."

"Tough," the technician said. "Where we goin'?"

"Upstairs," Bruno told him. "Four-oh-eight, I think. Fourth floor, anyways."

"Four-oh-eight's right," Jeffreys said. He watched the technicians carry their armloads into the elevator, heard it whoosh away, said, "What're we waiting for, Bruno?"

"Them plainclothes guys to come back down," Bruno said conversationally. "They'll wanta quiz you here before they take you in. The chief likes on-the-scene Q-'n-A's in the write-ups."

"That's fair," Jeffreys said, trying to shrug the cramps out of his shoulders and arms. "I wish they'd hurry. These damn cuffs aren't comfortable."

"Sorry," Bruno told him apologetically. "Can't help it. Regulations."

"I know," Jeffreys said. "Thanks for the thought."

The elevator whooshed, its gate clanged open and the car-coated detective stepped out. His hair, neatly in place when he had first come in, was tousled as though from finger-combing.

He walked to the desk, sat down on it facing Jeffreys, his feet flat on the floor. He laid a crumpled pocket notebook on his thigh, scribbled something into it with a chewed plastic ball-point pen. Eyeing Jeffreys, he asked, "You been read your rights?"

"Yes. Bruno took care of it."

"You understand 'em?"

"Sure."

"Good. You kill the guy upstairs?"

"No," Jeffreys said, trying to sound as casual as had the questioner. "I found him like that."

"One of the uniforms upstairs says the security guy told him he caught you with the gun in your hand."

"I picked it up off the floor," Jeffreys said. "The security guy didn't catch me with anything. I came into the room, saw the body, stepped on the gun, picked it up, and noticed it'd been fired. That's when the security guy came in."

"How'd you know it'd been fired?"

"It felt warm and it smelled fired."

"You know what a fired gun smells like?"

"Sure do," Jeffreys said. "I used to hunt a lot, practice shooting on the range a little, trail you guys around for a living."

"Us guys?"

"Homicide cops. I was a reporter for a lot of years, and police beat for some of 'em."

The detective made another scribble in his notebook, ran his fingers through his hair, stood up.

"Name?" he said, poising his pen.

"Jeffreys, Samuel, T for Thomas. I'm thirty-eight years old, an American citizen, Indiana resident. I live at seven-fifty-three Elizabeth, Crown Point, Indiana. I'm a freelance writer, retired from the newspaper business, a widower, father of one, no police record. I was visiting ... uh ... the deceased in connection with a book I'm writing. I understand I'm entitled to a lawyer and you'll provide me with one if I'm indigent. Well, thanks but no thanks. I'm not indigent and I do want to call my own. Lawyer, that is."

"Nice recital," the detective said, after a half-minute of silence while he scribbled. "I'm Sergeant Sankstone. Joe Sankstone. Sorry we can't shake hands. The rules say to keep you cuffed."

"I know," Jeffreys said. "No problem."

"What's the book about?"

"The life and times of a crooked politician."

"Won't sell," Sankstone said, scribbling. "Too ordinary. All politicians're crooked."

"It's already sold," Jeffreys said, stung. "In outline form, anyway. To Morrissey Publications, New York City, in case you're interested."

"Could have fooled me," Sankstone said, scribbling.

"You want to take me in so I can get decuffed and make my phone call?"

"Why not?" Sankstone said. "Let's go."

Jeffreys stood up and started out. At the foyer door, he turned back toward the security desk.

"See you around, Bruno," he told the uniformed cop. "Sorry you caught this goddam shift-break deal."

"Don't worry about it," Bruno said cheerily. "Happens alla time."

"Listen, Bruno," Sankstone said, pausing in the doorway. "Get the name of that security guard and a number where I can reach him. Put it in your report. Okay?"

"Okay," Bruno said. "Only you'll prob'ly see him out front, so's you can ask him yourself."

They didn't, though.

Now, at going on 6 o'clock in the morning, Jeffreys finally had the coffee he'd been wishing for the evening before. It was strong, black and hot, brought by the jail guard who'd locked him into this dingy holding cell in the municipal jail building after warden's office workers processed him, relieved him of all personal articles, including his belt, took his picture full face and profile, and recorded his fingerprints for posterity.

He'd used his obligatory phone call to roust Bartel Van Til from his bed back in Highland, Indiana. The lawyer answered on the fifth ring. Because it was an open call on a public telephone with a half-dozen police personnel within earshot, Jeffreys tried to be discreet. He said only that he was being held by Bloomburgh police as a witness in a fatal shooting. He didn't identify Cornie by name. Van Til promised to head for Bloomburgh as soon as he could rearrange his schedule and catch an airplane out of O'Hare.

Sipping at the coffee, Jeffreys tried to assess the situation objectively. True, he'd committed no crime, done no wrong, broken no law. Equally true, he was the only suspect in a temporarily on-hold investigation into the night-shift death of an unremarkable resident of the city.

The probe would be recommenced in a few hours by day shift police personnel who would routinely set about establishing the decedent's identity and the cause of death so that homicide proceedings could either be initiated or averted. The decedent's background would be checked so that known enemies and/or friends could be interviewed for establishment of a possible motive if —no, make that *when*—the case was labeled murder.

The coroner's report would list it *homicide by gunshot*, Jeffreys mused. It would identify the victim as Nicora, Cornelius, age 64, dead at—no, not so! The corpse would be labeled *Nelson, Charles,* age whatever was shown on the phony ID cards doubtless found on the body. *Dead of brain destruction from one or more of three .32 caliber bullets fired into the back of the head, penetrating the occipital lobe,* the report would say, *gangland-execution-style by a person or persons unknown.*

There would be other findings, Jeffreys' police-beat experience reminded him. They would record the presence or absence of powder burns from which could be determined the distance between the gun and its target. They would report the bullet entry-path angle trajectory and, thus, relative positions of shooter and shootee could be deduced. They would describe any collateral wounds and/or injuries denoting a struggle or lack thereof. They would include such gross details as weight, appearance and condition of the internal organs extricated for examination through the huge incisions the examiner would slash into the cadaver's chest and belly.

He suddenly realized he was considering the killing clinically, objectively, without emotion. His earlier reaction, thus, was repeated: he was devastated by the death of the book, but not saddened by the death of its subject.

Wow, he thought. *If a longtime acquaintance isn't upset at the killing, what about those overworked and underpaid strangers whose job it is to look into it?* What team of city-police investigators, given Jeffreys' gun-in-hand presence at the scene of the fatal shooting of one Charles Nelson, as testified to by three eye witnesses, would bother digging deeper for a suspect or looking further for a murderer?

Hey, wait, he corrected himself. *That might be okay for city cops.* But wouldn't the witness protection Federales be aware of the victim's real identity? If so, how would they feel about one of their wards getting knocked off? Indignant? Embarrassed? Would they want to cover it up and keep it quiet so other potential witnesses wouldn't be scared away? Would they charge in to get the guy who did it and thus vindicate the integrity of their witness protection program? Or was this maybe the first time they ever lost one of their protectees to an executioner?

Unable to answer his own questions, Jeffreys stretched out on the hard cot and tried to fall asleep.

After a time, he succeeded.

He had no idea how long he'd been sleeping when he was awakened by yelling.

"Hey," somebody was shouting. "C'mon, wake up. I ain't got all day."

It was the guard of the early morning coffee, Jeffreys saw, when his eyes came into focus. The cell door was open and the guard was standing in the doorway, glaring at him.

"What's up?" Jeffreys asked groggily, his eyes burning and his stomach growling. "Is it lunch time?"

"Ya missed lunch," the guard said. "Ya slept through it. Yer lawyer's waitin fer ya. C'mon, let's go."

"My lawyer?" Jeffreys said, climbing to his feet and following the guard's back down the corridor. "Already? What time is it, anyway?"

The guard didn't answer. He stopped before a door, opened it, stood aside, closed it behind Jeffreys.

Bart Van Til was sitting at a small table in the sparsely-furnished lawyer-client conference room.

"Thanks for coming," Jeffreys said, sticking out his hand.

"What the hell's going on?" Van Til demanded, shaking hands without getting up from his chair. He waved Jeffreys into the one across the table. "Why are they holding you as a material witness in a murder case?"

"Because they think I'm the murderer. Somebody killed Cornie Nicora, and they figure it was me."

Jeffreys considered his attorney and longtime friend Bartel Van Til unflappable, but now the former FBI agent showed shock.

"Cornie Nicora?" he echoed. "The dead guy's *Cornie Nicora?*"

"Shhh," Jeffreys said, fearful that the guard outside the door would overhear. "You suppose this room's bugged?"

"Doubtful," Van Til said. "Police departments don't risk blowing cases by unauthorized eavesdropping anymore. You said the decedent is Cornie Nicora?"

"Right," Jeffreys said. "Or *was,* anyway."

"Can't be. The feds flipped him. They've kept him hidden someplace. Nobody's seen him for months, except when the marshal's office sneaks him back to sing to grand juries or testify against the guys he used to steal with."

"Not quite true," Jeffreys said. "I have. Seen him, that is.

Last night. He was alive for a while, and then he ... wasn't."

"What's he ... what was he doing *here?*"

"The witness protection people set him up with a job and an apartment and a new identity as a Charles Nelson six, seven months ago. He's been working as an inventory clerk in a local factory. Marge is someplace else under a different name."

"So what're *you* doing here?" Van Til demanded.

"Chasing Cornie. I've been looking for him for more than a year."

"Why?"

Jeffreys told Van Til about the book, about his search for Cornie, about his post office snitch, about the prior chases ending in futile stakeouts, about the final, successful one, about the deal he'd struck with Cornie, his trip to the car, the shots heard from the elevator, his finding of the corpse, his arrest.

"That's it?" Van Til asked, when he finished.

"That's it."

"You didn't shoot him?"

"Of course I didn't shoot him."

"Any thoughts on who did?"

"You tell me," Jeffreys said.

"Okay. I will. A mob hit man. A contract killer sent to shut Cornie's mouth. Or maybe to convince other potential flippers that they'll live longer if they don't flip. More likely, both of the above."

"Hell of a happenstance that a hit man would find Cornie the same time I did," Jeffreys said skeptically.

"It wasn't a happenstance."

"Then what ... oh, boy. Are you suggesting I've had a professional killer trailing me around? Figuring I'd lead him to Cornie?"

"Betcha. That's just what I'm suggesting."

Jeffreys considered the idea, rejected it.

"No," he said. "Couldn't be."

"Has to be." Van Til eyed him across the little conference table. "When does the killing come? Right after you've located the victim. How does the killing come? By gunshots to the back of the head. Who fires gunshots to the back of the head? Professional hit men."

"Maybe. Only whoever did it, I didn't lead him to Cornie."

"Sure you did. He's been following you. When you found Nicora, he found Nicora. When you went out for your gear, he went in for the kill. Maybe he knocked at Cornie's door, pretended to be you, said he had his hands full, and Cornie opened it. Or maybe he let himself in, somehow. Either way, he got the drop on Cornie, took his gun away from him and executed him with it. That's how it had to be."

"It fits," Jeffreys said, dubiously. "Except I can't believe anybody was following me because nobody knew I was looking for him."

"How about your publisher's people?" Van Til demanded.

"No," Jeffreys said, thinking about that, "The only one I ever talked to was the editor assigned to my project. And I never told her I was looking for Cornie. I just said I intended to collaborate with him."

"How about your post office snitch? The guy who was feeding you the names and addresses on Cornie's daughter's outgoing mail?"

"Not a guy," Jeffreys said. "A girl. A woman, actually. I never told her what I wanted them for, though."

"So she figured it out," Van Til said, his lips pursed in thought. "Or somebody else did. Maybe she was snitching for that somebody else, too. Maybe that somebody else decided you knew what you were doing so he had you followed every place you went."

"I'd have noticed."

"Not necessarily. Your tail's a pro. And you better hope he knows you never noticed."

"What's that mean?" Jeffreys asked. Then he shook his head in reluctant understanding. "Oh, wow!"

"Betcha," Van Til said. "Oh, wow, for sure!"

There was a knock at the door. The jail guard stuck his head inside.

"They want ya in the dick bureau," he said.

Van Til said, "We need another minute."

"I'll tell 'em." The guard's head disappeared and the door closed.

"You think I'm in danger?" Jeffrey asked.

"Betcha," Van Til said, his lips pursed again. "If the guy thinks you might've made him, you are. Or even if he only figures you for a loose end."

"Thanks," Jeffreys said. "Just what I needed to comfort me in my time of trouble."

"That's for later, though. Right now we've got other problems. I think you better play dumb about who the decedent is. Was."

"You mean we think the dead guy is Charles Nelson?"

"Betcha. For starters, anyway. I'm curious whether the Marshal's Service keeps close enough tabs on its program people to know right away when one of their protected witnesses gets dead."

"Me, too," Jeffreys said. "If they don't, shouldn't we tell 'em? So they can start looking for the killer? To get me off the hook as a suspect? Maybe catch him before he decides I'm a loose end?"

"Let's find out where they're coming from," Van Til said. "I'm not sure if they want all the facts out. It might suit them better to let the corpse be buried as Charles Nelson so nobody knows that one of their protected witnesses wasn't."

"There's a fly in that ointment, though," Jeffreys said. "The killer knows."

There was another knock on the door. The guard's head

reappeared. "You guys ready?" it said.

"Ready." Van Til got to his feet.

Jeffreys stood up, too, flexing his arms to rid them of the ache he attributed to his handcuffing of a few hours before. Still hurting, he followed his lawyer out of the conference room.

III
THE PUNCH AND
JUDY SHOW

Sgt. Joe Sankstone, his hair neatly in place but his necktie off-center as though from a nervous yank, was the only one Jeffreys recognized as he followed Van Til into the interrogation room. Four other men, all in plain clothes, eyed them from chairs behind a long, narrow table. Sankstone sat at one end on Jeffreys' left, fiddling with a tape recorder. The others lined its far side, facing the door.

Van Til walked to the table and stopped. Jeffreys halted beside him. The guard who brought them shut the door behind them. Jeffreys glanced back to see if he followed them in. He didn't.

"Gentlemen," Van Til said, wearing his bland lawyer smile. Jeffreys saw the recorder's cassette spindle start to turn. "I'm Bartel Van Til. I'm an attorney. My practice is mainly in the Circuit and Superior Courts of Lake County, Indiana, and the U.S. District Court in Hammond, Indiana, although I'm also admitted in other jurisdictions. I'm here representing Mr. Jeffreys. I thank you for postponing his formal interrogation until my arrival."

Sankstone nodded. The others sat motionless and impassive. Van Til continued.

"I understand you may already have subjected my client to

possible Miranda violations, but we'll talk about that later. Right now, I'm here to see that his rights are protected while you do your jobs. Where do you want us?"

The recorder spindle stopped when Bart did, Jeffreys saw.

"Sit down any place," Sankstone said, waving the back of his hand at the row of chairs along the unoccupied side of the table. "I'm Sgt. Sankstone. Joe Sankstone." He jerked a thumb toward the man next to him. "Your left to right, Lieutenant Dudley, Corporal Carl Sileski, Jim Lichterman, our lawyer. At the far end, there, Stanley Quick."

Each man nodded as he was identified, stayed seated, made no effort to rise or to shake hands. Van Til nodded to each in turn. Jeffreys did too. Van Til pulled a chair out from the middle of the table, sat down. Jeffreys followed suit, seating himself on his attorney's right.

"This is Tuesday, October fourteen, at sixteen twenty-seven hours," Sankstone said, watching the recorder start up to digest that information. "Mr. Jeffreys, what was your relationship with the dead man?"

"Hold it," Van Til said. His right elbow touched Jeffreys' arm, pressed it as though in restraint. "Is this room wired, and do you have a court reporter somewhere making a record?"

"No and no," Sankstone said, a note of irritation in his voice. He jerked a thumb at the recorder. "Obviously, we're taping."

"I'd like the tape to show, then, that I'm requesting on behalf of my client a full, unedited, authenticated copy of the tape at your earliest convenience," Van Til said. "Further, I think we should start off here by identifying for the record the decedent concerning whose death you are interrogating my client."

"Okay," Sankstone said, combing his hair with his fingers to mess it into a tangled shock. "You want formal, you got formal." He stared at the tape recorder. "By the book. With the above named in the interrogation room, headquarters, Bloomburgh PD, are Samuel T for Thomas Jeffreys, J-E-F-F-R-E-Y-S, age thirty-eight, of Crown Point, Indiana. He is represented by his attorney, Bartel Van Til of ... ah ... Highland, Indiana. We are here to interrogate Mr. Jeffreys about his possible role in the death of one Charles Nelson, sixty-four, of Bloomburgh. The decedent died after sustaining multiple gunshots to the back of the head in his own residence, suite four-oh-eight, Garrison Arms Apartments, Bloomburgh, on or about twenty-three-thirty hours, thirteen October, this year."

Jeffreys felt Van Til's elbow press lightly into his arm at the mention of the Nelson name.

"So now, then, Mr. Jeffreys," Sankstone was saying. "What was your relationship with Charles Nelson?"

"I had no relationship with any Charles Nelson," Jeffreys said, speaking slowly and deliberately so Van Til could stop him. "I don't know any Charles Nelson." He paused, expecting the lawyer to intervene. He didn't. Jeffreys plunged on. "I've never known any Charles Nelson."

Sankstone pounced on the statements.

"Then what were you doing in Charles Nelson's apartment?" he demanded. "And why were you carrying a suitcase containing your clothes and personal possessions as though you were moving into Charles Nelson's apartment?"

"I knew the dead man from before," Jeffreys said, hoping for a Van Til interruption, at least for the pressure of an elbow on his arm in warning or in reassurance. There was nothing. "Only not as Charles Nelson. And not here. I knew him back in Indiana. I came here to see him on a business matter. He invited me to stay with him. I went out to the car to get my bag. When I got back, he was dead."

"Did you kill him?"

"No."

"Then who did?"

"I have no idea," Jeffreys said. The room was hot. He felt sweat moistening his forehead and the back of his neck. He wondered why Van Til wasn't helping him.

"Did you see anybody else in the apartment while you were discussing your business?" Sankstone asked.

"There wasn't anybody else in the apartment."

"How do you know that?"

"I was listening. For well over an hour, while we talked. I was listening for a footstep, a movement, breathing, any kind of a sound. There wasn't any."

"So you were the only one there?"

"Yes," Jeffreys said, realizing he'd talked himself into another corner.

"You were expecting somebody else to be there?"

"Sort of," Jeffreys said. "His wife, Marge."

"You knew the wife?" the number four man at the table interrupted. *Lichterman*, Jeffreys remembered Sankstone saying. *Jim Lichterman, our lawyer.* "You knew the dead man's wife, and her name was Marge?"

"Yes," Jeffreys said. He felt Van Til's elbow on his arm. He recognized it as a signal. He didn't know what the signal meant. "I knew her back in Indiana, too."

"When did you last see this Marge?"

"Two, two and a half years ago, I guess," Jeffreys said, recalling interviewing her in the corridor outside the courtroom just before Cornie was sentenced and sent away.

"Our records say Charles Nelson was a widower," Lichterman said coldly. "Our records say his wife died more than ten years ago. Our records say her name was Florence."

"Florence?" Jeffreys echoed, wondering if he should brand that information phony or leave it alone. Van Til gave him no help. "Her I didn't know."

The fifth man cleared his throat. He looked angry. Quick, Jeffreys remembered from the introductions. *Stanley Quick.*

"Mr. Jeffreys," Quick said brusquely. "What was the nature of your business with the late Charles Nelson?"

Jeffrey waited for Van Til to interrupt. He didn't.

"I'm writing a book about him," Jeffreys said.

"Hell of a book," Quick said. "Best seller! Can't miss! The life and times of Charles Nelson, inventory clerk! Who, Mr. Jeffreys, would want to buy such a book or read such a book?"

"You asked me, I told you," Jeffreys said, feeling rebellious.

Quick leaned across the table, stared into Jeffreys' eyes and shook a finger at him.

"Were you really interested in an unknown person named Charles Nelson?" he demanded. "Or was your interest in a notorious person named Cornelius Nicora?"

If they knew who Nelson was, Jeffreys wondered, his mind whirring, why did they play dumb?

"You knew Cornelius Nicora, didn't you?"

Jeffreys waited for a signal from Van Til. There was none.

"Yes, I did. I knew Cornie Nicora long before he became Charles Nelson. I knew him well enough to want to write his life story."

"Did you know he was in the federal witness protection program?"

"Yes."

"Did you know he was in hiding because there was a contract out on his life?"

"Yes."

"Of course, you did. And wasn't that the nature of your business with him? Didn't you hunt him down to collect on that contract? Didn't you shoot him three times in the head in its fulfillment?"

"Hold it," Van Til interrupted, shoving his elbow into Jeffrey's arm.

Jeffreys understood the signal but decided to ignore it. "No way!" he shouted. "I'm not a killer. I'm a writer. And I needed him alive, not dead!"

"Hold it," Van Til said again, more emphatically.

Quick leaned back in his chair, grinning nastily at Jeffreys. "So you looked up Nicora, Cornelius, AKA Nelson, Charles, in the city directory. You found his aliases and addresses cross-indexed there for your convenience. You drove over to his apartment to greet him. He welcomed you as a friendly visitor from the past he'd fled. The two of you discussed your writing of a book exposing his corruption. He agreed to publicly confess his evil acts for all the world to know. Then some third party came along and killed him while you weren't looking. Is that what you're asking us to swallow?"

"It's what happened," Jeffreys said doggedly.

"Hold it!" Van Til said again, shouting the message this time and slapping the table top with his palm. "It's my turn." His eyes flicked from man to man across the table. "We figured you people were probably holding out on us, but we couldn't be sure. If you'd leveled with us on the decedent's identity in the first place, this charade needn't have gone on so long."

"If we'd leveled with you?" Sankstone said. He combed his hair with his fingers. "How about the other way around?"

"Hey," Van Til shrugged. "For all my client knew, it could be a criminal offense to divulge the real name of a protected witness after he's been whisked off and given a counterfeit identity by the federal government."

"Even to homicide investigators?" Sankstone demanded.

"Betcha," Van Til told him. "Even to homicide investigators. I'm not sure what the rules are myself, and I'm a lawyer." He swung his head toward the end of the table, demanded, "What are you, Mr. Quick? FBI or Marshal Service?"

"FBI," Quick said.

"When I was with the bureau," Van Til said, his voice now cold and hard, "if we weren't undercover, we had to identify ourselves up front and produce our credentials whenever it was appropriate. Are you undercover, Mr. Quick?"

Quick glared at him, shook his head.

"Then I believe now is appropriate," Van Til said.

"Like the sergeant told you, I'm Stanley Quick." He produced a leather folder from his jacket pocket, flipped it open and held it at arm's length toward Van Til. "I'm a special agent with the Federal Bureau of Investigation on loan to the U.S. Marshal Service's witness protection program."

Jeffreys glanced at the ID. It appeared authentic. He looked at Van Til.

Van Til scanned the folder. Then he nodded. Quick put it away.

"So what about it, Special Agent Quick?" Van Til prodded. "Do your people take kindly to citizens who blow the covers of protected witnesses by blabbing their true identities and tattling their police records?"

"We want to know how your client found our protected witness," Quick countered. "Is he going to tell us?"

"Probably not," Van Til said. "I'm going to advise him not to, for now. I have a hunch that information might be good trading stock somewhere down the line. Unless ..." he paused, grinned at Sankstone, "unless, of course, my client is released, preliminary charges are dismissed with prejudice, and I'm assured on the record that he'll be granted immunity. If and when that happened, I probably would reconsider my advice."

Sankstone, his hair tousled and his tie now even more awry, looked at the man on his left. *Lieutenant Dudley*, Jeffreys remembered.

The lieutenant spoke for the first time. His voice was calm, unruffled.

"At worst, ridiculous, and at best, premature," he said. "Down the road a ways, possibly, but not now, for damn sure. We'd need to turn over some stones, first. And we'd need another suspect, because just now we have only the one."

"Suspect?" Van Til asked, his rising inflection making his point. "Or witness? You'd do better deposing Mr. Jeffreys than interrogating him."

"We aren't convinced of that," Dudley said. His demeanor told Jeffreys he was directing the investigation into Cornie's killing, not Sankstone. "We haven't finished checking the murder weapon's fingerprints. We need to be told by the FBI lab whether your client fired a gun around the time of the shooting. We have other hard evidence to consider, disinterested witnesses to question. I'm sure you're familiar with the way we work."

"As you wish, Lieutenant," said Van Til, with equal calm. "But let's not bullshit each other any more, okay? Let's tell it like it is. For instance, if there are fingerprints on the gun that aren't too smudged to identify, they'll be the decedent's, because he owned it, and my client's, because he picked it up. The killer's won't be readable, because he either wore gloves or he wiped off the weapon after he fired it. We all know that's how professionals operate, Lieutenant, and I believe we all recognize this as a professional hit."

Dudley sat mute, gazing at Van Til without expression.

Van Til said, "As for the FBI lab's report on my client's swab test, I have three comments."

He held up a finger. "One, you may have violated his constitutional rights of privacy and protection against improper search and seizure when your technicians without his permission took skin-surface samples from his hands with the swabs from their powder blast detection kit."

He flipped up a second finger. "Two, let's not hold our breath until the results come back from the FBI lab. You know better than I that we're talking weeks, maybe months, before the federal lab people accumulate enough such tests from local PDs around the country to make it worth their while to run a batch of them."

Van Til extended a third finger. "Three, when you do get the report, it can't prove anything except that my client's hands bore traces of antimony and barium products from the cartridge primer of a recently fired handgun. We already knew that, though, didn't we, because he told us he handled the murder weapon. Betcha. So the lab report at best can only corroborate such handling, not confirm whether he did or did not fire the gun."

Dudley still sat silent.

Van Til said, "Beyond that, I don't know what kind of hard evidence you have, but I do know it can't implicate my client in a shooting he didn't commit. Ditto for whatever witnesses you may have on the string. So why are we really stalling?"

"Nobody's stalling," Dudley said quietly, wearing an affable smile. "We're conducting a murder investigation. We have one suspect, caught at the scene of the killing with the death gun in his hand. Under the circumstances, you as a lawyer, and officer of the court, wouldn't really counsel us to cut him loose, would you?"

Jeffreys saw that Van Til was smiling back at Dudley and looking equally affable.

"Betcha I would," Van Til said. "Assuming you don't really think my client's a contract killer, what kind of a case can you build against him? What motive could he possibly have? Why would he want the decedent dead?"

"Crimes of passion don't need motive," Lichterman cut in. He stood up. "People kill other people in the heat of rage. Maybe your client's temper flared when the man he'd been hunting refused to cooperate after he finally found him, if his book-writing story checks out."

"That's pretty thin," Van Til said.

"It's what we've got," Lichterman said. "Please advise your client that the preliminary count of material witness to a homicide will be dismissed within the hour."

Jeffreys felt a surge of elation. He saw Van Til's face go grim. His own euphoria faded.

"Replaced by?" Van Til asked.

"Replaced by formal charges of first-degree murder," Lichterman said. "By the way, murder one isn't bailable in this state."

Jeffreys felt his stomach sink and his mouth go dry.

"Charges?" Van Til said, obviously surprised. "Plural?"

"Plural," Lichterman said. "Two counts. The second, of course, involving the death of Wallace Echols."

"Who the hell is Wallace Echols?" Van Til demanded, coming to his feet and swiveling his head back and forth from Lichterman to Jeffreys.

Jeffreys stared back, his thoughts jumbled.

"Was," Lichterman corrected. "Wallace Echols was the security guard at Garrison Arms Apartments."

Van Til digested that. Then he said, "How could my client be involved in the killing of the security guard who turned him over to your people? The guard was alive then, and my client's been in your custody and control ever since."

"Wallace Echols was the real security guard," Lichterman said coolly. "A janitor found his body in a basement supply closet the day after the Nicora killing. He'd been strangled and his uniform taken. The coroner placed the time of his death as maybe an hour before Nicora's."

"Then who was the guard that held my client at gun point until the police came?" Van Til demanded.

"Obviously an impostor," Lichterman said. "Maybe a colleague of your client's who helped him execute the decedents. He took off right after the police got there. We were hoping your client would tell us who he is and where we can find him."

Van Til swallowed, said, "My client stands mute."

"Fine," Lichterman said. "Then please advise your mute client that he is shortly to be charged with two counts of murder one."

"Betcha," Van Til said. "I will so advise him. Meanwhile, I remind you that the citizens of this community depending on you people for their security and protection have a *real* killer running loose out there among them."

"Lots of 'em, Mr. Van Til," Lieutenant Dudley cut in quietly. "Lots of 'em." He stood up. "Gentlemen, I think we're through here. Sergeant, will you summon a guard to escort the prisoner back to his cell?"

Sankstone did.

IV
LOUIS LEWIS

Jeffreys slept well despite the dismal surroundings of the cell and the hardness of the cot.

He awoke ravenously hungry. He remembered that he'd only picked at the jail food the night before. He wondered what time it was.

After a while, a guard brought him a tray. Jeffreys heard him coming. It wasn't the same guard who'd ushered him to the interrogation room and back again the previous afternoon. This one walked with a slap-slapping shuffle, as though he wore clown shoes or didn't pick up his feet.

"Hi," the guard said, shoving the tray through the crosswise slot in the barred door. "Eatin' time."

"I'm ready," Jeffreys told him, meaning it. The oatmeal looked dried out and lumpy, but there was milk to moisten it, sugar to sweeten it, a plastic spoon to eat it with, toast to eat with it, and coffee to wash it down. "What time is it?"

"Goin' on for seven," the guard said. "Give or take."

"Morning or evening?" Jeffreys asked, feeling silly.

"Mornin'," the guard said over his shoulder as he slap-slapped away. "Wednesday, October the fifteenth."

"Thanks," Jeffreys said. He sat down on the cot, held the tray in his lap, and went to work on the modest breakfast. It tasted great. The coffee was strong and bitter, but satisfying. He concentrated on eating, making an effort to blot everything else from his mind. Then the tray was empty, he yearned for a cigarette, and conscious thought returned.

Van Til had promised to visit him this morning. Maybe he'd have something to tell him when he came. Like when—and how—he could expect to get out of this cell and out of this predicament and out of this city and back to living his life again.

But if that seeming miracle were to come about, if he did get back to living his life again, what would he do with it? Spend it mourning the death of a biography that died with its subject? Or maybe trying to salvage it without the help of the man who knew its plot?

Was it salvageable? Would Fifi Malloy and her bosses settle for a third-party chronicle in lieu of the first-person epic he'd sold them on? Or was it time to forget the book, to think only about extricating himself from the jam that chasing Cornie had dumped him into, and to write off Cornie's life story as never to be written?

"An unwritten write-off," he said aloud.

His muse was interrupted by the slap-slapping of the approaching guard.

"You say somethin'?" the guard demanded.

"Not me."

"Gimme the tray," the guard said.

"You got it," Jeffreys said, tipping it to pass through the cell-door bars. "And thanks. I enjoyed it. When's lunch?"

"Around noon," the guard said, departing. "Give or take."

"Thanks," Jeffreys said, sinking back onto the cot and resuming his contemplation about whether he yet could put together a lively book on the life and times of a dead politician.

He was awakened by the guard again.

"You got company." The guard scraped a key in the lock.

"My lawyer, I hope," Jeffreys said sleepily. He stood up, stretched, followed the guard slap-slapping down the corridor. The man wasn't wearing clown shoes, Jeffreys saw. He just didn't pick up his feet. "What time is it?"

"Goin' on for eleven," the guard said. "Give or take."

Bartel Van Til and another man were waiting for him in the little conference room. They got up from behind the table, hands extended. Jeffreys took Van Til's, shook it, dropped it, reached for the other man's, wondering who he was and why he was there.

"Sam Jeffreys, meet Louis Lewis," Van Til said.

"Call me Louis," the stranger said solemnly. He squeezed Jeffreys' hand in an overly firm grip.

"Hi, Louis," Jeffreys acknowledged, eyeing him. He looked young, not much over 30, immaculately and conservatively dressed, dark-blue suit, white shirt, button-down collar, Windsor-knotted light-blue necktie. His smile seemed contrived, solicitous. Probably one of the junior members of a prestigious—and expensive—law firm, Jeffreys decided.

"We've retained Lewis as local counsel," Van Til said. "I've told him what I could about the case. He'll have questions for you."

"Right," Lewis said. His smile faded. He walked behind the table, sat down, waved at a chair in front of Jeffreys. "Let's talk."

Jeffreys seated himself, leaned his elbows on the table, and waited for Van Til to take a chair. He didn't. Instead, he stepped behind Jeffreys and patted him on the shoulder.

"I'll leave you two," he said. "I've got to get back to the office."

"Office?" Jeffreys echoed. "What office? Where office? Your home office? Your Highland office?"

"Betcha," Van Til said. "I've got a jury trial starting in federal court tomorrow."

"When'll you be back?" He felt abandoned.

"I'm not sure. The trial'll likely go two weeks, give or take. Meantime, Lewis'll be here for you." Van Til opened the door and started out.

"Wait," Jeffreys said, jumping up and following. He was surprised at the panic in his chest and the desperation in his voice. "Please. What ... How much can I ... Should I tell Mr. Lewis?"

"Louis," Lewis corrected from behind him. Jeffreys turned, saw that the solicitous smile was back. "You should tell me everything."

"Betcha," Van Til said from the open doorway. "Everything. He'll be defending you." And the door closed behind him.

Defending me! Jeffreys thought. *Nothing about springing me, cutting me loose, bailing me the hell out of here. Just, defending me.*

"Bartel and I didn't have a whole lot of time to review your situation," Lewis was saying. He picked an attaché case off the floor, removed from it a legal-sized yellow pad, replaced it on the floor. He took an expensive-looking gold fountain pen from his breast pocket. "He outlined the broad picture, but I'm not firm on the details."

"Me either," Jeffreys said dispiritedly, sitting down again. His feeling of abandonment was total.

"I've read the charge affidavits. One says you knowingly, willfully and with premeditation killed and murdered one Charles Nelson, also known as Cornelius Nicora, by shooting three bullets into his head with a certain .32 caliber firearm. The other says you strangled to death one Wallace Echols after administering a blow to his head with a blunt instrument."

"Not so," Jeffreys said dully. "I didn't shoot Cornie and I didn't choke or bash what's his name ... Echols. I never even *saw* Echols."

"Bartel tells me you were at the scene of the shooting at

the time of the shooting."

"Wrong. I got there afterwards."

"How long afterwards?"

"I don't know. Minutes, maybe. No, more like seconds."

"Tell me about it," Lewis said. His pen was poised over the yellow pad. "*All* about it. What you saw, what you heard, what you felt."

Jeffreys sighed, and remembered Bart's advice to tell Lewis everything.

"I'd started up from downstairs with my bag from the car," he said. "I heard three shots while I was in the elevator. Cornie's door was open. He was on the floor, dead. I went in and picked up the gun. A woman showed up out in the hall and stood there staring at me. An old man in a bathrobe was peering out of another apartment behind her. He called the police. Then the guard came in."

"The guard?" Lewis asked, looking up from his note-taking.

"The security guard."

"Would you know him if you saw him again?"

"Probably," Jeffreys said, thinking about that. "He had a walrus mustache and a heavy beard. He was huge. His uniform was way too tight ... Hey, sure, he must have taken it off of the *real* guard ... unh ... what was his name?"

"Wallace Echols," Lewis said.

"Wallace Echols had to be a smaller man. That'd explain the tightness. And if he took the real guard's keys, that'd explain how he got into Cornie's apartment."

"Perhaps," Lewis said. "You said two witnesses saw you holding the gun, a woman in the doorway and a man across the hall, when the man in the guard suit came in?"

"Right," Jeffreys said, trying to visualize that confused moment and realizing something didn't fit. "No, wait. He didn't come in. He couldn't have. The woman was in the doorway, blocking it. I could only see the old guy in the bathrobe over her shoulder."

"So what are you saying?"

"The guard ... unh ... the man in the guard's uniform, must've already been in Cornie's apartment. Maybe in one of the other rooms. When I first saw him he was standing beside me. I was facing the body, with my back to the door. I turned my head to look behind me at the woman in the doorway and the man across the hall, and that's when the guard—the guy in the uniform—suddenly appeared. Beside me."

"Splendid," Lewis said, writing. "That seems to put him at the death scene before you got there. We'll depose those witnesses about where he was when they first saw him. Their testimony may be extremely useful."

"The guy in the guard suit's got to be Cornie's killer," Jeffreys said. "The real guard's, too."

"Not necessarily," Lewis said, looking up again. "But we'll adopt the theory as a working hypothesis. Tell me about the victim, the man you call Cornie."

"He was a crooked politician. I covered his rise and fall when I was a reporter. The feds got him for evading taxes on kickback and bribe money plus misuse of campaign funds. They convicted him under RICO ... uh ... the Racketeer Influenced and Corrupt Organizations Act. He got twenty years, actually served a few months, decided he didn't like prison, and cut a deal to flip ... uh ... turn government witness."

"Flip," Lewis said, unsmiling. "I know the vernacular, including RICO. I flipped a few RICO candidates myself as a deputy prosecutor."

"Bully," Jeffreys said. "Anyway, when Cornie started blowing the whistle on his crooked cronies, I decided he and they would make a hell of a book. But then they put him into the federal witness protection program and hid him out under a new identity. They only brought him back under heavy guard to testify from time to time, and I couldn't get at him."

"I'm familiar with how the program works. Go on."

"So I decided to find him. I hunted for a long time, traipsing all over the country in the process. The other night I caught up with him. I told him I wanted to ghost-write a book under his byline that could make us both some money. He was always interested in a buck, and decided to play. I was to move into his apartment with him so we could get started right away. That's when I went out to get my things and somebody killed him."

"How did that somebody find him?" Lewis asked.

"Beats me," Jeffreys said.

"How did you find him?"

"It wasn't easy."

"Tell me about it."

"I'd rather not."

"Why?"

"I'm not sure why," Jeffreys said. "Maybe because it's the only piece of private information I have."

"You lost me," Lewis said. "I don't follow that."

"I can't explain it. I just have this feeling I shouldn't tell people how I found Cornie."

Lewis looked upset. "I'm not people. I'm your lawyer. I need to know everything you know."

"You already do," Jeffreys said. "Everything else, anyway. And this seems ... ah ... irrelevant."

"Perhaps, perhaps not." Lewis shrugged. "So tell me about the security guard. Echols, I believe. Wallace Echols. You claim you didn't know him?"

"What's to tell? I never even heard of him. Cornie's killer obviously knocked him off, too."

"Why?"

"How the hell do I know why? To get him out of the way, maybe. To wear his uniform as credentials to roam the building. To use his pass keys. Maybe all the above. What really bugs me is how the phony guard had the balls to hang around after he shot Cornie and then herd me downstairs at gun point to turn me over to the cops."

"He may've hung around because he was looking for something, only you interrupted his search," Lewis said thoughtfully. "And he may've herded you downstairs so he could kill you without witnesses, only your execution was interrupted by the arrival of the police."

"You think?" Jeffreys asked.

"Maybe," Lewis said solemnly. "I'll ask you again, would you recognize him if you saw him?"

"I think," Jeffreys said, trying to picture the bearded man in the guard's uniform. All he could see clearly was the muzzle of the .357 pointing at him.

"Could you pick him out of a mug book?"

"Maybe. Big and bearded is what I recall."

Lewis reviewed the scribblings on his yellow pad. He looked Jeffreys in the eyes. "I guess that's all we can do for now. Arraignment's set for Tuesday. I assume we'll plead not guilty?"

"Damn right," Jeffreys said. "Because we are not guilty. Tuesday? You said Tuesday? And today is Wednesday?"

Lewis looked pleased.

"We managed to hurry it up," he said. "My firm is not without influence."

"So what do I do between now and Tuesday?" Jeffreys demanded. "Sit here in the slammer?"

"I'm afraid so. I suggest you relax and get used to it. We'll try for an early hearing on a motion to let to bail soon after your arraignment. Courts here don't much believe in bonding out murder defendants, though, particularly when they're charged with double counts."

"Thanks for sharing that comforting thought," Jeffreys said.

There was a knock at the door behind him. The guard stuck his head in.

"You got more company," he said. "Wanta see her?"

"Me?" Jeffreys countered, staring at the guard over his shoulder. "Her?" He looked at Lewis, shrugged, said, "I guess."

The guard's head disappeared. A woman stepped into the room, shutting the door behind her. She walked to the table and stood there, looking down at the seated men. She was wrapped in a double-breasted trench-style raincoat, hatless, peering at one and then the other.

Jeffreys decided she reminded him of Edie—the same chestnut curls, the long oval face, the tall slender body. Only this one was even slimmer, and she stood straighter, her shoulders thrust back like a British sergeant-major's. She'd be about Edie's age, too, if Edie had lived, mid-thirties, probably. He rose from his chair, saw that Louis Lewis had risen too.

"Sam?" the woman said. "Is one of you Sam Jeffreys?"

He said, "I'm Sam Jeffreys. Were you looking for me?"

"Damn right." The woman turned toward him.

"Fifi Malloy?" Jeffreys blurted, his mind racing. It sounded like her, the female phantom from the publishing house, the self-assured, mildly profane, disembodied voice over the telephone that badgered and cajoled him into repeated revisions of his proposal; that finally announced acceptance of the latest version; that promised a contract and an advance; that came through with both. It sounded like that Fifi Malloy. It was her voice and her speech pattern. It couldn't be, though, of course. Could it?

"You got it," the woman said, her smile widening. She thrust out her hand. "It's nice we finally got together, Sam. Only this's a hell of a place for it."

Jeffreys took the hand. It was warm and moist. He shook it, dropped it, said, "Fifi Malloy, meet Louis Lewis."

"A pleasure, Miss Malloy," Lewis said. His face was expressionless.

"Mrs. You're Sam's lawyer?"

"Just so," Lewis said. "And you're?"

"Sam's editor. What can we do to help him the hell out of jail and back to his damn word processor?"

"We?"

"Morrissey Publications. Sam's writing a book for us, if you didn't know. I'm here to do whatever I can to expedite it."

"The autobiography of Cornelius Nicora?" Lewis said.

"Sam!" Fifi Malloy exploded, glaring at Jeffreys. "Damn it to hell, that's confidential!"

"Not any more," Jeffreys said. "Confidentiality ended around eleven-thirty the night before last."

"When you got busted for witnessing a murder?"

"How did you know that?" Lewis cut in. "And how did you know Sam was in jail here?"

"The Bloomburgh police called my office," Fifi said. "A Sergeant Sinkstone, I think it was, checking on Sam. He said Sam claimed we were publishing his book and wanted to know if it was true. I answered his damn questions, asked a few of my own, and here I am. Aren't you damn people going to ask a lady to sit down, for Christ's sake?"

"Sorry," Jeffreys said, pointing to his chair and pulling it back from the table for her. "Please."

"I'll take his chair so I can look at you." She walked around the table, waited for Lewis to seat her, motioned for Jeffreys to sit down across from her. He did. Staring into his eyes, she asked, "So why'd you blab about the damn premise of the damn book?"

Jeffreys started to answer, but Louis Lewis interrupted.

"I have a few questions for you, Mrs. Malloy, if you don't mind."

"Damn lawyers," Malloy said. "Everybody's a damn witness they've got to voir dire. Okay. Shoot."

"Why are you here?" Lewis demanded.

"Because I bought his damn book, because that makes me responsible for it, and because it's my ass if he doesn't get the damn thing written."

"The life and crimes of Cornelius Nicora?" Lewis pressed.

"The working title's Protected Witness," she said, evading the question. "We'd appreciate your not using any names at this time. We think it's going to be a damn blockbuster."

"You've read it?"

"Hell yes, I've read it. I bought it! The outline, that is."

"But not the book itself."

"Of course not. It isn't written yet."

"That's what puzzles me. What did you buy?"

"A proposal. Sam's manuscript-in-preparation, his outline, his formal summary of what the damn book'll be."

"Publishers pay for things that don't yet exist?"

"Sure. We bet on the come. Advances against expected earnings."

"What if the book turns out to be an unsalable stinker? Or never gets written?"

"Tough shit," Malloy said, shrugging philosophically. "That seldom happens, though. Publishers know what the hell they're doing. They—we—usually get what we pay for."

"Like an unwritten book on the life and times of one Cornelius Nicora?"

Fifi Malloy looked upset again. "Quit saying that. It's confidential."

"Was," Lewis corrected. "Do you know why Mr. Jeffreys is in jail?"

"He's a witness in a damn murder case," Malloy said. "That's what the damn sergeant said when he called, anyway."

"Try suspect in a murder case," Lewis said. "Did the sergeant tell you who the victim was?"

"The name didn't mean anything to me."

"It was phony. Who got killed was Cornelius Nicora. Does that mean anything to you?"

Fifi Malloy's face reflected shock.

She fixed her eyes on Jeffreys. "You killed him? You killed the son of a bitch the damn book's about? The viewpoint guy who's supposed to be telling the damn story?"

"No," Jeffreys heard himself say. "I didn't."

Louis Lewis cut him off. "Mrs. Malloy, in the light of all this, just what do you propose to do that could, as you put it a while ago, help Sam the hell out of jail and back to his damn word processor?"

She didn't answer. She sat mute, her mouth open, staring at Jeffreys. Lewis shrugged, walked to the door and opened it. He told the guard they were ready.

Following him out, Jeffreys turned to see Fifi Malloy still staring after him as the door swung shut.

"What time is it?" he asked the slap-slapping guard escorting him back to his cell.

▼
WANT TO CHAT?

It was a long, hungry afternoon.

Jeffreys napped. He dreamed of Cornie alive, dictating details of dirty dealings into the tape recorder, and of Cornie dead, staring at him from sightless eyes. Finally, he heard the guard's shoes slap-slapping along the corridor.

"Eatin' time," the guard said, sliding a tray into the horizontal slot in the cell door.

"I'm ready," Jeffreys said. "Boy, am I ready. You still on overtime?"

"Sure am. My relief ain't showed."

"What time is it?"

"Goin' on for six," the guard said, slap-slapping off in the direction he had come. "Give or take."

Jeffreys dug into the food. There was a thick slice of fat roast beef in the sectioned plastic plate alongside the paper napkin atop the tray. There was a mound of mashed potatoes in the next compartment, its top cratered to contain a little lake of dark brown gravy. Next to it was a tangled pile of green beans. There was a smaller plastic dish holding a squarish piece of yellow, icingless cake. There was a saucerless mug of very black coffee.

The beef was tough. The potatoes were lumpy. Or were the

lumps in the gravy? The beans were stringy, tasteless.

"The hearty man ate a condemned meal," he told himself.

He finished it and attacked the cake. It was dry and crumbly, but sweet. On the third cut, his plastic fork hit something hard. It proved to be the stub of a pencil.

Jeffreys withdrew it from the middle of the cake, wiped it clean with his napkin, set it on the tray and stared at it. Just over an inch long, it was yellow like the cake except for the black lead at one end and the red eraser at the other. Its point was machine sharpened, not whittled. Its eraser was pristine. The metal band crimping it to the wood was unmarred. It showed neither teeth marks in the wood nor use marks in the rubber.

A spanking new pencil deliberately sharpened down to a nub so it could hide in a square of cake? Why? Jeffreys shrugged, addressed himself to the remainder of the cake, finished it, reached for the coffee mug.

He saw a folded piece of paper under it when he picked it up. It was a square of whitish note paper. Unfolding it, he saw words on it in black ink: **Want to chat?**

There was no signature.

Jeffreys thought about that, sipping the bitter, lukewarm coffee and feeling panic creeping into his chest again.

The note had to be from someone with access to the jail kitchen. Or maybe from someone with access to his meal tray after it left the kitchen. Or maybe just with access to the guard who brought it from the kitchen.

That could be anybody, he told himself, screening the video tape his memory played back from his inquisition in the interrogation room. Left to right there were Sergeant Sankstone, Lieutenant Dudley, Corporal ... uh ... Corporal what's-his name, Carl something? Then Jim ... uh ... Lichterman, our lawyer. Finally, there was Quick, Special Agent Stanley Quick.

Which one? he asked himself.

Sankstone? A hard-working street cop who maybe bought his story and wanted his help in digging up a lead to chase toward the real hit man?

Lieutenant Dudley? A desk cop interested in getting the witness protection Federales off his back by handing them Cornie's killer, hog-tied and convictable? Looking for a chat without a lawyer around to see if he could leverage something useful? No. Desk-rank cops knew better than to risk cases killed in court or convictions overturned by improperly prying information from defendants.

Corporal what's-his-face, Carl something? Not likely. He was probably at the interrogation only as the low-level cop who would take the stand at trial time if the questioning led to a confession, thus springing Sankstone and Dudley from such dull though necessary duty.

Lichterman? Doubtful. Hard telling whether he was the PD's legal advisor-liaison with the prosecutor's office or a ranking deputy prosecutor. Likely that, though, the way he apparently made the decision switching Jeffreys from material witness to double defendant. Either way, legal eagles seldom involved themselves in the investigation phases of murder cases except on TV shows.

Quick? Could be. As an FBI agent assigned to the Marshal Service's Witness-Protection program, Cornie's killing likely left him with egg on his face. He might even have been Cornie's personal bodyguard, officially responsible for keeping Charles Nelson alive to testify in other seventh-circuit criminal proceedings against other seventh-circuit criminals.

I vote for Quick, Jeffreys mused, finishing his coffee. But whoever, what should he do? Meet with the guy? Listen to what he had to say? Or ignore the note?

He heard the guard slap-slapping down the corridor toward him and knew he had to decide in a hurry.

Suppose it wasn't Quick, Jeffreys thought. Suppose the note

was from Cornie's killer, wanting Jeffreys dead to cover his own ass or just to tie up the loose ends. Suppose he slipped a sawbuck to the guard or a kitchen trusty to smuggle in the pencil and the note. Or maybe sneaked them onto the tray himself, somehow. Or perhaps even dumped a little cyanide into the coffee while he was at it. But then there'd be no need for the pencil and the note, would there?

"Gimme the tray," the guard said, shuffling up to the cell door.

"You still here?" Jeffreys asked, rising from the cot. He left the tray atop it. The sharp end of the pencil stub pricked the palm of his left hand as he made a fist to conceal it and the note.

"Still here," the guard said. "How was the grub?"

"Just what I needed," Jeffreys said, watching the man's face. "Food for the body and a message for the mind."

The guard's expression didn't change. "Gimme the tray," he said.

"Of course," Jeffreys said. He turned his back, scribbled a tiny *yes* on the note cupped in his left hand, folded it in four along the original creases, picked up the tray, slid the paper under the coffee mug, turned back to the guard and pushed the tray through the door slot. "You get paid for working over?"

"Time'n a half," the guard said. "We got a better union than them outside guys."

"Bully," Jeffreys said. "What time is it?"

"Goin' on for half-pas'-six," the guard said, slap-slapping down the corridor. "Give or take."

Jeffreys unclenched his fist and put the pencil stub into his left-hand pants pocket. Then he sat down on the hard cot, wondering whether the little *yes* was a good move or a bad one.

"Anything beats sitting here waiting to be tried as a double murderer," he reassured himself, under his breath. Then he added, "Well, almost anything."

⬛

"You got a visitor," the guard said, shuffling up to the cell door with a key extended.

"You still here?" Jeffreys asked, scrubbing the sleep out of his eyes with the backs of his hands. "What time is it?"

"Goin' on for 'leven," the guard said. "Give or take." His key grated in the lock, and he swung the door open. "I hope my damn relief busted his damn leg or somethin'."

"Look at all the money you're making," Jeffreys said, stepping out into the corridor and stretching.

"Oh yeah," the guard said. "Couple more o' these an' I c'n retire. Wanna follow me?"

Jeffreys did. The route was familiar. It ended outside the door of the same small lawyer-client visitation room he'd first seen when he was ushered into the presence of Bartel Van Til the day after Cornie's killing a century or so ago, and later shared with Louis Lewis and Fifi Malloy.

The guard opened the door. Jeffreys walked into the little chamber.

"I wasn't expecting you," he said, sitting down across the table from Corporal What's-his-face.

"Sileski," the man said, making no move to shake hands. "Corporal Carl Sileski." He looked embarrassed. He said, "You wanta tell me how you found the dead guy?"

"Be glad to," Jeffreys said, wondering whether so low-level a cop who appeared so fumbly-bumbly could manage the note-sending, and why he'd want to lure him out of his cell in the middle of the night. "I found him dead."

"I meant ... how you located him," Sileski said.

"You think I ought to tell you?"

"Sure." Sileski's eyes darted from Jeffreys' eyes to his mouth as though to read his lips.

"Why?"

"Couldn't hurt. Might help."

Was he hinting at a deal? Ah, no, Jeffreys decided. He wasn't hinting at anything. He was just trying to make conversation. Why? Because this was a nice-cop, nasty-cop setup, of course. The nice cop was this schmo across the table hoping to con him into saying something useful while the nasty cop listened—maybe even watched—from somewhere else. He looked around the little room for a one-way window or a mirror. There was none. There wasn't even a big enough blemish on any of the dirty plaster walls to mark the hiding place of a camera lens or a peephole.

"You're wired," Jeffreys said. "You're a puppet. Your string-puller's listening from somewhere."

"Wired?" Sileski said, looking more flustered. "Puppet? Whattaya talkin'?"

"It's Quick, isn't it?" Jeffreys persisted. "He's on the other end, right?"

"Whattaya mean?" Sileski spluttered. "Quick who?"

"Go get him," Jeffreys said, leaning back in his chair and feeling suddenly calm, self-assured, in control. "Come on in, Quick. If I'm going to chat, it won't be with the corporal."

Sileski stood up, looking distressed. The door behind Jeffreys opened. A familiar voice said, "Okay, Corporal, you can go." Sileski walked around the table without looking at Jeffreys. He left. The door closed. Quick stepped around Jeffreys and the table, sat down across from him and smiled. It was a cold smile.

"So let's chat," he said.

"That was dumb," Jeffreys said. "The poor guy's way out of his depth."

"I suppose," Quick said. "It was a worth a try."

"So what happens now?"

"Up to you."

"Me? What do you expect from me?"

"Some answers."

"What are the questions?"

"How'd you find Charles Nelson?"

The question was a demand, Jeffreys decided. Quick seemed suddenly intense. Obviously, he really cared. His eyes were narrowed and fixed on Jeffreys' eyes. His mouth was small and tight, with little crease-lines radiating from its corners.

"By tracking down Cornie Nicora," Jeffreys said. He felt unaccountably at ease.

Quick nodded almost imperceptibly as though weighing the answer and finding it sound. Then he tried again.

"How'd you know where to look for Cornelius Nicora?"

Jeffreys considered, decided, plunged. "I had a tip," he said. "No, a dozen tips. More, maybe. One of them panned out."

"All from the same tipster?"

"Yes."

"Who?"

"The name wouldn't mean anything to you."

"Try me."

"Sometime, maybe. Not now."

"One of our people? Witness protection?"

"No."

"Is that straight?"

"It's straight."

"Good," Quick said. "And thanks." Jeffreys decided he looked relieved. "What's your connection with Chris Landgrebe?"

"Who?" Jeffreys asked, surprised.

"Christopher Landgrebe."

"Never heard of him."

"Sure?"

"Positive. Who is he?"

"A lawyer. Mostly defends heavies, mob people and such. Maybe your lawyer from Indiana hired him?"

"No. You probably already know he dug me up a local named Louis Lewis. Unless this Landgrebe's with the same firm."

"Nuh uh," Quick said. "He's not."

"So what makes you think I'm connected to him?"

"One of Landgrebe's investigators spent the afternoon checking you out. Female type named Shirley Holmes. Know her?"

"Shirley Holmes?" Jeffreys said, grinning. "An investigator? Really?"

"Really. She spent hours in the courthouse reading the charge affidavits and everything else in your file. Then she had the prosecutor's office PR people track down Lichterman so she could ask him personally whether your lawyers had filed a motion to let to bail that wasn't yet entered of record."

"Had they?"

"No. Lichterman says Lewis told him he will, but not until after arraignment. You didn't know that?"

"I wasn't sure," Jeffreys said. "Nobody tells me anything." Now he was feeling bitter again. "So what's with this Landgrebe? Why his interest in me?"

"I was hoping you'd tell me," Quick said. "Any thoughts?"

"Maybe," Jeffreys said, thinking about it. "My lawyer thinks whoever killed Cornie Nicora probably wants me dead, too. If so, maybe he hired this Landgrebe to keep him posted on where I am so he'll know where and when to run over me if and when I get out of the pokey."

"Makes sense," Quick said, digesting that. "Assuming, of course, you're not the killer." His eyes came up to meet Jeffreys' again.

"I'm not. Cornie was worth a whole lot to me alive and not a damn thing dead."

"I know," Quick said, waving a hand as though to dismiss the topic. "You told me."

"Van Til thinks the killer's been trailing me for months, hoping I'd lead him to Cornie."

"Interesting idea," Quick said. "You buy it?"

Jeffreys shrugged, said, "I can't believe I wouldn't have noticed a tail. But the timing of the killing makes me wonder."

"If your lawyer's right, you're better off in jail than running around loose."

"I thought of that," Jeffreys said. "Only I'm not sure the security's worth it. See, I don't like bars on my bedroom."

"I don't suppose."

Both men sat silent for a moment. Then Jeffreys said, "You have more chatting in mind?"

Quick shrugged, said, "Guess not. You told me what I came for. Your tipster wasn't one of our people, and you can't explain the Landgrebe interest in you unless somebody hired him to keep track of you. Right?"

"Right," Jeffreys said. "You didn't have a deal in mind?"

"A deal?" Quick looked blank.

"You didn't lure me here to offer me something?"

"Like what?"

"Like asking me did I want to be a decoy," Jeffreys said. "Like offering me a pass out of this dump to play bait for the guy who killed Cornie."

Quick sat silent, apparently considering the thought. Then he said, "How would I manage that?"

"Beats me. You're the government guy. I'm just a citizen caught in the system. You mean a federal agent can't pry a local prisoner loose from a local slammer?"

"Not from a murder rap. Not directly, anyway."

"What's that mean?"

"It means you've got an idea there," Quick said, thoughtfully. "Would you be willing? If I could arrange it?"

"Spell it out," Jeffreys said. "Drop the other shoe."

"Suppose I pulled some strings and got you rebooked from defendant back to material witness, like your lawyer suggested the other day? And then arranged your bail?"

"That would be nice. Can you do it?"

Quick shrugged. "Probably. Understand, you'd be a sitting duck if you're not Nicora's killer and whoever is really wants you dead."

"True," Jeffreys said, hoping his voice didn't betray the chill raising the hairs on the back of his neck. "I could live with that, no pun intended. You need a decoy so you can bag the guy that offed your witness. I need Cornie's killer caught so I can go back to Indiana and brood about my dead book. Sounds like there's something here for both of us. What I haven't heard you say, though, is that while I'd be playing bait, you and your people'd be covering my butt."

"We'd be trying," Quick said.

Jeffreys got the message. No guarantees. It'd be another witness protection attempt, akin to the one that hadn't worked for Cornie.

"When?" Jeffreys asked.

Quick studied the table between them for a full minute. Then he said, "Maybe soon, if I can sell the idea to Lichterman and he can sell it to his boss. You want your lawyer in on it?"

"Louis Lewis? No."

"It's your call," Quick said. "You don't want him involved, fine, but I'd need that in writing to cover my butt if ... unh ... things didn't work out."

"I understand," Jeffreys said, picturing what Quick meant by things not working out. He saw himself lying on a floor, like Cornie, with holes in the back of his head. He visualized a solemn assemblage of people at a formal inquiry investigating how a murder suspect had been sprung from jail to wind up a corpse himself. He sighed, erased the picture and said, "Let's do it."

Quick rose. He reached across the table to shake hands. His grip was not warm, Jeffreys decided. Firm, but not warm.

"We'll find out how good a salesman I am," Quick said, departing. "And how big a sucker, maybe, too. See you later, I hope." He left the door open.

"Goin' on for one, give or take," the guard said, in response to Jeffreys' question, slap-slapping back toward the holding cell. "I'm too damn old for this extra-duty shit."

VI
MANSLAUGHTER

Jeffreys was awakened by the stomp of heavy shoes clump-clumping down the corridor toward him.

Must be a different guard, this clump-clumper, he thought, sitting up on the cot and rubbing the sleep from his eyes with the backs of his hands. *He's not slap-slapping.*

"Mornin'," the clump-clumper said, pushing the tray through the horizontal slot. "Chow time."

"Morning," Jeffreys said, rising from the cot to take it. "What time is it?"

"Little after six."

"So it'll be a while," Jeffreys told himself, parking on the cot with the tray across his knees. Dried-out oatmeal again, he saw, and cold toast and black coffee. He lifted the mug to look for a note. There wasn't one.

The guard came back, after a time, clump-clumping to the cell door, halting, eyeing Jeffreys without apparent interest.

"I'll take the tray," he said.

Jeffreys stood up, shoved it through the slot.

"Any messages for me?"

"How would I know?" the guard said, turning away and heading back down the corridor. "I ain't no messenger boy."

Jeffreys shrugged, sank back onto the cot, tried to doze.

Then there were two guards outside the cell door, opening it, staring in at him. Neither was the clump-clumper. One
was bald, black, monstrous. The other was a bearded, long-
haired Latino of normal size.

"Hi," Jeffreys said, getting up and stepping through the
doorway. "What time is it?"

Neither man answered. Jeffreys fell in behind the giant
and trailed him down the corridor. The bearded guard followed. The three of them, Jeffreys decided, resembled a two-
man military escort marching a prisoner-of-war to a firing
squad.

The patrol dropped him off in the interrogation room
where he and Van Til met the inquisition team the afternoon
of his first day in jail.

Quick sat at the head of the table looking grim. The creases
showed prominently at the corners of his mouth. He waved
at a chair alongside him. Jeffreys dropped into it, wondering
why the solemnity.

"I couldn't get it done the way we agreed," Quick said, his
eyes boring into Jeffreys'. "Best I could do was deal the charge
to involuntary manslaughter with a recommendation for reasonable bail."

"You said—" Jeffreys started.

"—I know what I said," Quick cut him off. "Lichterman
wouldn't buy it. He said his boss'd eat him alive if he re-filed
you back to material witness." He shrugged, added, "I pushed
hard, but no go."

"What happens now?"

"Up to you," Quick said. "If you accept involuntary,
Lichterman asks the judge to set bail, and if it works, my
people bond you out, providing it isn't too steep for our
petty-cash fund."

"Otherwise?" Jeffreys asked.

"Otherwise you sit."

"My arraignment's Tuesday," Jeffreys said, thinking aloud. "I plead not guilty then, and I sit some more, at least until Louis Lewis gets the court to set bail, which is a low-probability shot on two murder counts. And if it works, maybe I still sit some more even after that if the judge puts my bond so high I can't make it."

"It's a rotten world," Quick said.

"Damned if it ain't."

"So what'll it be?"

"Involuntary," Jeffreys said. He stood up, thrust out his hand. "I may live to regret it. Or I may not."

"Vive la Jeffreys," Quick said without apparent humor. He took the outstretched hand, shook it. His clasp wasn't warm, Jeffreys told himself.

Quick said, "Now I need your disclaimer, in writing. It'll say you've decided to cooperate with federal and local authorities participating in an undercover investigation involving the killing of a protected federal witness. It'll say you make that decision of your own free will without coercion, threat, or promise of reward. It'll say you understand the risks involved, accept full responsibility for your own safety, waive all claims against and hold harmless the federal and local government agencies with whom you are cooperating. It'll say you chose not to discuss it with your attorney of record, Louis Lewis. And it'll say you instructed us not to advise him of your action."

"Draw it up," Jeffreys said.

"I already did," Quick said, taking a folded sheaf of papers from his pocket. "In quintuplicate. One for you, two for Lichterman, two for me." He unfolded the sheets, smoothed them out on the table, and shoved them toward Jeffreys.

Jeffreys read the typewritten top sheet carefully. Then he scanned the next four pages. They were copies.

"Got a pen?" he asked.

"But not a witness," Quick said. He stood up, walked to the door and opened it. The guards were lounging in the hall outside, Jeffreys saw when he turned his head.

"Get Lichterman," Quick told them. The Latino guard walked briskly off. Quick closed the door, came back, sat down.

"Listen," Jeffreys said, wondering if he was doing the right thing. He held a copy of the disclaimer. "I don't want Louis Lewis in on this, but can I mail my copy to Van Til?"

"Your lawyer in Indiana?"

"Right."

"I'd have no problem with that."

"He needs to know, just in case," Jeffreys said. "Somebody on my side needs to know."

"I'll tell you something," Quick said softly. "As of now, I'm on your side."

"Thank you for that," Jeffreys said.

"But don't be misled," Quick said. "You're still the enemy. One way or another, I consider you responsible for the death of a witness I was assigned to protect."

"Understood," Jeffreys said. "Only now we have the same goals of catching the SOB who killed him while keeping me alive."

The door behind him opened. Lichterman swept past him and walked around the table. He sat down next to Quick.

"Involuntary?" he asked, eyeing Quick.

"Involuntary," Quick said. "And reasonable bail."

"We'll recommend a hundred thou to the court."

"Make it ten. Our budget's tight."

"Fifty," Lichterman said. "Twenty-five per count. At ten percent, that means your guys post five thou, if the court approves. There's no guarantee of that, of course, and I'm not sure I like the idea, anyway." He eyed Jeffreys coldly. "Cutting this cat loose doesn't make sense to me, bait or not. If he gets snuffed or if he skips, I've got egg on my chin both ways."

"Fifty," Quick said, sounding resigned. "It's my job to see there's neither snuffing nor skipping. When?"

"Soon as we can make it," Lichterman said. He leaned back in his chair, ticked off the steps on the fingers of his left hand with the index finger of his right hand. "An hour or so for our paperwork. A half-hour to explain to the court in closet why we're doing this. A few minutes for the court to rule one way or the other. A half-hour to get the record brought up to date, if the court approves. A half hour for your people to go through the bond-posting procedures. An hour for the warden's office to check the paperwork and issue the release. That makes it noon or thereabouts."

"Let's get started," Quick said. He looked at Jeffreys. "You want to sign those disclaimers?"

"Why not?" Jeffreys said. He scrawled his name across the bottoms of the five sheets, shoved them towards Quick.

"You witnessed the signatures," Quick told Lichterman. "Want to initial them with me?"

"No way," Lichterman said. "I'm stuck with the arrangement if it backfires, but I'm not putting it in writing."

"Suit yourself," Quick said, initialing the papers. "Anyway, we've got a deal." He extended his hand. Lichterman took it, shook it perfunctorily. Both men stood. Lichterman walked around the end of the table, past Jeffreys, out the door and slammed it behind him without another word.

"I don't like him," Jeffreys said.

"I'm not wild about him myself," Quick said. He eyed Jeffreys. "Any questions?"

"Lots," Jeffreys said. "I've never been bait before. What do I do to attract the shark? How do I know when I'm about to be eaten? Do I get a gun to protect myself?"

Quick shrugged. "You do like I do," he said. He sat back down. "You play it by ear. And no gun. What would you do with a gun?"

"Protect myself."

"I'll be protecting you."

"Like you did Cornie?"

"Give me a break," Quick said. "I never lost one before."

"Was Cornie the witness-protection program's first casualty?"

"Classified," Quick said, the crease lines deepening around his mouth. "Need-to-know basis only."

"I need to know," Jeffreys said. "Who better?"

"I suppose," Quick said, the lines softening. "Okay. We lose one now and then. But not often."

"Thanks," Jeffreys said. He sighed. "So what's the plan?"

"No plan." Quick's eyes bored into Jeffrey's. "You leave here, and I keep track of you. With backup."

"Where do I go?"

"Other than staying in town, no rules. You're a citizen out of the slammer awaiting arraignment, remember? So you do what any citizen would do. You find a hotel or a motel or whatever. You eat, you sleep, you read the papers, you go for walks, you take in a movie maybe. You belly up to a bar if you're a drinking man, or not if you're not. Meanwhile, we'll be watching you wherever you go and whatever you do."

"Can I call home to see if everything's all right with my son and his Gramma?"

"Wouldn't any citizen do that?"

"I guess," Jeffreys said uncertainly. "And Bart Van Til?"

Quick shrugged. "Be careful what you say, though."

Jeffreys digested that. "You think my hotel phone might be bugged?"

"Your home phone, more likely. And your lawyer's, too. Depends on how the killer works."

"I don't understand," Jeffreys said, "but thanks for referring to the killer as a third party. It's your first time."

"What don't you understand?"

"You said depending on how the killer works."

"Oh. Well, if he's a contract man who works alone, the phones are probably secure. But if he's part of a mob operation, they've probably got taps on whatever lines you or somebody connected to you would use to contact your people or your lawyer or anybody else they figure you might call."

Good Lord, Jeffreys told himself, thinking about that. He'd thought a guy with a gun maybe looking for him to ... uh ... tie up loose ends was a rough go. But a group operation with his ... uh ... departure as its specific goal? He decided not to think about it.

"Do we know who it is I'm baiting?"

"Probably the guy in the security-guard uniform. Would you recognize him if you saw him again?"

"I'm pretty sure," Jeffreys said. "Huge guy with a walrus mustache and a heavy beard."

"Then," Quick said. "Maybe not now."

"Oops," Jeffreys said, getting the message. "Without the hair it could be tougher."

"We think he has a sidekick."

"Great."

"But maybe not."

"Nice you're so definite," Jeffreys said, "So I gather I'm to head for a hotel and check in and hang around and wait for a guy or maybe two guys to try to kill me? Is that about it?"

"That's about it," Quick nodded, his eyes still boring into Jeffreys'. "What we want is for our target or targets to find you and make his or their move against you so we can grab him or them."

"Alive?"

"Preferably," Quick said. "We'd like to talk to him or them."

"I'd like that, too," Jeffreys said. "Furthermore, I'd like to talk to him or them myself, if only to prove I can still talk."

"Let's plan on that," Quick said.

"Yes, let's. Have you done this before?"

"Done what?"

"This bodyguard gig. Following somebody around waiting for executioners to show up so you can interrupt the foul deed and save a valuable and deserving life."

"Never have," Quick said, dropping his eyes and rising from his chair. He came around the table. "See you noonish, Jeffreys."

"Sam," Jeffreys said, standing up.

"Sam," Quick said. "Oh, and if we run into each other, if you see me, that is, don't recognize me. Remember, I'm a stranger."

"A stranger?"

"A stranger," Quick said. He opened the door and started out.

"Wait a minute, Stranger," Jeffreys said. "I have another question."

Quick came back in, shut the door. "Shoot."

"Something's happened," Jeffreys said. "What is it?"

"Happened?"

"Happened. Until last night, you figured me as maybe a contract killer. Now you seem to have changed your mind. Why?"

Quick walked around the far side of the table, sat down again. "Maybe my people checked you out," he said, his eyes into Jeffreys'. "Maybe they gave me good reports on you from back in your bailiwick. Maybe they said your reputation labels you a straight though pushy newspaperman. Maybe I go along with the old saw that most leopards don't change their spots."

"Maybe," Jeffreys said, feeling the veteran reporter's sixth-sense conviction that there was more to be mined from this lode, and boring in to dig it out. "But that's not enough. You're hinting at a two-man murder team hired to exterminate Cornie Nicora and run some other errands. What's happened to make you think it may be a team? And what other errands?"

Quick sat silent for a moment. Then he dropped his gaze and sighed.

"I hate pushy newspapermen, but I guess you're entitled," he said. "Maybe my people have a mob informant in your bailiwick. Maybe he passed along some information on a couple of soldiers calling in back there to report a score on a contract hit here in Bloomburgh. Maybe he said they were then given further orders to find the contractee's stash."

"Aha," Jeffreys said. "A stash. That makes sense. The word was when Cornie disappeared into the witness protection program he had more than a million bucks salted away."

"So doesn't it figure that the people who wanted him dead also want his ... ah ... estate?"

"It figures. Did your informant ... Do we maybe have a line on who the two soldiers are?"

"I'm told they're out of East Chicago," Quick said. "I'm told they're called 'The Poo Boys', a couple of hoodlums named Alex Pucci, with a street name of 'Big Poo', and Sylvester Poodle, known as 'Little Poo'. I'm told they're tough customers, known to the local PDs back in your bailiwick, but with only minor rap sheets and no photos on file."

"Thanks for sharing that. You really think they're looking for me?"

"You're what we've got," Quick said. "And we see you as a double-dipper lure. We figure the killers want you dead so you can't identify Big Poo as the man you saw in Nicora's apartment, but first they want you to lead them to Nicora's stash like you led them to Nicora's hideout."

"You're pretty certain I was followed, then?"

"Aren't you?"

"I guess," Jeffreys said. "You said stash. Are we talking cash or jewels or securities or what?"

"Unknown," Quick said, getting up. "Money and or valuables. We think real valuable valuables, but we don't know."

"You didn't find anything in the apartment?"

"Right," Quick said. "We didn't find anything in the apartment. See you noonish." He left.

"Noonish," Jeffreys said. The guards were eyeing him. He sighed, fell in between them, headed back toward his cell.

No, they're not escorting you to a firing squad, he told himself, grinning at the way the three of them were marching in single-file lockstep again. *Or not directly, anyway.*

VII
THE ESCAPING

"You got a visitor," the voice said. A guard Jeffreys hadn't seen before scraped a key into the lock. "You wanta come outta there?"

"Gladly," Jeffreys said. "What time is it?"

"Ten, maybe. Somethin' like that."

It's too early, Jeffreys told himself, an alarm bell ringing in his head as he followed the new guard down the corridor towards the visitation room. There had to be a screw-up. Lichterman said noon or so. Quick said noonish. Being summoned two hours earlier must mean the deal fell through. Probably Quick was here to tell him no dice. Maybe the judge wouldn't go for involuntary manslaughter. Or maybe Lichterman's boss balked.

It wasn't Quick waiting for him in the little conference room. It was Fifi Malloy sitting there on the far side of the table.

"Hi," she said, smiling brightly as Jeffreys pushed through the door. "We need to talk." She was wearing the raincoat again, a khaki-colored, double-breasted affair. Its cut emphasized her slimness and its epaulets exaggerated her erect, almost military posture.

"So let's talk," he heard himself saying. He sat down across the table from her, saw water droplets clinging to the rain-coat. "Is it raining out there?"

"Yes, it is, if we have to make small talk about the damn weather." Fifi Malloy lowered her voice to a conspiratorial whisper. "You didn't really kill anybody, did you?"

"Of course not."

"The dead guy really is ... was Cornelius Nicora?"

"That's who he was, all right."

Fifi Malloy looked distraught. "So what the hell happens now?"

"Unknown," Jeffreys said. He fixed his eyes on hers. They were brown, he saw, not hazel like Edie's. "Maybe they catch his killer, maybe they don't. Maybe they can hang it on me, maybe they can't."

"I meant to the damn book," Malloy said, tossing her head setting her chestnut curls oscillating. "What the hell happens to it?"

"Thanks for your heart-wrenching concern," Jeffreys said. "I should've known it was the book you're worried about."

"Don't get touchy," Malloy snapped. "I'm here for you, too, Buddy. But you're damn right I'm worried about the book. I've ... we've got an investment in it."

That's true, Jeffreys decided. Aloud he said, "That's true."

"And in you."

"True again. I'm grateful for your interest. Got any ideas?"

"Just one. And I don't like it. Looks to me like the damn book's dead. Can you tell me I'm wrong?"

"Sure," Jeffreys said. "You're wrong."

"I mean can you convince me I'm wrong?" Malloy's eyes were into his again.

"The protagonist's dead, but his story isn't," Jeffreys said, trying to put conviction into his voice. "I'll write it without him."

"Shit," Malloy said. She shook her head. "Ordinary damn

third-party biographies of ordinary damn rotten bastards are a dime a damn dozen. Looks to me like we paid you a wad of money for something you can't deliver. So do we just write it off and forget it? Or is there some way to salvage the damn project?"

"Who says I can't deliver?" Jeffreys was still both as amused and repelled by her unladylike stringing of mild profanities as he'd been the first time she telephoned to tell him he had a damn good idea for a damned interesting book and Morrissey might be damned interested in his damn proposal.

"The coroner, for one. He says Nicora's too damned dead to collaborate. The criminal justice people for another. They say you're a damn killer they intend to keep in the slammer."

"Short term, maybe, no pun intended," Jeffreys said. "Not forever. If you're looking for a refund, forget it. First place, I already spent most of it. Second place, I still intend to write the book, as promised."

"As told to you by a damn dead man?" Malloy demanded.

"Could be. Who knows what Cornie confided to me before he died? I may have notes and tapes and memorized confessions that'll blow your mind when you read them."

"Great," Malloy blurted, looking pleased. Then her expression changed. "Wait a damn minute. Morrissey Publications does not publish phony quotes or made-up shit. If that's what you had in mind, forget it."

"Perish forbid," Jeffreys said. "My integrity's as good as Morrissey's, any day. What I'm saying is, I'm under contract to deliver Morrissey a book about the life and times of Cornie Nicora, and by God I'm going to fulfill that contract."

Malloy shrugged out of her raincoat, let it fall onto the back of her chair. She had great breasts, Jeffreys decided, striving to keep his eyes on her face. "That's a neat speech, but the fact is the damn book may not be worth publishing."

"I've got notebooks and tapes full of Cornie Nicora lore,"

Jeffreys said. "I covered him for ten years while he was a public official before the feds got him. I'm an experienced researcher, an expert interviewer, and a competent journalist. I intend to submit a manuscript faithfully chronicling the life and death of one big-time crooked bastard."

"But not the first-person story of a certified son of a bitch turned protected witness as told by him, alive and in his own words, to a former newspaper reporter who used to cover him."

"Not quite," Jeffreys acknowledged. "We'll have to settle for the former newspaper reporter's third-person version."

"Which at best might be marginally acceptable," Malloy conceded, her mental wheels obviously turning. "Only I happen to believe you don't have enough facts and figures and dates and details for a respectable novella, let alone a man-sized book-length."

"I've got a lot," Jeffreys said, hoping he sounded convincing. "And I'm planning on getting more."

"Where are the notes and tapes and files you've already collected?"

"Some are impounded," Jeffreys said, "in the suitcase the cops grabbed when they booked me. The rest of my material's safe at home."

"How about if you authorize me to collect the damned impounded stuff and get it all organized for you to write from when they let your ass out of here?"

"No need," Jeffreys said, a warning bell sounding in his head. "I won't be here that long."

"Your stuff at home, too," Malloy persisted. "I could catalog all your damned material and get it ready for you."

"No need," Jeffreys said again. "It's already in good order."

"I think I should go through it anyway. That way I could give you the benefit of a fresh damn perspective on whatever the hell's in it."

"Maybe," Jeffreys said, thinking about what else she might do with it. She could show her bosses at Morrissey what he had. If they considered it insufficient, they could write off the book and him. If they found his files did support a book, they could farm it out to another writer, maybe even to Fifi herself. "I'll get back to you on that. Meanwhile, thanks for coming."

"My damn job, man," Fifi said. She stood up, shrugged into her raincoat, walked around the table to pat him on the shoulder. "I'm only trying to help." She knocked on the door behind him. It opened immediately. "See you," she said, and left.

"Wanta head back?" the guard asked from outside the door.

"Why not," Jeffreys said, and followed his escort down the corridor to his cell.

⬛

Lunch came, a bologna sandwich on stale white bread, a cup of bitter, tepid coffee, and three pretzels.

"Noon, maybe," the guard said when Jeffreys asked, pushing the tray through the slot. "Somethin' like that." He slouched away silently, his shoes neither slap-slapping nor clump-clumping.

Jeffreys ate the sandwich dutifully, enjoyed the pretzels, washed everything down with the bitter coffee, and waited. And waited. And waited.

The noiseless guard came back, after a while, suddenly appearing at the cell door without betraying his approach.

"Wanta hand me the tray?" he said.

"Sure," Jeffreys told him, getting up off the cot and pushing the tray through the grill. "What time have you?"

"Lotsa time," the guard said. He chewed a toothpick. "One-thirty, maybe. Somethin' like that."

"I'm expecting callers," Jeffreys explained.

"Good luck," the guard said, and departed silently.

Jeffreys stood at the bars for a while. Then he sat on the cot again, wondering if his release had been sabotaged.

"I'd kill for a cigarette," he said aloud.

"Can't help ya," the silent guard said, clanking a key into the cell door lock. "I ain't a smoker."

"Me either," Jeffreys said, pretending he wasn't startled by the man's materializing. "I quit a long while ago, but every now and then I really miss that old nicotine boost."

"Tough," the guard said, swinging the door open. He was still chewing his toothpick. "C'mon out. Warden wants ya."

Jeffreys stepped through the doorway. He followed the guard down the corridor, hearing his own shoes tapping the concrete floor and marveling at the guard's silent walk. It reminded him of another hike behind an Indian guide trailing a herd of mule deer through Canadian Jack Pine deadfalls and fallen leaves that constantly crackled and crunched under his boots to spook the animals ahead, but gave off no sound at the passing of the Indian.

At the end of the corridor, the guard turned into a cross hall and stopped at a huge, barred, sliding door. He pressed what looked like a bell button alongside it. Beyond the door was a glass-enclosed room above floor level. Inside it were several desks topped with what appeared to be radio-control consoles, switching panels and a cluster of television monitors. Two uniformed policemen were chatting inside the room, their backs to Jeffreys and the guard. A third sat before one of the consoles talking into a hand-held microphone.

The guard pressed the bell button again. One of the chatterers looked around, nodded in acknowledgment, and moved to a switching panel. The door slid silently open. Jeffreys followed the guard through it, sensed the door sliding shut behind them.

The guard knocked at a conventional door, pushed through it, and led Jeffreys inside a smallish office filled with steel filing cabinets and a battered desk. The man behind it wore civilian clothes. He looked up, scowling. His suit jacket was rumpled, his shirt wrinkled, his necktie askew. There was a half-smoked cigar in his mouth. It had gone out.

"This Jeffreys?" he asked the guard.

"Right, Major," the guard said. "Want me to wait?"

"No need," the rumpled one said. The guard left, silently. "You Jeffreys?"

"That's me," Jeffreys said. "Sam for Samuel. Middle initial T. You would be the warden?"

"Affirmative. Major Hathaway. I've got a release order with your name on it."

"And about time, too," Jeffreys said. "You've got a lovely jail, Warden, but I've been looking forward to escaping."

The warden frowned. "Don't get smart with me, Mac. He rolled the cigar to the other side of his mouth.

"Sorry," Jeffreys said. "I was just trying to be pleasant."

"You find this a pleasant place?" Hathaway demanded. The cigar rolled back again.

"Negatory," Jeffreys said. "I find this a nasty place. See, I've never been locked up before. That probably explains my happiness at the imminence of my escape."

"Ummm," Hathaway said, the cigar clamped tight.

"It is imminent, isn't it?" Jeffreys said. "You are about to cut me loose, aren't you?"

Hathaway stared at him a moment, his eyes narrowed and his cigar sticking out of the middle of his mouth. Then his jaw softened, and he dropped his gaze to a stack of papers atop the desk.

"Damned imminent," the warden said. He rolled the cigar to the left corner of his mouth. "I get your John Hancock, you get back the personals we impounded when we booked you in, I issue the release, and you're outta here." He shoved the papers to Jeffreys' side of the desk, pointed to a signature line, held up a pen.

Jeffreys took it, bent over the desk, started to read the fine print on the form above the signature line, decided it was legal mumbo-jumbo certifying and attesting that he was who he said he was and that he was receipting for his personal valuables. He signed it, and straightened up again.

"Two more signature lines," Hathaway said. "Same places, next two pages. Did you really think I'd turn your stuff over to that woman just on her say so?"

"What woman?" Jeffreys asked, signing.

"The woman you sent to collect your gear."

"Dark-haired female in a double-breasted raincoat? Chestnut curls, brown eyes, big boobs?"

"That's the one. Swears a lot."

"Never heard of her," Jeffreys said, shoving the papers back.

The warden stared at him a moment, shrugged, picked up his telephone, punched a button on its base, and said into the mouthpiece, "I've got Jeffreys, Samuel T in my office. Bring me in his personal effects." He hung up.

A door opened behind Hathaway. A uniformed policeman came in carrying Jeffreys' trenchcoat, his hat and a paper bag. He cast an incurious look at Jeffreys, laid the items on the warden's desk, departed.

"How about my suitcase?" Jeffreys demanded.

"What suitcase?" Hathaway countered. He opened the paper sack, upended it, spilled out its contents, pushed them toward Jeffreys.

"I had a suitcase," Jeffreys said, wondering if Fifi Malloy had managed to get her hands on it somehow. "It had clothes, tapes, notebooks and a tape recorder in it." He began stowing the items from the paper bag in his pockets. The chain of keys, with Cornie's still on it, went into his left trouser pocket;

the penknife and coins into the right; the comb into the inside suit-jacket pocket. He picked up the wallet, unfolded it
to glance into the money compartment, saw bills, refolded it,
and stuffed it into his left-rear pants pocket.

"Never saw a suitcase," Hathaway said, the dead cigar jut-
ting from the right corner of his mouth. "No suitcase listed
on your inventory. Not going to count your money?"

"Do I need to?"

"Don't matter," the warden said, chuckling around the cigar. "You already receipted for it."

"My mom always warned me never to sign anything without reading it carefully," Jeffreys grinned, shrugging into his
coat.

"You shoulda listened to your mom," Hathaway said, grinning back. He stood up, took the stub of a cigar from his
mouth, pointed it at the door the guard had brought Jeffreys
through, said, "That's your way outta here."

"Thanks, Major," Jeffreys said, and headed for the door.

He expected to find Quick waiting outside it. Instead, there
was a cop he hadn't seen before. He was in full uniform,
including a visored cap. There was a nightstick in his belt, but
his holster was empty.

"Mr. Jeffreys?" the cop asked.

"That's me. Samuel T."

"This way, Sir." The cop headed off up the hall away from
the direction the guard had brought him.

Jeffreys followed. The hall ended at a locked and barred
door. The cop unlocked it and led Jeffreys into a chute he
recognized as a metal detector. It began boinging when Jeffreys
entered it. The cop stopped at the far end of the chute and
looked back questioningly.

"Keys," Jeffreys said. He took the key chain and penknife
from his pockets, tossed them to the officer from inside the
chute. The boinging ceased. He stepped out of the chute,

pocketed the keys and knife the cop gave him and looked around.

They were in a huge room lined with counters and alive with people. The cop stopped at the first counter. A young girl in a skirt and blouse smiled at him and handed him a revolver. He slid it into his holster, snapped the flap, headed away again. Jeffreys followed.

There was another door flanked by a row of floor-to-ceiling windows looking out onto the street. The cop shoved it open. They were outside. Jeffreys savored the sunshine, the fresh smell of the chilly wind, the sounds of the passing traffic.

The cop stopped on the sidewalk and looked him in the face. "Do you know where you are, sir?"

"Bloomburgh?" Jeffreys countered, feeling stupid.

The cop smiled. "Yes, Sir. But I meant are you oriented? I'm told you were brought here at night. In the dark."

"Ah," Jeffreys said, comprehending. "I see. No, I guess I don't know where I am."

"This is Pierre Street," the cop said, sweeping his hand toward the passing traffic. "It runs north and south. Two streets south there's a traffic light where Pierre intersects Highway Avenue running east and west. The downtown district starts four blocks west on Highway. Our parking lot is a block south of here on Pierre. Your car is in the far southeast corner."

"I see," Jeffreys said. "That's helpful. You're not coming with me?"

"No, Sir," the cop said, still smiling. "This is as far as I go." He turned and disappeared inside.

Jeffreys watched him go through the door. Then he stood there for another full minute, staring around, eyeing the passing cars and trucks in the street, scanning the sidewalk traffic for the familiar figure of Quick. He saw no one he recognized. He turned south. As he walked, the chill wind in his face, his back felt cold, naked, exposed. He glanced frequently behind him. There were people following him, hurrying along, heads down to protect their faces from the cold breeze. Were they on private errands? Or were they trailing him as benefactors, guardians, protectors, good guys? And might others, also on errand bent, be bad guys anxious to tie up a loose end or to trail him to Cornie's stash?

The parking lot was vast and filled with autos, pickup trucks, vans, recreational vehicles and a mini-bus. He spotted his car—in the southeast corner, just as the cop promised—from a long way off, zeroing in on the yard-long whip antenna standing up vertically from the hinge-crease of the trunk lid.

It took a while to get the engine going. The starter ground futilely. He hoped the battery wouldn't too quickly lose its oomph. A cylinder fired, and suddenly the motor caught, roaring in response to his foot upon the accelerator.

He dropped the gear-shift lever into drive and moved toward the parking lot's exit onto Pierre street, scanning the rearview mirror as he went. Nothing stirred behind him. He left the lot, turning southbound onto Pierre. From half a block away, he caught the flash of another car rolling out of the parking lot and turning onto Pierre. Was it a killer following him? A defender? Or was it just another motorist with problems and plans of his own who happened to be heading in this same direction with no interest in Jeffreys' course, destination, future or fate?

Jeffreys stopped for the light on Highway, turned west when it came green. Traffic was relatively light. He speeded up to pass a few cars, slowed again to be passed. His rearview mirror showed nobody behind him that stood out from the others. None seemed to match his pace before, during, or after the speed changes.

There was a Holiday Inn ahead on the right. He worked his way into the right-turn lane, drove into the entrance. Parked, he sat for a minute, watching. No car drove in behind him. Sighing, he climbed out and hit the door-lock button.

"AMEX," Jeffreys told the desk clerk. He flipped the gold card from his wallet, watched while the clerk ran it through the machine, slid it back into the wallet. He nodded in acknowledgment when the clerk penciled the route to his room on the paper map of the premises and drew a circle around the separate building housing 612.

On his way back to the car, map in hand and the room key in his pocket, Jeffreys thought about his suitcase and its contents. He was carrying it when the presumed security guard at Cornie's apartment had turned him over to the Bloomburgh cops. He still had it, he remembered, when Sankstone took him in. He unlocked his car trunk and raised its lid. There was the suitcase. He grinned in recognition of Quick's professionalism, and slammed the trunk lid shut again.

The map was easily followed. He drove to the second building on the left, parked near the entrance close to the covered walkway connecting it to the main building, locked the car, retrieved the suitcase from the trunk and pushed through the unlocked door.

There was nobody in sight when he entered the near elevator and punched the 6 button. There was nobody in the sixth-floor interior hallway when he disembarked. He found 612, unlocked the door, stepped inside and flipped the wall switch. The room looked familiar. But it wasn't *deja vu*, Jeffreys realized with a grin. It was *Holiday Inn*. He locked and chained the door, dropped the suitcase on the floor, walked over to the nearer of the two double beds, and collapsed onto it.

"I don't know if I'm bait," he said. "But I do know I'm beat."

VIII
MENTHOLYPTUS

It was dull in the motel room.

There was nothing worth watching on the swivel-based TV set bolted to the dresser, he decided, setting down the remote controller after punching his way through all the channels. So maybe a drink and a non-jail meal would be in order.

He felt his spirits lift at the thought.

He'd napped for a half-hour after locking himself in the room. Then he'd stripped off his clothes and stood for another half-hour in the shower, letting the hot water flow over him to wash away the grime and the sweat and the aches of recent days and a hard jail cot.

The call home had been awkward.

He told Serena where he was, assured her all was well, asked her how Geoff was handling high school, said to tell him he'd be home in a week or so, admitted he'd been saying that every time he called for the last month, insisted that this time he meant it, and hung up, feeling guilty. It wasn't as though he were intentionally neglecting his son, though, he consoled himself. It was just that he'd had to be out on the road as if he were a traveling salesmen or a professional ballplayer. Meanwhile, he told himself, his widowed mother-in-law made as good a home for him and the boy, whether

Jeffreys was there or off plying his trade, as any father and son could hope for after the death of their wife and mother.

Jeffreys' call to Bart didn't reach the lawyer.

"Mr. Van Til isn't available at the moment," Cile said. "May I take a message?"

"It's Sam Jeffreys, Cile. Is he out of the office, or just closeted with a client?"

"Oh, I'm sorry, Mr. Jeffreys. I didn't recognize your voice. Mr. Van Til's in court. Can I have him call you back when he comes in? I've no idea when that might be."

"No, thanks," he said. "Just leave him a note that I've been bonded out. Oh, and tell him I'm mailing him a memo he may find interesting."

He fished his copy of Quick's disclaimer from his coat pocket after he hung up, stuck it into an envelope from the nightstand drawer, scrawled Bart's name and office address across its front and sealed it.

Then it was time to leave the security of the locked motel room to enter the world of the killer that his release from jail was intended to flush out and upon whose successful baiting his future depended.

"Good luck, Quick," Jeffreys whispered, unchaining the door. The hair stood erect on the back of his neck. "And good luck, Sam."

The corridor was empty. He rode the elevator alone. There was nobody in sight when he stepped out on the ground floor and traversed the covered walkway to the lobby. He sensed nobody watching when he got there. He handed the envelope and a dollar bill to the desk clerk, raising his eyebrows to ask a silent question. The clerk, a telephone handset clamped to his ear, accepted it, answering the unspoken question with a nod and a grin.

In the shadowy cocktail lounge, Jeffreys followed a short-skirted, bosomy hostess to a corner table and sank gratefully into it with his back to a wall.

"Manhattan, rocks, please," he said, and began surveying the room for a familiar-looking figure or a sinister-looking one. In the semi-darkness, he saw neither.

The manhattan was nectar of the gods. The cheese spread and crackers on the snack tray accompanying it were ambrosia. The 1940's musical selections drifting softly from the piano bar at the far corner of the room were pleasantly nostalgic and soothingly melodious. The low hum of conversations among traveling men exchanging the vesper banter of a fading business day was soothing. Jeffreys sat back, sipping and chewing and listening, eyes half-closed in appreciation, enjoying.

Eventually, the glass was drained and the snack tray was empty and the pianist had switched to 1990's non-musical selections. The banter grew louder and coarser. No predator had moved to his table, but neither had a rescuer. Suddenly it was lonely and dull and time to escape the gloomy lounge with its clangorous non-music and its raucous laughter and its conversational din.

Jeffreys left a dollar tip, dropped a five at the cash register with the check, pocketed his change, asked directions to the dining room and headed toward it.

The glare of lights outside the lounge hurt his eyes until his pupils contracted to accommodate.

He squinted at the menu, seated in the overly bright dining room. He ordered a combination shrimp-and-steak dinner—medium-rare on the meat, tartar sauce with the shrimp—plus a second manhattan on the rocks. Then he looked around. There were no familiar figures and no sinister ones, he decided. He grinned, realizing he was disappointed at spotting neither threatening predator nor hovering rescuer.

The second manhattan wasn't as good as the first. Their combined buzz was dissipated by the meal, which was adequate but not great. The cherry pie was satisfactory, though nothing like Serena's. The coffee was hot and plentiful, but weak.

The check was modest. He counted out fifteen percent, left it on the table, surrendered his ticket and a twenty-dollar bill to the cashier, stared longingly at the cigarette packs stacked behind her, pocketed his change, and headed for the lobby. He bought a newspaper at the magazine stand and sauntered through the walkway to the elevator. He saw no followers and there were no fellow riders. He stepped out into a deserted sixth-floor corridor.

Feeling neglected, Jeffreys unlocked the door to his room. He pushed it open and stepped into darkness, fumbling along the wall for the light switch. The smell of eucalyptus and menthol assailed his nostrils.

Hall's Mentho-Lyptus lozenges, he realized in a sudden burst of recognition.

He dove backwards out onto the corridor floor, hauling the door shut as he dropped.

He rolled to his feet, raced down the hall to the elevators and stood there with his finger on the call button, staring back toward his doorway. His lungs heaved and his heart pounded.

Nothing stirred in the hallway. His door stayed quietly closed. The newspaper he had dropped in his hasty retreat lay crumpled in front of the doorway. The elevator came. Its doors shooshed open. He stepped inside, his eyes still on his doorway, his finger holding in the door-open button. After a time, he stepped out again. The elevator doors shooshed shut and the cage started down. He stepped slowly, quietly, deliberately back toward his room, his heart pounding and his neck hairs quivering, wondering what kind of an idiot would do what he was doing.

He stopped at the door. It showed no sign of forcible entry. He listened intently, hearing only the low background noise of a busy motel. Analyzing the meld of sounds, he separated them into discrete entities, inventoried them—the buzz of heating-cooling machinery, the hum of electrical transformers and fluorescent-fixture ballasts, the murmur of distant voices, the tangled cacophonies of TV musicals and talk show programs—all filtering together through the floors and the ceilings and the walls. From inside his room came only the sound of silence.

Taking a deep breath, Jeffreys picked up the newspaper. He fit the key into the lock as quietly as he could. He turned it, pushed the door open, and reached inside to snap the wall switch. The room flooded with light. It smelled of mentholyptus. He saw no occupant. There were only the beds, the nightstand between them at their heads, the dresser with the TV set bolted to its top a yard beyond their feet, the table, the chairs, his suitcase.

It was on the near bed, open. He had left it on the floor, closed.

Jeffreys took another deep breath, his heart still racing. He stepped inside, leaving the door open. He turned left into the tiny dressing room-bathroom area and flipped the switches on its wall. The overhead lights came on, illuminating the countertop sink, the mirrored wall, the closet alcove, the bathroom beyond. He saw no one. The only hiding place was behind the shower curtain in the tub. He walked to it, his throat tight. He thrust it aside with the rolled-up newspaper. It was empty. He felt a surge of relief.

Back at the bed, with the door closed, locked and chained, he saw that someone had pawed through his suitcase. The shirts, underwear, socks and pajamas were in disarray.

"Looking for what?" he asked himself, dumping the contents of the bag onto the bed. The tape recorder tumbled out atop the pile of wrinkled clothing, its loading door ajar. The cassette that had been in it was gone. So were the spares. Jeffreys felt through the little pile of clothes, didn't find them. Where were his notes, the three crumpled and creased spiral-bound stenographic notebooks into which he had for the past two years scribbled names and addresses and ideas and thoughts and remembered incidents of Cornie's career before his disappearance into the witness protection program?

"Ah, no," Jeffreys said aloud. "Not my goddam notes, yet."

He decided he needed Quick.

He sat on the bed, flipped the telephone directory from the night-stand drawer, thumbed through it to *United States Government*. He ran his finger down the listings to *Justice Department*. He looked under it for *Federal Bureau of Investigation*, didn't find it. He tried *Marshal*, found a number, dialed it. It rang in his ear, monotonously. He hung up.

"That was dumb," he told himself. "Quick's got to be right here, close by, waiting for the shark to take the bait."

He walked to his door, unlocked and opened it, peered down the hall in both directions. It was empty. He stepped out into the corridor and looked at his watch. It was 9:35.

"Help," Jeffreys shouted, at the top of his lungs. "HELP!"

Doors opened up and down the hall. People stared at him. A man in a green plaid sport coat and a yellow bow tie ogled him from 618. A woman holding a robe in front of herself peered from 621. Quick was framed in the doorway of 609.

"Hey, there, Stranger," Jeffreys said, pointing at him. "Could you help me get the alligator out of my bathtub?" He went back into his room, leaving the door open, and sat down on the near bed.

"What the hell was that all about?" Quick demanded, walking in and slamming the door behind him. There was anger in his voice.

"Somebody searched my room and rifled my bag and walked off with my things," Jeffreys told him. "Hell of a guardian, you are."

"What's missing?" Quick demanded.

"Audio tapes. Notebooks." Quick walked to the far bed and sat down on it, apparently digesting that. "Who'd break into my room to steal blank tapes and personal notes?"

"Somebody who didn't know they were blank tapes and personal notes," Quick said without looking at him. "Somebody who chose burglary over robbery."

He had a point, Jeffreys suddenly realized. If the thief wanted him dead, he might well have done him in, and then taken his things. Could the fact that the intruder hadn't done so mean he had no interest in killing him?

"You figure I'm not a loose end for Cornie's killers after all?"

"Not yet, probably," Quick said, shrugging. "Not until you lead them to whatever they're looking for or they find it without you." He fixed Jeffreys face with his eyes. "We're guessing, of course. But why the hell else was that lawyer's investigator so interested in you unless he's got clients who want something they think you either have or can lead them to?"

"Like Cornie's money," Jeffreys said.

"Makes sense," Quick said. "Did I tell you that high-living Charles Nelson had only six hundred and eighty bucks in his checking account? And less than a hundred in his wallet?"

"You didn't tell me anything," Jeffreys said bitterly. "You mean your people didn't find a safety-deposit box full of Cornie's cash someplace?"

"Negative," Quick said. "We found his lockbox, all right. It had his birth certificate in it, and his army discharge papers. Period."

"Aha," Jeffreys heard himself saying. "What is it your narcotics people are always reciting? Look for the money?"

"Follow the money."

"Follow the money. Right. But if Cornie's killers figure he had a wad hidden somewhere, and if they thought I might know where, and if they wanted to rifle my bag looking for a clue to its whereabouts, why didn't they do it before?"

"They couldn't," Quick said. "We had your bag. I personally put it back in your trunk just minutes before you walked out of jail and headed for your car."

Jeffreys thought about that. "You didn't check out what was in the bag?"

"Of course."

"Did you by any chance make copies of my notes?"

"As a matter of fact, we did."

"Could I maybe get copies of your copies when this thing is over?"

"Shouldn't wonder," Quick said. His smile faded. "Now it's my turn for the questions. Why'd you dive out of the room when you came back from dinner a while ago?"

"You saw that?"

"Let's say I know about it."

"How?"

"Never mind how. But try to understand that my mission is to protect you, not your room and not your belongings."

Jeffreys digested that. "I wouldn't have it any other way," he said.

"So why'd you dive out of the room?"

"I smelled him."

"Who?"

"The security guard. I mean the guy dressed like the security guard. The bearded monster we figure snuffed Cornie."

"You smelled him?"

"Right. I smelled eucalyptus and menthol in the room, like those super-strong cough lozenges guys with head colds suck to open their sinuses, or guys with liquor on their breath chew to cover it up. You can still smell it."

"True," Quick said, sniffing. "So? What's that got to do with the security guard?"

"He smelled like that in Cornie's apartment."

"You didn't mention it before."

"I didn't remember it before."

Quick got up from the bed, his forehead creased in thought. He sauntered over to a chair, sank down on it. "That might be helpful. If the guy's addicted to cough drops, maybe we can smell him coming. Meantime, though, he may've made a mistake. That could mean our bait-and-grab game is over."

"Care to explain that?" Jeffreys asked.

"Sure. People have been following you, presumably assuming you aren't aware of it as you weren't when you led them to Nicora. But now they've tipped their hand by tossing your room and lifting your tapes and the notebooks they saw you writing in while they were trailing you around. Was that a mistake? And will they quit following you when they realize it, figuring you're onto them now? Or will they keep on tailing you anyway, because you're their only lead to Nicora's goodies?"

Jeffreys thought about that. Then he said, "I bet you're a hell of a chess player."

"Nope," Quick said. "The game's too complicated."

"Hah," Jeffreys said. "So what do we do now?"

"What I do is fade out of here," Quick said, standing up and making for the door. "What you do is wait a few minutes and then head for the bar."

"The bar? What do I do in the bar? Have a drink and sniff around a little?"

"Why don't you have a drink," Quick said, letting himself out. "And sniff around a little."

IX
THE BETTER MOUSE-TRAP

The lounge was louder now. The piano was banging and its banger was belting out a show tune. Talentless patrons joined him in bellowing the lyrics. Talkative non-singers shouted their conversations over the unmusical cacophony.

Jeffreys stood inside the entrance letting his eyes accommodate to the gloom. There were as many empty stools as occupied ones at the bar. None of the people atop those in use looked familiar.

He walked to an empty stool, sank down on it, and eyed his bar mates. He counted seven lone male guzzlers scattered along the curved counter, plus a man and woman near the far end who were grinning blearily at each other. All seemed as uninterested in him as he in them.

"Jim Beam and water," Jeffreys told the bartender, dropping a five on the countertop. He accepted the glass the bartender placed in front of him, sipped, and swiveled on his stool to look around the room.

A man entered. He paused inside the doorway to peer about in the semi-darkness. Jeffreys recognized the green plaid sport coat and the yellow bow tie. It was the starer standing outside the doorway of ... 618, wasn't it, when he'd yelled for help a while ago? Could this be one of his followers? Not

Big Poo, from the size of him, but maybe Little Poo? It made sense the Poo Boys would be nearby, staking him out. This man didn't look much like a killer, but then, he asked himself, who does?

Jeffreys saw the man's eyes focus on him, saw the head bob and the grin of recognition, saw him start toward him.

Surely even a cold-blooded contract killer wouldn't try anything in a public place like this, Jeffreys thought. Would he?

He squeezed his glass, hefting its weight, wondering how effective it would be as a weapon smashed across the bridge of an attacker's nose in case the improbable actually were to occur, like if a gun or a knife were suddenly menacing him.

"Hi," the man shouted over the noise of the crowd as he reached the empty stool alongside Jeffreys. He grinned wider, sat down, asked, "Did you get the alligator out of your bathtub?"

"Sure," Jeffreys said, managing to grin back. He sniffed the air, testing it for mentholyptus. He got a whiff of cheap after-shave. "Only it turned out to be a crocodile."

"Scotch, rocks," the newcomer told the bartender. He thrust his hand at Jeffreys, said, "Lukeman, Herb Lukeman. I'm in office supplies. What was that all about, up there?"

"Jeffreys. Sam Jeffreys. I was hoping for somebody to play a little gin with. You'd be surprised how yelling for help turns up warm bodies."

"But you aren't playing gin," Lukeman pointed out.

"I picked the wrong guy to help me with the alligator," Jeffreys explained, sipping his bourbon. "No sense of humor and wouldn't play cards."

"Woods is fulla clowns like that," Lukeman said, sipping at the glass the bartender slid him. He seemed to be scanning the room.

"I guess," Jeffreys said, wondering what Lukeman was looking for. Big Poo? Quick? "You come here often?"

"Now and then." Lukeman's eyes were patrolling the lounge like a radar dish.

"Where's home?"

"Indianapolis," Lukeman said, his head swiveling.

"Nice place," Jeffreys said, feeling an alarm sounding in his stomach. Indianapolis? Headquarters for a salesman in the office-supplies field? Possible, but improbable, he decided. He stared at Lukeman, memorizing the V-shaped bare spot in the middle of his left eyebrow. A scar from some prior encounter with a sharp blade or a blunt object?

"I like it."

"Used to spend a lot of time there as a reporter," Jeffreys said, mentally groping for the names of some non-Indianapolis newspapers. "I covered eleven straight sessions of the Indiana legislature. Ran around with a couple of guys from the Indianapolis Inquirer and the Morning Bulletin."

"Small world," Lukeman said, sipping. His eyes stopped roving, settled on Jeffreys' face. "Buy you another drink?"

"No, thanks," Jeffreys said. "Bob Harper and Steve Dallas. Thought you might recognize their bylines."

"Don't think so," Lukeman said, sipping. "Know their papers, of course."

"Of course," Jeffreys said. He stood up, raked his change off the bar, pocketed it. Faking a yawn, he managed a grin at Lukeman, muttered, "My bedtime," said "good night," and departed.

Past the lobby, through the walkway, into the elevator, down the hall, and into his room he saw no followers.

There was a red light flashing on his telephone. He picked it up, wondering why Quick would be calling at this time of night.

"Sam Jeffreys in room six-oh-eight," he told the deskman who answered. "I think you have a message for me?"

"Yessir," the deskman said. "It was logged in at ten-ten.

You're to call room four-twelve. The calling party didn't leave a name."

"Thanks," Jeffreys said, wondering why Quick had moved two floors below the decoy he was supposed to be protecting. "Would you ring four-twelve for me, please?"

It wasn't Quick who answered.

"Fifi Malloy," her voice said in his ear.

"Hi," Jeffreys said, trying to cover his surprise. "You rang?"

"Damn right, I rang. Nearly an hour ago. You know what the hell time it is?"

"Elevenish," Jeffreys said. "How'd you find me?"

"By calling around. Did you know you were getting sprung when we talked this morning?"

"Yes. I thought I was, anyway. It wasn't certain, though."

"Why the hell didn't you tell me?"

"It was confidential," Jeffreys lied. "I couldn't—didn't—even tell my lawyer."

"I found that out. I called Louis Lewis when they told me you were gone. He's madder'n hell."

"When who told you I was gone?"

"Warden's office people. I went to visit you with a damn steak sandwich in my purse and found out you weren't there. Had to eat it myself."

"Thanks for the thought. When was that?"

"Around dinner time. Sevenish, maybe. I wanted to talk to you about the damn book."

"I'm sure. So how'd you trace me here?"

"I told you I called around. I started with Louis Lewis, tried your lawyer in Highland. I called your home to see if you'd checked in there. Then I started in on hotels and motels here in town, alphabetically, from the yellow pages. Would you believe there's a dozen of 'em before you ever get to the damn H's?"

"You called my home?" Jeffreys felt his blood pressure rise.

She'd bothered Serena, probably upset her, maybe even had Geoff worried. "And Bart Van Til?"

"I got a damn recording at your lawyer's office," Malloy said. "So I hung up. I talked to a woman at your house. I thought your wife was dead."

"She is. I hope you—"

"—You've got a damn roommate?" Malloy demanded.

"A housekeeper," Jeffreys said. "My mother-in-law. She keeps house for my son and me. I hope you didn't upset her. She's—"

"—Hell, no," Malloy cut him off. "I said I was an old friend wondering how you were, and she said you were out of town but expected home soon, and that was that."

"So you called around, and you located me, and then you moved into my motel," Jeffreys said. He heard the anger in his voice and didn't bother trying to cover it. "Too bad you couldn't get the room next to mine so you could really keep track of me."

"Just a goddam minute, Buster," Malloy said, and now he could hear the anger in her voice, too. "I've been living here since I hit town, if you call this living. You checked into my motel."

"Aha," Jeffreys said. "Sorry. I thought ... How about I buy you breakfast? We can talk then. Meet you in the coffee shop around eight?"

"Deal," Fifi Malloy said.

There was a knock on his door while he was in the bathroom.

"Who is it?" he called. "Fifi?"

"You wish," Quick's voice filtered through the portal.

Jeffreys let him in and shut the door behind him.

Quick was carrying a paper-wrapped package the size and

shape of a large cigar box. He parked on the far bed beyond the TV set, setting the package alongside him. Jeffreys peeled off his suit jacket, tossed it onto the near bed, plopped down beside it.

"Speaking of Mrs. Malloy," Quick said, "I don't like her hanging around you."

"Me either," Jeffreys said. "The woman's a nuisance. The problem is, she's got a legitimate interest in me and my future."

"I had in mind we don't need a jealous husband poking around," Quick said. He seemed embarrassed. "If we catch some guy following you, how do we know whether he's our mobster or her mister?"

"Ah," Jeffreys said, grinning at Quick's discomfiture. "No problem. The lady and I don't much like each other, but there won't be any jealous husband even if we did. She's a widow."

Quick digested that, looking relieved. He changed the subject. "It's not working," he said. "Nobody's chasing the bait."

"Maybe it is working," Jeffreys countered. "The guy in six-eighteen could be looking it over."

"Your drinking buddy? Forget him."

"How did you know I had a drink with him?"

"My spies are everywhere," Quick said, grinning.

"You were watching me?"

"Of course."

"I didn't see you."

"Of course not."

Jeffreys thought about that, shrugged, said, "He says his name's Lukeman. Herb Lukeman. He claims to be a traveling salesman from Indianapolis, but he isn't."

"Isn't what?" Quick demanded.

"Isn't from Indianapolis."

"Ah. And he isn't huge. And he doesn't smell of cough drops."

"True. You know him?"

"Shouldn't he smell of cough drops, if he were the one?" Quick persisted, ignoring the question and grinning at Jeffreys. "Wouldn't the guy you sniffed in your room a while ago still smell like cough drops?"

"Maybe this is the other guy."

"What other guy?"

"You said there's a team of them, Big Poo and Little Poo, like the big guy I saw and smelled when Cornie was shot and the little guy I didn't see."

"That's our information," Quick said. "It's not gold-plated, certified, and cast in concrete, though. We won't know whether it's solid until and unless they make their move on you."

"I suppose," Jeffreys said, feeling the frustration that Quick was implying. "You have any suggestions for hurrying them up?"

"Thought you'd never ask," Quick said. "As a matter of fact, I do. I believe we can force their hands with a better mousetrap."

"A what?"

"A better mousetrap. Tomorrow you'll go into the bank where Nicora had his safety-deposit box. You'll go in carrying only a newspaper, but you'll come out carrying something wrapped in it."

"What something?" Jeffreys demanded.

"This something," Quick said, pointing at the parcel on the bed alongside him. He picked it up, unwrapped a big cigar box, tossed its paper packaging into a wastebasket. "It's your better mousetrap, guaranteed to make a couple rats beat a path to your door."

"Aha," Jeffreys said, comprehension dawning.

"You'll smuggle it in under your coat, and then you'll carry it out for all the world to see."

"I dig," Jeffreys said. "If I'm being trailed, my trackers'll figure I've found Cornie's money and they'll knock me off and take it away from me, and that'll bring them out in the open so you can nab them and send my remains home for Christian burial. Right?"

"Partially right," Quick said, not smiling. "Hopefully, the knock-you-off and home-for-burial parts are wrong. Hopefully, we'll grab your assailant or assailants before he or they can hurt you."

"A situation greatly to be desired," Jeffreys said.

"More realistically, though, you likely won't even be on the scene when they grab the box. What we expect is for them to snatch the box from your room while you're out of it."

"Only this time you'll be watching it," Jeffreys said. "I'd like that. Can you arrange it?"

"I can wish it, and you can make it possible," Quick said, getting to his feet. He picked up the cigar box, handed it to Jeffreys. "This is the mousetrap." He took a key from his jacket pocket. "This fits safety-deposit box eleven-thirty-seven in the Edgewater Bank on Highway Avenue and Eighteenth Street. You will arrive there at eleven a.m. carrying the mouse trap under your coat and a newspaper in your hand. You will sign the register and go into the vault. When the clerk gives you the lockbox you will take it into one of the privacy rooms. You will wrap the mousetrap in your newspaper. You will leave the bank carrying the newspaper-wrapped package— out in the open for all to see—and bring it here."

"I hope I get this far with it," Jeffreys said, taking the package and the key. The number 1137 and the maker's name, MOSLER, were stamped into it, he saw. It bore no bank name or other identification.

"We think you will. We don't believe they'll bother you in public, but we'll be there watching, just in case. Drive back to the motel and bring the package up here to your room. Then leave it here and go out for some lunch."

"Sounds simple," Jeffreys said. "I hope I'll be in condition to eat."

"Plan on it," Quick said. He started for the door, stopped,

said, "Any questions?"

"A couple," Jeffreys said. "Whose name do I sign on the lockbox register? Mine? Cornie's? Charles Nelson's?"

"Good catch," Quick said. "I guess I'm getting old. You'll sign in as Charles Nelson. Anything else?"

"Yes. Isn't that box kind of small for a million-dollar stash?"

"Maybe. Or maybe it's full of ten-thousand-dollar bills. If you were trailing a man you figured just picked a money tree, would you pass up a package that size?"

"I guess not," Jeffreys said. "Is it true Cornie entered your program with a million-plus stashed away?"

Quick shrugged. "The IRS boys thought so, but they didn't find it and neither did we. The way he lived, though, he had to have lots of big bucks available."

"How about his job here. Didn't it pay well?"

"Peanuts. His salary covered his apartment rent and not much more. Yet he ate in fancy restaurants, bought five-hundred-dollar suits, even dropped a bundle now and then on high-priced female companionship."

"Sounds like the Cornie I knew, all right," Jeffreys said, grinning. "He was a big spender, but only on himself. Tightest man I ever knew, otherwise. Did he ever buy you coffee?"

"You kidding?" Quick shook his head. "If we had coffee, I paid. Cheapest SOB I ever met." He strode to the door, opened it a crack, peered into the hall. "Remember, we're still strangers, you and I. If you pass me on the street or anywhere, you don't know me."

"As you wish."

"And no more yelling for help to get alligators out of your bathtub, either."

"If you say so," Jeffreys said.

"I say so," Quick said. "Let's get this over with."

"Right," Jeffreys agreed, nodding vehemently. "Let's."

X
THE BAITING

Traffic was heavy. He drove past the bank. There was no place to park. He drove another two blocks, conscious that he'd have to hurry to make his 11 o'clock arrival deadline, and turned off Highway Avenue onto a street whose sign read 18th. Cars filled every parking site on both sides of the street. There seemed to be nobody following him, neither killers nor guardians. There had to be both, though, unless he was wasting his time. So, assuming he managed to find a parking spot, where would they park?

They wouldn't, he answered himself. They wouldn't have to. The killers and the guardians were teams, each with a designated driver to drop off the walkers and then circle the block as long as necessary before picking them up again. *Only you are alone,* he reminded himself, *required to drive, park, walk, pose as bait for one of those teams, and hope to hell the other team doesn't blow it.*

Maybe he should've brought Fifi Malloy along to chauffeur him, he mused. That would've solved his parking problem. She could drop him where he wanted to go and pick him up whenever he was ready. She'd have been willing if he'd asked her, eager to keep track of him and his activities. She'd admitted as much at breakfast.

She'd beaten him to the coffee shop.

She was chatting with the cashier when he got there, leaning on the steel stand supporting the cardboard sign directing patrons to Please Wait to be Seated. It was the first time he'd seen her standing up without the figure-shrouding raincoat. She was wearing a green sweater over a red skirt. The sweater was well filled, drawn taut across her breasts by the up-and-back thrust of her sergeant-major shoulders. The skirt was tight across her hips.

"About time," she said. "Where the hell you been?"

"It's just eight," he said, looking at his watch.

"So why wait until the last damn minute?" she said, winking at the cashier.

They followed a waitress to a table. Jeffreys held a chair for Malloy, pushed it into place and sat down facing her. Ignoring the enormous menus the waitress left on the table, he asked, "What sounds good?"

"I'm a ritual breakfaster," Malloy said. "Ever since college."

"I guess we're all creatures of habit," Jeffreys said. He nodded to the waitress coming up beside him with a coffee carafe, her eyebrows raised in question. She filled his cup, set the carafe down in response to Malloy's negative head shake, eyed Malloy expectantly, pencil poised over her pad.

"Rye toast, peanut butter, and a pot of green tea with a lemon slice, please," Malloy said.

"Yuck," Jeffreys said. "I'd like orange juice, please. Two eggs over easy, bacon, white toast buttered. With honey if you have it or jelly if you don't."

"We do," the waitress said, and departed.

"So," Malloy said, leaning her chin on her hands, her elbows on the table top. "How the hell'd you get out? The jail people said you made bond, but Louis Lewis told me you weren't bondable."

"I wasn't," Jeffreys said, sipping his coffee. It was too hot to drink. "Not until they reduced the charges from murder to manslaughter, that is. Then I was."

"How big's your damn bond?"

"Fifty thousand."

"Jesus. You carry that kind of money?"

"No. But it's only five thousand cash."

"You carry that kind of money?"

"No. It was posted for me."

"By whom?"

"Government people," Jeffreys said, wondering if it was supposed to be confidential. It wouldn't be a secret in Indiana where bail bonds were matters of public record, but here?

"Government people?" Malloy echoed. She seemed upset. "Why the hell would government people bail you out of their jail?" Her voice rose. "What the hell's going on?"

Jeffreys saw heads turn their way at her outburst. He decided to explain.

"Shhh," he said. "Different government people. Not the locals. There's a federal agent believes my story. He went to bat for me."

Fifi Malloy's eyes showed her interest. They fixed on his and stayed there while the waitress set down their dishes.

"Are we talking about Quick, the federal guy that was supposed to protect Nicora but didn't?" she demanded, when the waitress left.

Jeffreys nodded, impressed at the way she'd done her homework. He sipped his orange juice. It tasted fresh-squeezed.

"Why'd he go to bat for you? What the hell's in it for him?"

"Maybe he likes me."

"Bullshit. Sankstone says Quick got his tit in the wringer with his own people over Nicora's killing and blames you for it, even if you weren't the actual shooter."

"Eat your breakfast," Jeffreys said, setting down his glass and picking up his fork. "If you can stand it, that is. Rye toast and peanut butter. Yuck." He dug into his eggs.

"What kind of a damn deal have you got going?" Malloy demanded. She picked up a piece of toast, knifed a dab of peanut butter onto it from the paper cup on her plate, and bit into it, her eyes never leaving his.

Jeffreys decided not to postpone the unpleasantness any longer.

"Look, Honey," he said, his eyes boring back into hers. He laid down his fork, leaned closer to her and lowered his voice. "I'm glad to see you're not the innocent little cutesy foul-mouthed bubblehead you'd like the world to think. I'm impressed with the way you've worked the news sources and pieced the facts together since you got here. But get off my back and get off my case and get back to your desk and your computer and your telephone. I owe you and your people a book. I'll do my best to get it to you. Meanwhile, I'm in big-time trouble, I'm doing what I can to get out of it, and what I don't need is you following me around asking me what I'm doing every step of the way."

"It's my job," Malloy said, her eyes in his.

"So do it someplace else."

"I can't. Wherever you are is where it is. You're my job, Buster. Like you said, you owe me and my people a damn book. I'm the horse's ass who bought that damn book. Ergo, if my people don't get what they paid for, I'm screwed, too."

"They'll get it," Jeffreys said.

"Damn right they will," said Fifi Malloy. "One way or another."

"Meanwhile," Jeffreys said, "you could louse me up."

"How?" Malloy demanded, a chunk of peanut-buttered toast poised halfway to her mouth. "What's to louse up?"

Jeffreys sighed. He decided a fragment of an explanation wouldn't hurt anything and might scare her into backing off. "We're hoping the killers are still around."

"Why?"

"We want them to show themselves."

"Why should they?"

"Because they think I've got something they want."

The toast moved into Malloy's mouth. She chewed quietly, apparently digesting his comments. She swallowed, took a sip of tea, set her cup down. "You keep saying killers with an S, and they and them. It's not just a him?"

"We think two guys. We don't know for sure."

"And you're *bait* for them?"

"You could say that."

"You're hoping they'll try for you, too?"

Jeffreys nodded, took a swallow of coffee, his eyes on hers.

"Jesus. If they get you, how're you going to deliver me my goddam book?"

"If we get them, I'll have a better shot at writing it," Jeffreys said.

"I see," Malloy nodded. She looked grim. "Quick's got you out on a damn string hoping the turkeys that killed Nicora'll try to do you, too?"

"Something like that."

"And you're gambling that the goddam wimp who couldn't protect Nicora can protect *you*."

Jeffreys nodded.

"Jesus," Malloy said again. She smeared peanut butter carefully, deliberately, onto half a slice of rye toast. She picked the toast up, stared at it, put it back down on her plate. She looked into Jeffreys' eyes, shook her head. "Jesus. You need a goddam *keeper!*"

"Maybe," Jeffreys said. "What I don't need, though, is you hanging around to maybe scare off the killers and maybe screw up the deal and maybe get yourself killed doing it."

"And what I don't need is a stupid damn jerk who owes me a book crossing streets in heavy traffic wearing a blindfold," Malloy said, her eyes into his. "Get used to me hanging around, Buster. I've got an investment in you."

"Conceded," Jeffreys acknowledged, his voice rising. He stood up, aware that heads were turning their way again. "But I've got a bigger one. Leave me the hell alone so I can do what I need to do to stay alive and out of prison and have a shot at writing your goddam book."

He dropped a twenty-dollar bill on the table, tossed his napkin atop it, and strode to the doorway. When he looked back, Fifi Malloy was dabbing peanut butter onto rye toast.

Coming around the block onto 18th Street for the third time, Jeffreys spotted a car pulling out into traffic on his side of the street. He speeded up, braked past the vacancy, and backed into it.

Sighing, he clamped the cigar box between his left upper arm and his chest under his trenchcoat, plucked the folded newspaper from the car seat, shoved it into his coat pocket, climbed out of the car, locked the door, pushed a dime into the parking meter, and started hiking back.

It was cold walking. The wind was in his face, stiff and chill. The sidewalks on each side of the street were peppered with people heading in both directions, all bowing into the breeze or away from it. Jeffreys kept sneaking looks behind him for followers. Nobody seemed to be paying any attention to him. The box under his arm pressed into his chest, its corners biting his flesh.

It was a bit warmer on Highway Avenue where store buildings blocked the wind. He walked on, wondering if he were heading into danger as his instincts told him, or not, as Quick had assured him.

He entered the bank. A blast of hot air washed across his face. He started to unbutton his trenchcoat, thought better of it, squeezed the box tighter under his arm and looked about

for the safety-deposit area. It was in the far corner of the squarish building, an overhead sign told him. He headed toward
it, conscious of the steady flow of people around him. He
flipped his wrist up to look at his watch. It read 11:01. He
hoped he wasn't too late.

"I need to get into eleven-thirty-seven," he told the lady
clerk who eyed him quizzically when he stopped at the desk
under the sign.

"Would you register, please?" she said, pushing a card into
the slot of a time-and-date stamping device and then handing it to him. He did, scrawling *Charles Nelson* with the ball-
point pen at the end of a chain attached to the desk.

The clerk looked at the signature, nodded to herself, looked
at him expectantly, her hand extended toward him.

"Something wrong?" Jeffreys asked.

"I'll need your key."

"Of course," he said, feeling foolish. "I'm sorry." He fished
the key from his trouser pocket and handed it to her, squeezing the cigar box more tightly against his chest.

"This way, please," the clerk said, turning toward the grilled
gate behind her. She pushed a button on her desk. The lock
chattered, and the gate went ajar. She retrieved a set of keys
from a bin atop her desk and walked into the vault.

Jeffreys followed her inside. He felt the hairs rising on his
neck, imagined eyes burning into his back.

The clerk stopped before a wall of numbered steel pigeon-
hole doors. She ran her eyes up and down their ranks. She
pushed Jeffreys' key into a keyhole, stuck a second key into its
twin, turned both, swung a little door aside on its hinges.
She slid a covered steel box out of its recess and handed it to
Jeffreys.

"You'll want to take it into a room?" she asked.

"Please," he said. The steel box was unexpectedly heavy.
He stuck it under his left arm, squeezing it against the wooden

box concealed beneath his coat.

Inside the little room with the door closed, he set the lock box on the table fastened to the wall, lifted the lid, peered inside. There was a brick in it. Grinning, he fumbled the cigar box out from under his coat, opened it, stuck the brick inside, closed it again, and wrapped it in the newspaper. He counted to fifty. Then he opened the door and paraded self-consciously out into the vault area, carrying the lock box with the newspaper-wrapped package clearly visible atop it, wondering who was watching.

The clerk took the lock box from him, slid it into its slot, shut the little door, withdrew the keys, and handed him one.

"Will there be anything else?" she asked.

"No, thanks," he said, He pocketed the key, stuck the package under his arm and started for the door, wondering who was watching.

He stepped outside into the sudden chill of the cold October air, wondering who was watching.

The sidewalk traffic was heavy. The traffickers were anonymous. They passed him, preceded him, followed him with their heads down, their faces expressionless, their features unfamiliar as he retraced his steps toward his car, wondering who was watching.

Over his shoulder he saw a fast-walking fat man in a leather jacket and a corduroy hat seemingly intent on overtaking him. Jeffreys decided this would be the package grabber. He steeled himself to drop, jab a knee into the groin, punch a fist into the face, whatever seemed appropriate when the attack came.

It didn't come.

The fat man jostled him in passing, mumbled an apology, made no move to snatch the package, and hurried on through the crowd ahead.

Jeffreys felt the cold wind whip him from behind as he turned the corner onto 18th and left the protection of the buildings lining Highway Avenue. He drew his coat closer around him, squeezed the package more tightly under his arm, and walked steadily toward his car, his eyes scanning the faces of pedestrians approaching him, the backs of those ahead of him. *Strangers,* he told himself, *all strangers,* at the same time relieved and disappointed.

The parking meter showed six paid-for minutes remaining when he reached his car. He fumbled the key into the door lock, climbed in, tossed the package onto the seat beside him and shut the door. Then he surveyed the street.

Pedestrians continued to plod past, their heads down. None paid any attention to him. Cars rumbled by, their drivers braking, accelerating, honking. None looked at him.

He started his engine, flipped on his left-turn signal, waited for a break in traffic, and pulled out into the stream of cars. Only one driver seemed to notice him. That one waved from behind his windshield, grinned, and pulled into the parking place Jeffreys vacated.

Jeffreys drove to the motel without incident. He parked, took the newspaper-wrapped package from the seat beside him, climbed out, and peered about the parking area for watchers. He saw none. Vacillating between relief and disappointment, he walked into the building, into the elevator, out of it, down the hall, and paused before his room to fumble the key from his pocket. Swinging the door wide, he looked inside. It was empty. He sniffed the air. It smelled of nothing.

He tossed the package onto the dresser alongside the television set. He shrugged out of his overcoat, hung it in the clothes rack. He went into the bathroom. Emerging, he took the package from the dresser and placed it on the near bed to be easily visible from the hallway outside the room. Leaving, he closed the door loudly behind him for the benefit of any possible listeners, and went to lunch.

The bean soup was good, the corned beef on rye excellent.

He washed the last morsels down with the final swallow of coffee, paid his check, looked for followers, recognized none and headed for his room. His watch told him he'd been gone just over a half hour.

A half hour isn't a lot of time in the eternity of the universe, he mused, riding the elevator upwards. But maybe it was enough. In that fractional flash of cosmic infinity, the bait could have been taken, the takers grabbed, the ordeal ended, his life put back on track.

He flicked his eyelids shut in silent prayer as the elevator cage opened. Stepping out into the empty hallway, he walked expectantly to his room.

His door was closed. He took a deep breath, unlocked it, pushed it ajar, reached inside to snap on the light switch, and sniffed. There was no scent of mentholyptus.

He swung the door wider, peered in. The package lay on the near bed, exactly as he had left it.

"Well," Sam Jeffreys said. "Shit!"

XI
THE POO BOYS

Sam Jeffreys lay on the bed nearest the door, trying to keep his mind on the college football hoopla displayed on the TV screen. His necktie was pulled down, his shirt collar unbuttoned, his suit coat bunched up under his shoulders.

"Who?" he challenged, muting the audio with the remote controller when he heard the knock.

"Me." It was Quick's voice.

Jeffreys let him in, glanced both ways down the hall, saw nobody, swung the door shut.

"Nothing?" he asked. "No takers? No followers? Nothing?"

"Nothing," Quick said. He went to the far bed, peeled off his suit jacket, tossed it at the headboard and settled his shoulder holster more comfortably under his left armpit. He collapsed onto the bed. Bunching the pillows up behind him, he leaned back against the headboard and closed his eyes.

"So what do we do now?" Jeffreys demanded, sitting down on the other bed again.

"We wait," Quick said.

"For what?"

"For our guys to make their move."

"Or not," Jeffreys said, letting his fears surface. "How do we know they're still around?"

"We don't, for sure."

"That's great," Jeffreys said, pulling his feet up onto the bed. He leaned back on his arms, his elbows locked, sitting spraddle-legged, his head twisted to glare at Quick. "That's really neat. They're probably long gone."

"I don't think so," Quick said calmly. He opened his eyes, fixed them on the TV screen. "It doesn't figure they'd leave with Nicora's stash still unfound and you still around to identify his killer."

"That's not real comforting. Do you realize my whole future hangs on the stupid hope that two hoodlums'll show up to either kill me dead or steal a stupid cigar box it was your stupid idea to have me haul back from the stupid bank?"

"It wasn't stupid."

"Hah."

"Listen," Quick said. "I'm betting they watched you pick the package up at the bank, trailed you back here with it, and then called their people for instructions."

"Balls. That's wishful thinking."

"These guys are professionals. They're disciplined. They keep in touch with their bosses, report in when anything changes. Right now, I'm betting they're on the telephone getting new orders even as we speak."

"You wish."

"I'm reasonably sure. When you go to supper tonight, they'll probably pop in here looking for the package and we'll nab 'em and that'll be that. Meanwhile, get off my back. I want these guys as much as you do. Maybe more. So relax and shut up and watch the football game."

"Maybe you can relax," Jeffreys said. "I can't. I'm too ..." He didn't finish the sentence or the thought, interrupted by the sudden sound of the door bursting open.

He turned his head to face it and went rigid.

Two men lunged into the room, slamming the door shut behind them. One was huge, tall and heavy. The other was smaller, short, almost skinny. Both brandished automatic pistols. Their muzzles were pointed toward him and Quick.

Reflexively, Jeffreys leaned forward in his sitting position to take his weight off his arms and raised his hands over his head. The scent of mentholyptus assaulted his nostrils. His brain raced.

The Poo Boys, he told himself. *These are the hoodlums from East Chicago, these characters in rumpled suits and wrinkled neckties and shapeless hats. The huge hunk of meanness on the right is Big Poo, the guy in the too-tight guard suit at Cornie's apartment, only now without the beard. And the little guy with the two-day whisker stubble and the grease stain on his shirt has to be Little Poo.*

The pair strode toward him, their guns leveled. Little Poo took two steps for each of Big Poo's, Jeffreys noted.

"Hey," the little man yelled. He jerked his gun at the dresser. "Ain't that it?"

"Grab it," the big man said. "And haul ass."

Little Poo dove toward the dresser, seized the newspaper-wrapped cigar box from alongside theTV set, turned, and ran for the door. It swung forcibly inward just as he reached it, knocking him backwards onto the floor.

Through the doorway came Jeffrey's drinking companion of the previous night. He was brandishing a snub-nosed .38.

Little Poo fired from where he lay, three times in quick succession. The reports were loud. Lukeman's face showed surprise, distress, went blank. His eyes glazed and he pitched forward onto the floor.

Little Poo scrambled to his feet, ran out the open door, his gun in one hand, the package clutched in the other.

"My God!" Jeffreys heard himself yell, his hands still over his head. "He's killed him!"

"Don't," the big man rasped, looking beyond Jeffreys. His gun exploded twice.

Jeffreys' mind went blank. Propelled by his hands and his legs, he launched himself at Big Poo standing alongside him.

His knees caught the big man in the midsection, knocking him over backwards. Jeffreys' elbow bumped the pistol, knocked it free. He hit the floor hard, feeling the gun beneath him pressing into his back. Grabbing it, he swung himself into a sitting position and raised it to shoot.

There was a momentary glimpse of a moving body and then it was gone, vanished through the open door beyond the prostrate form of the man he'd known as Herb Lukeman. He heard running footsteps pounding heavily down the hall toward the elevator.

Jeffreys climbed to his feet, clutching the gun. He turned toward Quick, still on the bed with his back against the headboard. Quick's right hand clutched the butt of his gun, half withdrawn from its holster. His eyes were closed. There were two holes in the front of his shirt. Blood was seeping from them. He didn't seem to be breathing. Jeffreys ran to Lukeman, bent over him, felt for a throat pulse. He found none.

Faces stared in at him from the hall. Fingers pointed. There were voices, running footsteps growing nearer. A bareheaded man in a wrinkled suit burst into the room. His eyes were wide and his face was pale.

"Jebbens, hotel security," the man panted. "Put down the gun." He reached inside his jacket.

"Freeze," Jeffreys said, pointing the pistol at the newcomer. He raised his voice, shouted, "Out there in the hall. Somebody call an ambulance and the police. Do it now!"

"Don't shoot," Jebbens cried, his arms raised obediently. "Gimme the gun and I'll testify you—"

Jeffreys didn't hear the rest. He bolted from the room, down the hall, past wide-eyed gapers, looking for Big Poo's running figure, not seeing it. The elevator door stood open. He ran into it, punched the 1 button. Downstairs, there was no Poo in sight, Big or Little. Jeffreys slid the gun into his jacket pocket, raced out the door fighting panic. He looked for a car speeding out of the parking lot, didn't see one. He ran to his own car, unlocked it, climbed into it, started it, squealed his tires on the way out of the lot and into the early afternoon traffic. He scanned the cars ahead of him, looking for ... what? He was blocks away when he met an incoming ambulance and two police cars, their emergency lights flashing and their sirens screaming.

Fifteen minutes later, his gas-gauge needle flickering over the empty mark, he pulled into a Howard Johnson parking lot, still fighting panic.

"Just one night," he answered the clerk. He started to write *Sam* on the guest-record card, changed it to *Steve*, added *Jefferson*, and dropped three twenties onto the counter top.

After a short elevator ride, with the door to room 316 locked and chained behind him, Jeffreys collapsed into the only easy chair, his mind a blur.

Four people dead, he screamed silently. *They'd all be alive if I'd stayed home and minded my own business and never met Cornie or tracked him here or thought about the book, the goddam book.*

After a bit, he started asking himself quiet questions.

Did Quick and Lukeman have families, kids, dependents?

Would Sankstone or Lichterman believe his story of the hotel-room shootings?

How long could he survive as Steve Jefferson with twenty-two dollars in his pocket, his only liquid assets the credit cards of a wanted man named Sam Jeffreys?

How interested were the Poo Boys in tracking him down for stiffing them with a boxed brick, or in trailing him to Cornie's stash, or in erasing him as an eye-witness to their multiple murders?

After a time, he forced himself to stop thinking. He got up from the chair, sat down on the bed, took the pistol from his jacket pocket and examined it.

It was a lightweight, blue steel, hammerless model, nicely

made, well balanced.

He worked the clip release on the bottom of the grip, removed the magazine and pulled the slide back to eject the shell in the firing chamber.

The ejected round was a .22 caliber long-rifle cartridge capped by a hollow-point lead bullet. It was the kind of ammunition he'd loaded into the long-barreled Colt Woodsman automatic handgun he hunted squirrels with as a kid on the farm. The slug made an entry hole only twenty-two hundredths of an inch in diameter, but the cratered perforation in its tip caused it to mash out to double width or more when it hit bone. Had the two bullets puncturing Quick's shirt encountered bone? He aborted the thought with an effort of will.

Jeffreys put the gun atop the Gideon Bible in the drawer of the nightstand alongside the bed, shook his head at the irony and shut the drawer.

He turned on the television set.

The local news program carried a confused report of a fatal shooting at the downtown Holiday Inn. A deep-voiced anchorman with wavy hair and a simpering smile said in a single breath that police sources declined to identify the victims, one dead and the other critically wounded, pending notification of their next of kin, but promised early arrest of the fled suspect, a former Hoosier newspaperman, one Samuel T. Jeffreys, 38, of Brown Point, Indiana.

The news segment ended with display of a photograph of the wanted man, a pronouncement that copies of his picture were being distributed to area newspapers and TV stations, a warning that he was considered armed and dangerous, and a solicitation for calls to the Bloomburgh PD by anyone spotting him.

Jeffreys recognized the picture as a cropped version of the shot the police photographer took of him in the Bloomburgh jail at his mugging and fingerprinting five days ago,

Or was it five years ago?

XII
THE FUGITIVE

Sam Jeffreys was hungry again.

The bean soup and corned beef on rye he'd wolfed down in the Holiday Inn coffee shop were long digested, and hunger pangs were building.

When was it he had eaten that lunch, light-heartedly, hopefully? Was it only seven hours ago that he was a reasonably happy, relatively confident man posing as prey for some sharks, expecting them to solve his problems by biting on the bait set out to trap them? Whenever it was, his stomach was calling for replacements.

Staring at his reflection in the bathroom mirror, he tried to change his appearance by combing his hair differently with his fingers. He gave it up as a waste of time.

Thrusting his shoulders back and pulling his stomach in to bolster his self-confidence, he let himself out of his room and headed for the lobby, forcing himself to walk slowly and hold his head high.

Nobody seemed to be noticing him. Where was the ubiquitous sign directing newcomers to the cocktail lounge, the dining room, the reservation desk and the rest rooms, always in that order? Spotting it, he followed its lead to the dining room. On the way, he pulled up before a newspaper dispenser trumpeting the legend, *EVENING HERALD*, plugged a quarter into its slot, opened its cover, withdrew a paper and resumed his walk without looking at it.

There was a seat-yourself placard on the cashier's counter just inside the dining room doorway and nobody manning the cash register.

"Thank you," Jeffreys said under his breath. He surveyed the dining room. A vacant table along a far wall away from the windows looked inviting. He started toward it, forcing himself to walk slowly, casually. There were a dozen diners scattered about. His route didn't take him close to any of them. He made it to his destination without incident, sat down facing the entrance and looked about again. There was a single waitress in view, pouring coffee at one of the occupied tables. She looked up at that instant and caught his eye.

"Be with you in a moment, Sir," she called, smiling.

He forced a return smile, saw with relief that nobody else seemed interested in him, opened the newspaper.

The story of the shootings started below the fold on page one and jumped inside. There was no picture out front. He turned to the jump and saw himself looking out of page five. It was the jail shot again, but only one column wide and two inches deep, neither all that noticeable or recognizable.

The waitress bustled up carrying a glass of water and a menu. He refolded the paper and laid it down.

"Evening, Sir," the waitress said cheerily. "Can I get you something from the bar while you're deciding?"

"I'd love a manhattan on the rocks," he said.

"Coming right up."

She bustled off, and he picked up the paper again.

A shootout in Bloomburgh's Downtown Holiday Inn killed one FBI agent and critically wounded a second today, triggering a citywide manhunt for a former Indiana journalist already charged in an earlier gun-slaying here.

"So they weren't both dead," Jeffreys told himself. "That's something."

> Police sources identified the wanted man as Samuel T.
> Jeffreys, 38, of Crown Point, Indiana, and warned that he
> is armed and dangerous.
>   Pronounced dead at the scene from multiple gun-
> shot wounds to the chest and abdomen following the 2 PM
> shooting was Special FBI Agent Herbert Lukeman, 47, of
> 5723 Tyler, Bloomburgh.

Jeffreys felt his pulse quicken. So it was Quick who survived. He read on.

> Reported in critical but stable condition at
> Bethany Hospital late this afternoon after surgical removal
> of two bullets from his right lung was Special Agent Stanley
> Quick, 46, of Roanoke, Va.

"Damn," Jeffreys said under his breath. "Critical." So even if Quick survived, it didn't sound like he'd be testifying anytime soon about who shot him and Lukeman. His eyes went back to the story.

> Police investigators reconstructing the incident
> said the wounded man apparently was the victim of a
> surprise attack by someone he trusted, reporting that he
> had taken off his jacket and was lying on the bed in Jeffreys'
> motel room when he was shot. His service revolver was
> partway out of his shoulder holster, the investigators said.
> Lukeman apparently burst into the room after hearing
> gunshots, the investigators theorized, and was killed as he

came through the door. He was found face down just inside
the doorway, his service revolver in his hand.

It was the first fatal shooting of FBI personnel
here since the 1957 killing of two federal agents outside
the now defunct Tivoli Tap, a notorious gambling and girlie
joint on Smith Street allegedly operated by then mob-boss
Frankie Stifetti. That double-slaying has never been solved.
Turn to page five.

Jeffreys did.

Bloomburgh Det. Sgt. Joseph Sankstone told the
HERALD that Jeffreys had been released from city jail here
only Thursday, a scant 24 hours before the double shooting. He had been held under preliminary charges accusing
him of two gangland-style executions last Monday night,
Sankstone said. Killed in what Sankstone labeled "professional hits" at the Garrison Arms Apartments were resident Charles Nelson, 64, dead of three bullets fired from
close range into the back of the head, and the building's
security guard, Wallace Echols, 59, clubbed and strangled.

Jeffreys' picture interrupted the text, a bold-faced caption
beneath it announcing that he was Sought in FBI Shootings.
Underneath the picture, the story ran on.

Sankstone said the suspect was freed on $50,000
bond set by Criminal Division Judge Farley Bigler after he
approved reduction of the charges against Jeffreys from
murder to involuntary manslaughter.

Bigler wasn't immediately available for comment,
but Sankstone told the Herald, "The arrangement smells
like a plea-bargain agreement that backfired."

Bloomburgh Police Chief Harold Baumgartner,

noting that his entire department was mobilized for the
manhunt, said he was "confident of an early arrest."

The waitress returned, setting down his drink. Jeffreys
dropped the newspaper onto the table and managed to smile
at her. "Know what you want?" she asked, smiling back.

"Five minutes alone with this manhattan," Jeffreys said.

"You got it," the waitress said.

Jeffreys sipped the manhattan. It was made with bar whis-
key. Aside from its consequent harshness, it was great.

After two swallows, he picked up the menu, ran his eyes
along its entries, nodded to himself, set it down, and concentrated on the manhattan.

"Ready?" the waitress asked, standing alongside him again.

"Yup. The Veal *Parmigiana* with spaghetti."

"It looks real good tonight. Another manhattan?"

"No, thanks. Coffee, please. Black."

"Coming right up," the waitress said. She left.

He picked up the paper again. The rest of the story reported that there was an all-points bulletin out on the wanted
man. It added that local police in his home bailiwick of Lake
County, Indiana, were alerted to watch for him there. And it
said Chief Baumgartner had called a press conference to assure shocked citizens that everything was under control.

Jeffreys refolded the paper.

His food came. It was good. He ate ravenously. The coffee
was hot and strong.

"Dessert?" the waitress smiled from alongside him as he
washed down the last bite with the last swallow.

"Believe not, thanks. But a touch more coffee, please."

"Just happened to bring my music," she grinned, pouring
from the carafe she carried. "And your check, Sir. Come back
and see us again."

"Plan on it," Jeffreys said.

The check was $12.85. He left three ones on the table, picked up the newspaper, walked slowly with his head up and his shoulders back to the cashier's counter, dropped a ten and a five on it, grinned dutifully at the money taker and pocketed his change.

"Great," he told himself under his breath, as he marched sedately toward the elevator. "The hunted man has six dollars and silver to his name."

In his room, he turned on the television set, switched off the lights, flipped through the channels. Friday-night fare, he saw. Junk. Sitcoms, old movies, no newscasts, not even a football game.

He hit the remote controller's Off button. He stared at the screen for a long time after it went dark, still seeing pictures in its blankness.

Quick's likeness was there, his face pale, his eyes glazed, two red-rimmed holes in his white shirt.

So was Lukeman's, a slow-motion version, erect and wearing a look of surprise, falling forward, then lying inert and quiet.

Cornie was there in a series of stop-action replays, his revolver pointed at Jeffreys' belly, his hand proffering Jeffreys door keys, his lifeless eyes staring at nothing from the apartment floor.

The Poo Boys were there, big thug and little thug in wrinkled suits, their guns extended, one of them exuding the odor of mentholyptus.

"Balls," Jeffreys said under his breath. "That's four down and me to go."

He lapsed into muse mode, wondering whether he was safe for the moment. From the Poos, probably. They had no way to track him down. Did they? No, none that came to mind. How about the police? Did they have ways? Sure, they did. They had *manpower.* They had door knockers, picture passers, telephone answerers. They had beat cops, patrol cops, informants, tipsters, desk cops, manpower. They would ... They would find his car! Its Indiana license would stand out from local plates in the parking lot like a liver sausage in a wiener display. It would be spotted, once daylight illuminated the lot, and identified. And when they knew it was his, locked and left outside a Howard Johnson, where would they look for him?

Jeffreys sighed, abruptly aware that he had to leave this warm, secure sanctuary. He must reenter the cold world outside and move the damn car. He had to ditch it someplace where its location wouldn't so obviously point to his location. He looked at his watch. It was going on for midnight. It would be light in five or six hours.

Yawning, Jeffreys reached for the telephone to leave a wakeup call. Then he snatched his hand back in dismay, and pondered again the power of habit. Conditioned reflex, his psych professor termed it. But what it really was, he realized, to a former police-beat reporter anyway, was MO for Modus Operandi, the way a person reflexively reacted, instinctively performed, did his thing.

"Got to change my MO," he whispered into the darkness, still unnerved by his instinctive move toward the telephone.

Shaking his head, he lay down on the bed in the darkness, told himself he had to be up by four o'clock, and went instantly to sleep.

Sam Jeffreys opened his eyes unto blackness, wondering where he was. Memory flooded back and he wished he were elsewhere than sprawled atop a Howard Johnson bed, fully dressed, cobwebby, vaguely aware of an urgent need to flee.

He climbed to his feet, fumbled the nightstand lamp alight and stumbled to the bathroom. He splashed cold water on his face, brushed his teeth with a finger, combed his hair with his hands.

His wristwatch read 4:45. When did daylight come? Too soon, for sure.

He looked around the shadowy room, uncertain of what he'd brought that he now should take. He saw nothing, remembered he'd fled the Holiday Inn without luggage or trenchcoat.

Wishing for a cigarette, he started for the door, remembered the gun, retraced his steps to the nightstand, and stood over it for a moment, undecided. He slid open the drawer. He took the little automatic from atop the bible. He stuck it into his jacket pocket.

Dropping the room key onto the rumpled bed, he headed for the door again, peered out into an empty corridor, stepped into it and closed the door behind him.

He rode the elevator downstairs. The lobby was deserted except for a desk clerk slumped in a chair behind the counter, mouth open and eyes closed, breathing deeply.

Jeffreys walked quietly to the exit, forcing his shoulders back and his stomach in. He pushed through it into the world outside, the cold air shocking him into full wakefulness. Wishing for his trenchcoat and a hat, he headed for the car.

It was where he'd left it. As he unlocked its door, he realized he'd been subconsciously fearful it might not be there and felt relief that it was. He climbed in, started the engine, flipped on the lights and steered out of the lot into the nearly deserted street.

"So now where?" he said aloud, glancing at the fuel gauge. It showed empty. He groaned, answered himself, "Someplace close."

He passed an all-night self-serve gasoline station, thought about turning in, remembered the six dollars in his pocket, and drove on.

He flipped the heat control to high, shivering in the chill

breeze set in motion by the fan.

Where in a strange city do you ditch a car? he mused. Where would an abandoned auto bearing an Indiana license plate be least likely to attract attention and least likely to direct tracers to its owner once it did attract attention? A junkyard? Probably not. Probably the operators would be as instantly aware of an addition to their inventory as of a theft from it. Anyway, weren't junkyards always patrolled by watchdogs, mean, noisy watchdogs?

"Right," he said aloud, and drove on.

So how about a parking lot adjacent to a factory or a refinery. Didn't big-industry employees work rotating shifts so there always were cars nearby the clock around? Sure, but weren't their parking lots guarded, patrolled, at least gated, with uniformed security people also on watch the clock around?

"Right," he said, and drove on.

Traffic was sparse. The fuel gauge needle hovered over the "E". A Greyhound bus overtook him, its left-turn signal flashing as it passed, replaced by the right-turn light as it pulled back into his lane ahead of him, going dark again.

"Hey," he said. "A bus depot parking lot." An army of cars would be left there while their owners headed for Chicago, Detroit, New York, Boston, wherever. His would be unremarkable among theirs. If it were spotted and identified, it would send an implied message to Sergeant Sankstone and his colleagues that he was headed for Chicago, Detroit, New York, Boston, wherever.

But was this bus heading for the depot or leaving it? And if it were headed in, did he have enough gas to follow it there?

Jeffreys shrugged and followed the bus.

It was breaking dawn, the blackness of the night sky settled over the city's lights beginning to pale a bit. The bus turned right, then left and cruised toward an island of illumination two blocks ahead.

"If the depot comes," Jeffreys rejoiced, "can the parking lot be far behind?"

With a whoosh of air brakes, the bus stopped in front of a building through whose grimy windows showed white marble counters, brown Naugahyde stools, coffee tanks, smoking griddles, people. Adjacent to it, a pair of monstrous sliding doors stood open on their overhead tracks to display the gloomy tunnel of an entrance to a dimly lighted garage and loading area.

Jeffreys drove on past the bus looking for a turnoff leading to a parking lot. He found it just beyond the restaurant. He swung into it and saw his headlights reflecting back at him from a sea of windshields ahead. The cars they belonged to stood side by side in rows and ranks and files, with here and there a vacancy. Their tops were splashed with yellow puddles of feeble light leaking from a dozen dirt-spattered globes suspended from the tops of utility poles marking the boundaries of the parking arena.

He steered to the far end, turned left, drove halfway along the huge lot, swung into an entrance road leading toward the center of the clot of cars. He pulled into a spot between an ancient Cadillac with a crumpled front fender and a battered Ford pickup truck. He switched off his lights, noticing that the fuel gauge needle was quivering at the left of the "E", and cut the ignition.

"Thanks," he said under his breath.

He climbed out into the cold of the dawning morning, snapped the locking button and closed the car door. He unlocked the trunk, raised the lid, and peered inside as the dim light came on to partially illuminate the interior. Maybe there was an old coat in there, or a jacket, possibly a rain slicker, something to protect him from the chill air. There wasn't. There was just a jack, a tiny doughnut of steel and rubber pretending to be a spare wheel and tire, and a hat, a silly, shapeless, fisherman's hat of light-weight tan poplin with a floppy brim.

Jeffreys seized it and pulled it onto his head, feeling the slight comfort of its slight warmth. He slammed the trunk lid and began walking briskly toward the back end of the lot, away from the bus and the restaurant and the depot, striding ... elsewhere.

It was full daylight of a gloomy, chilly, cloudy, windy morning when he slowed, stopped and looked around, shivering in the cold and needing a restroom.

He cataloged the neighborhood as the depressing kind whose dwellers, according to Thoreau, live lives of quiet desperation.

His side of the street was lined with single-story houses, mostly frame, but a few of dirty brick. They were old, close together, shabby. Their little lawns were littered with leaves, stones, shards of broken bottles, tin cans, torn pieces of newspaper, all the debris of cities. The sidewalks were cracked, broken and uneven.

Across the street were live-in commercial buildings, smallish, similarly shabby. There was a mom-and-pop grocery store with a cracked front window; a shop whose painted sign was so faded he couldn't read it; a tiny barber shop squeezed between a liquor store with steel gratings across its windows and a boarded-up store front; a two-story building leaning drunkenly to its left, one of its upstairs windows partly open, the bottom of a protruding curtain waving outside it in the wind; an off-level neon sign downstairs proclaimed, *Jim's Telev sion Sho pe.*

Street traffic was desultory. A car or truck passed him now and then. Half a dozen scattered pedestrians plodded along the sidewalks of this block and the next. Yellow light filtering through the grimy windows of the grocery store suggested that mom and/or pop already was on duty, though no customers were in evidence. The liquor store, the haircut emporium, the shoemaker's establishment and Jim's Telev sion Sho pe were dark.

Farther down, a solitary light showed through the gloom on the other side of the street. Jeffreys walked toward it, drawing his suit jacket closer around him, pulling the collar more tightly against his neck. There was a neon sign hanging in the window. *AFFORDABLE EATERY,* it read.

He crossed the street, looked in both directions, saw nobody, walked to the door, pulled it open and stepped inside.

There was a counter lined by six bar stools. There were four square tables, each surrounded by four straight-backed chairs. Behind the counter stood a short, heavyset, bespectacled woman wearing a ballooning chef's hat and a full-length apron. Both were starched stiff and glistening snowy white.

"Mornin'," she said, eyeing him up and down. "Nice outfit."

"Forgot my overcoat," Jeffreys said defensively, catching a glimpse of his reflection in a stainless steel coffee urn behind the woman. The cylindrical mirror made him a fat man in a ridiculous hat, his inside-out coat lapels turned up to hide his neck and chin. He looked, he decided, like the second banana in a burlesque routine. Peeling off the hat, he crumpled it into a ball and shoved it into his coat pocket, bumping the gun. He turned down the coat collar, smoothed it behind his neck and across his shoulders. Palming his lapels flat, he sank onto the stool farthest from the window. It felt good to get off his feet and out of the chill wind.

"Whatlya have?" the woman asked.

"I was thinking of coffee."

"Can't beat coffee for starters, but dassn't stop there," she said, grinning. She produced a white china mug from beneath the counter, held it under the spigot of the gleaming

tank behind her, set it down steaming in front of him. "Cream
'n sugar?"

"Neither, thanks," Jeffreys said, tasting it gingerly. It was
hot, strong, and good. He had another scalding swallow, felt
its warmth begin to flow through him.

"How's about panny cakes?" the woman asked, her grin
still there. "Or a waffle? Eggs? Hamburg? Chili Dog? Steak an'
spuds?"

Jeffreys realized he was hungry, thought about the six
dollars in his pocket, decided he wouldn't eat.

"Just coffee," he said, sipping.

"No way," the woman said, shaking her head. She continued to grin. "Can't start a cold day 'thout somethin' solid in
your belly. How about if I order fer ya? I say eggs. Like three
of 'em, scrambled in butter. An' toast alongside. With orange
marmalade. Sound good?"

"Sounds good," he said.

It *was* good, he decided, after he returned from a welcome
visit to the tiny restroom and the woman swung around from
the griddle behind her to slide the plate in front of him and
he began digging into its contents. *No*, he amended the
thought. *Not good. Great!*

He was getting warm, now, and his bodily needs were
satisfied or being satisfied, and the world was suddenly a
slightly better place.

Then his breakfast was gone, and his third cup of coffee.
Two sleepy-looking men came in, their hands huddled in
their zippered-up jackets, their baseball caps pulled low on
their heads. They sat down on the stools nearest the window.
The woman grinned at them, asked, "Whatlya have?" They
ordered coffee and eggs-over-easy-with-hash-browns. Jeffreys
sighed, dropped his five on the counter, and sat there, wondering how much change she would give him and what he
would do with the rest of this already long day that was only
just begun.

"Two-fifty," the woman said, snatching up the five, leaning under the counter with it, and dropping two ones and two quarters in front of him. "Have a nice day."

"Thanks," he said, leaving the quarters. "The same to you."

He headed for the door, stuffing the bills into his pants pocket.

Bringing out his keys to make room for the money, he dropped them. When he retrieved them from the floor, his eyes lighted on the two Cornie had given him.

Suppose I could hole up there for a while? he asked himself.

He pocketed the chain and stepped outside. At once the cold wind penetrated his suit coat and refrigerated his body. He extricated the hat from the pocket, unfolded it, pulled it down over his head, and turned up his coat collar.

Worth a shot, he answered himself. *Where else is there?*

XIII
THE REFUGE

It took him hours to find the Garrison Arms Apartments. When he did, he wasn't sure he should have.

Twice he walked past the building on the far side of the street, unable to see whether the security guard station was occupied, sauntering past with all the put-on nonchalance he could manage while shivering in a fisherman's hat and no topcoat on an Arctic October day.

Then he saw him, a uniformed guard inside, sitting behind the security desk beyond the foyer.

"Damn," said Jeffreys, pondering how to lure or chase or frighten the guard away from his station. After a while he figured it out. "I only have to wait. Everybody's got to go to the toilet sometime."

He picked a spot where he could stand at the curb in front of the apartment facing oncoming street traffic and glimpse the guard from the corner of his eye without actually staring in.

He hoped he looked like an innocent citizen casually waiting to be picked up by a friend or a taxicab or a bus or a carpooler rather than like an accused murderer waiting to invade an apartment building if and when the security guard headed for the john.

Nobody bothered him. Nobody entered or left the building to stare at him standing there. The few pedestrians passing by paid him no attention. The sparse motor traffic speeding past didn't slow for him. No police cars sirened up to whisk him off to jail. No watchers from the windows yelled down at him to be on his way.

After a while, he needed a bathroom himself. He walked back to the gas station he had passed earlier, used the facilities and returned to his post in time to glimpse motion in the hallway beyond the foyer door. Peering directly in, he saw a uniformed back disappearing into the elevator.

It was delightfully warm inside the outer door. Cornie's name was still on the card atop the bell push, Jeffreys saw. He snatched the hat off his head, bundled it into his coat pocket atop the gun, turned down his collar, smoothed his lapels, eyed his reflection in the glass of the inner door, and reached for his key chain. It was the brass-colored key of the pair Cornie gave him that fit this door, he remembered. It turned easily. He pulled the door open, took a deep breath, forced his shoulders back and his head up and stepped inside.

Everything was as he remembered it, the security guard's desk, chair, telephone, the elevator ahead. Jeffreys headed for the steel door alongside it with STAIRS painted across it.

The elevator started humming, whooshed, bumped to a stop. Its gate started to open.

Jeffreys dove to the door, pulled it open, leaped through the doorway, hauled it shut against its hydraulic closer, and stood there panting, praying he hadn't been seen.

Through the door, faintly, he heard footsteps. The sounds faded, moving away. He breathed a sigh of relief and looked around.

He was on a landing. Stairs went down to his left and up to his right. There was no sound from either direction. He started up.

He was panting again by the time he reached the fourth landing. He eyed the FOUR painted on the door, sat down on the top step, and rested, visualizing the corridor on the other side of the door. Cornie's apartment would be at the far end to his left.

How many doors between here and there, he asked himself. Three? Or was it four? Weren't there two on Cornie's side of the corridor opening into apartments occupied by unknowns, plus two more across the hall? One where lived the lady in the dressing gown and curlers who saw him standing over Cornie's body with a gun in his hand and the other occupied by the old man in the bathrobe who'd probably saved his life by calling the cops?

His breathing back to normal, Jeffreys got up and put his ear against the inside panel of the fire door. He heard nothing. Forcing his shoulders back and his head up, he pushed the door carefully open, stuck his head through the doorway and looked left and right. The hallway was deserted.

Taking a deep breath, he stepped into the corridor, turned left and walked sedately toward the end of the hall, pulling his key chain from his pocket as he went. Five paces from Cornie's door, he had the silver-colored key isolated, poised. Filtering through the door behind which the old man in the bathrobe had disappeared the other night were music, laughter, voices. A television program, Jeffreys decided, fighting panic.

There were three strides to go. Two. One. His key in his fist, he prayed Cornie's door didn't have a police lock, a seal, or a sign forbidding entry to non-authorized persons.

It didn't. His key fit, he turned it, the lock unlatched and the door snicked open.

Jeffreys pushed through into grey semi-darkness. He swung the door shut behind him, turned to latch the lock and slide home the burglar bolt. Then he leaned against the panel and stood there in the warm sanctuary of the darkened room, quivering.

It was a full five minutes before he stopped shaking. By

then his eyes were accustomed to the murky light filtering through the curtains covering the windows. Now he could see the outlines of the furniture, darker grey against the lighter grey background of the carpet and the walls. He walked to the sofa where he and Cornie had sat. He lowered himself onto it and stretched out full length in the soft warmth.

After a minute, he decided he could do better.

Getting up, he padded carefully through the murky semi-darkness toward the left-hand archway he'd earlier figured led into a bedroom. It did. He plopped onto the bed, stretched out on his back. It felt luxurious.

He sat up again, kicked off his shoes, shrugged out of his jacket, pulled the hat and the gun from his side pocket and tossed the coat and the hat onto the floor alongside the bed. Lying back down, he shoved the gun under the pillow.

"So now I'm ready to wake up shooting," he said aloud, grinning into the gloom, "like a two-bit hoodlum in a TV movie," and went instantly to sleep.

###

The readout on his watch glowed 1:24 P SA 18 when he opened his eyes to look at it.

"That was a neat nap," he told himself, sitting up in bed and staring around the room. He could see quite well in the weak daylight penetrating the drawn window shades. There was a nightstand alongside the head of the bed, a mirror-topped dresser across from its foot. Two chairs flanked the dresser, a straight-backed one to its left and a rocker to its right.

Sliding doors along the left wall suggested that a closet was behind them.

Clambering out of bed, he retrieved his jacket and the hat from the floor and tossed them onto the seat of the rocker. He found his shoes, slipped into them and walked through the doorway toward the living room. The bathroom loomed to his left. He went into it. It was darker, windowless. He shut the door, found the wall switch, flipped it up. Eye-searing light blazed overhead.

He intended only to sponge bathe, fearful that the sound of the shower, noticed elsewhere in the building, could call attention to this supposedly vacant apartment. But the temptation for a real bath was too great. Stripping and dropping his clothes into a heap on the floor, he stepped into the tub, pulled the plastic curtain shut and fumbled with the faucets until the water temperature was right. Then he stood motionless in the stream and luxuriated in the warm wetness flowing over his head, his shoulders, his body.

After a while he sudsed himself with the bar of soap stuck to the tub top, rinsed, shut off the shower, stepped out, and dried himself on the thick, fluffy towel hanging on the towel bar.

There was an electric shaver on the countertop, its cord plugged into a wall socket. He found its switch, turned it on, ran it over his face and neck until the two-day growth of whiskers was wiped away. He helped himself to the after-shave lotion also on the countertop, poured a palmful, rubbed his hands together and patted his face and neck and forehead with them, enjoying the scent of the pine forest and the bite of the astringent.

"All the comforts of home," he told himself. "Thank you, Cornie."

Stepping back, he stumbled over the wrinkled pile of soiled clothing on the floor. It gave him another idea. He flipped off the light, opened the door and trotted naked into the bedroom. Sliding open the closet door, he saw in the murky light what he was hoping for: a dozen suits and a row of hangered shirts. He checked the legend printed inside the collar of the first shirt in the line, read 16 33.

"Wow," Jeffreys said aloud, almost giddy at the prospect

of clean, fresh clothing. "A half inch too big and an inch too long, but I'll force myself."

The underwear in the dresser drawer was a sloppy fit, the Jockey shorts a bit loose at the waist, the T-shirt a trifle large across the shoulders and chest. The black, calf-length socks from another drawer clung properly to his legs. The short-sleeved white dress shirt at the far end of the shirt line was a fair fit with its collar left unbuttoned. The grey flannel slacks on the hanger under the blue blazer would need a belt to snug them around his waist. The blazer, though its shoulders were a bit wider than his, didn't look too bad, his image in the dresser mirror told him.

He found a black leather belt in the top dresser drawer, slipped it through the trouser loops to encircle his waist, cinched it snug and grinned back at his reflection.

"So who needs a necktie?" he asked himself. "The open-throated image suits me fine."

He retrieved his own clothes from the bathroom floor, slipped into his shoes. He fished his wallet, knife, keys and change from the pants pockets. He folded the pants and his suit jacket onto a hanger, shook them to dislodge the worst of the wrinkles, hooked the hanger over the closet rail. The shirt, socks and underwear he tossed onto the closet floor.

"Laundry comes later," he whispered. "Right now we go exploring."

In the murky light from the curtained living room windows, it looked as he remembered it. Here was the sofa on which he and Cornie sat. There were the chairs. Behind him was the archway to the bedroom. Across from it was the other archway. There, between the sofa and the door, was the carpet stained with Cornie's blood.

Jeffreys shrugged, trying to erase the picture of Cornie's corpse from his mental screen and padded toward the second archway he presumed was the entrance to what Cornie referred as the "shitty little kitchen" whose inadequacy he blamed for eating out.

It was indeed a shitty little kitchen, Jeffreys told himself. It had a single window opposite the entrance archway. The closed slats of the Venetian blind excluded most of the outdoor light, keeping the room in semi-darkness.

"No light in, no light out," Jeffreys told himself, fumbling for the wall switch. A circular fluorescent tube came alive in a light fixture on the ceiling.

There was a miniature refrigerator in the far corner to his left, a three-foot stretch of countertop alongside it with cupboards above and cabinets below, a tiny electric range, the archway, then another three-foot run of counter, cupboards and more cabinets to his right. Across the room, with a four-foot walkway between, was another stretch of the same countertop, cupboards, and cabinets butting against a diminutive double sink, the smallest automatic dishwasher he'd ever seen, and a waist-high breakfast bar. There was nothing on the stove or any of the countertops.

Even a shitty little kitchen ought to have some kind of a coffee pot in it, he told himself.

The refrigerator, when he opened its door, was empty, warm and unlighted, evidently unplugged. There was no coffee pot. Jeffreys found coffee in one of the upper cabinets, a one-pound can of Hills Brothers drip grind, nearly full judging by its weight. There was also an empty sugar bowl, a box of dishwasher detergent, dusty dishes and glasses. He found silverware in one of the drawers, pots and pans in the lower cabinets, but no coffee carafe, no pot, no percolator, no dripmaker.

"Okay," Jeffreys said aloud. "So I'll use a pan."

There were several suitable pans. He chose a two-quart, copper-bottomed, stainless-steel pot. While the water was heating in it, he poked through cabinet drawers for a strainer, found one, and set it aside. He located a cup and saucer in one of the upper cupboards, washed the dust from the cup at the faucet. The water on the stove began to bubble. He took the lid off the coffee can, expecting to find a plastic measuring spoon inside. There wasn't one. Digging a tablespoon from one of the cupboard drawers, he filled it from the can and emptied it into the pan five times, then used it to stir the muddy-looking water it created. After it boiled a while longer, he poured a cupful through the strainer, carried the cup to the breakfast bar, sat down on the stool, and, hoping for a miracle, sipped the steaming concoction.

There was no miracle. It was coffee, but it was stale coffee, weak coffee, rotten coffee, non-miracle coffee. It wasn't the worst coffee he'd ever tasted, maybe, but it certainly wasn't the best. No matter though, because it was, recognizably and indisputably, coffee.

He swung around on the stool to rest his back against the breakfast bar, sipping appreciatively.

The cup was nearly empty when the thought came.

Cornie said he ate all his meals out. Cornie had no coffee pot. Yet Cornie, stingy Cornie, tightwad Cornie, had a nearly full can of coffee that had cost several bucks. What for? Why?

Jeffreys set the cup down, crossed the room, picked up the coffee can, peeled off its plastic cover and peered into it. He saw coffee, dark brown, sawdust-textured, stale-smelling, drying-out, ground coffee. He set the can down, dropped to his knees to pull a largish aluminum cooking pan from a cupboard shelf, set it on the counter and slowly poured the can's contents into it. Watching the brown granules sift from the upper vessel to pile up in the lower one, he felt like some medieval soothsayer tipping a misshapen hour glass to read the passage of time from its spilling sands.

The can was nearly empty when its prize appeared like a toy from a Crackerjack box. A red rectangle dropped onto the

conical pile of coffee in the pan. It was immediately covered
by more of the loose brown particles.

He dug the object out, shook it free of the coffee dust
clinging to it and stared at it. It was two inches by three, a
tiny envelope of colored cardboard, its flap secured with a
metal snap. He could feel something inside it. It felt like a key.
It *was* a key, he saw when he pulled it from its covering, a flat
plate of brass with the numbers 914 stamped into one side of
its head, MOSLER pressed into the other.

Jeffreys eyed the envelope. There were faint markings on it.
He held it up, moved it to catch the full light of the overhead
fluorescent fixture. The pale blue tracks of a ball-point pen
pressed lightly against the cardboard had embossed them into
the red background. He read the line of tiny, connected, erect
letters marching across the envelope. *Clem Nathan*, they read.
Mdtwn Indstrl.

"Bingo," Jeffreys said, his stomach churning. "Eureka."
Could this be the key to the stash the Poo Boys were trailing
him for? Money, maybe, the million bucks the IRS looked for
and didn't find? Or diaries detailing the story of Cornie's rise
and fall, the makings of a book? Maybe both of the above?

Euphoric, he shoved the key inside its envelope, snapped
its flap closed, pocketed it. He dumped the coffee back into
its can, covered it, replaced it on the cupboard shelf between
the box of dishwasher detergent and the empty sugar bowl.
He shook coffee particles from the aluminum pan into the
sink and returned the pan to its resting place. He strained
another cup of the non-miracle coffee, snapped off the kitchen
light, carried the cup into the gloom of the living room and
sank down on the sofa to enjoy it.

When it was almost gone, another thought came.

Cornie always ate out. Cornie didn't make even coffee at
home. So why would Cornie, stingy Cornie, tightwad Cornie,
buy dishwasher detergent?

He raced back into the kitchen, snapped on the light, set down the coffee cup, flung open the cupboard, grabbed the detergent box off the shelf and eyed it.

CASCADE the legend on the box read. The paper patch covering its tin fold-out pouring spout was whole, untorn. The box had been opened, though. Three sides of its top were cut through so it could hinge back on the fourth side. Judging from its heft, little or none of the contents had been used.

Jeffreys dug out the aluminum pan again, set it down on the counter, lifted the top of the detergent box, and peered inside. He saw yellow-green granules. He upended the box over the pan and poured. Yellow-green granules trickled out in a stalactite stream to form a growing yellow-green stalagmite in the pan below. The soap-smell irritated the lining of his nose. He sneezed.

The trickle slowed, stopped. Jeffreys shook the box. It was lighter, but not empty. Something rattled inside it. He reached in, felt something taped to the box bottom. He peeled it loose. His hand came out into the light bearing a roll of paper money.

"Wow," Jeffreys said aloud, his stomach churning again. "There must be ..." He stopped and opened the roll of bills into a stack. They seemed to be hundreds, mostly, with a few fifties and some twenties. He began counting, whispering the running totals, "Forty eight, forty nine, five, five one, five two ..."

"Wow," Jeffreys said again, staring at the stack. It added up to nine thousand dollars. Cornie's walking-around money. What he kept at home between visits to his stash. Quick said he had six hundred in his checking account and less than a hundred in his pocket when he died. He didn't need any more. He just tapped the cookie jar—the detergent box—probably a grand at a time, and then refilled it from the bank box whenever the home roll got thin.

"So now I can do that," Jeffreys told himself, his spirits soaring. Nobody else knew about the stash, obviously. So it was his, all of Cornie's money, with nine grand up front for starters, hard telling how much more in the stash, and maybe a diary or tapes or notes or a journal to write a book from to boot.

Reality flooded back.

"Except I can't show my face," he said.

The euphoria faded.

Except he was due for arraignment in criminal court Tuesday—day after day after tomorrow. Except he'd be back in jail if he showed up for his court appearance and sought all the harder if he didn't. Except it wasn't his money, anyway, not this in the detergent box nor that in the bank.

Jeffreys sighed, shook his head, peeled five twenties off the stack of bills and set them on the counter. He rolled the rest into a bundle, replaced it inside the detergent box and began pouring the yellow-green granules back into it from the aluminum pan. He poured slowly, carefully. The soap smell of the yellow-green granules sifting into the box irritated the lining of his nose. He sneezed.

"Not what it looks like," he said aloud, closing the box, replacing it on the shelf and shutting the cabinet door. He picked up the little stack of twenties from the counter top, folded them, shoved them into his pants pocket. "Consider it a loan, Cornie, this hundred bucks, along with the clothes and the apartment. I need it for eating money. I'll see Marge or Angie gets it back, if I can stay alive and out of jail long enough."

He poured himself another cup of non-miracle coffee through the strainer. Then he headed back to the living room, telling himself he would sit down and get comfortable while he waited for ... while he waited.

XIV
THE FOREBODING

The afternoon died slowly, its lingering demise marked by the progressive fading of the daylight filtering through the window curtains from yellow-orange to grey to purple and finally to black.

Jeffreys sat in the softness of the sofa, only vaguely aware of the changing colors, of the darkness creeping over his portion of the world, of the long-empty coffee cup atop his left thigh, of still steadying it there with his left hand.

He had a key to a bank box that likely held a lot of money and maybe something more. He knew the name of the bank and the phony name used by the box's renter. But did he have the balls to march into a strange place, sign in as somebody else, and play out the charade? If he tried, would bank personnel recognize him as a newspaper-and-TV-billboarded fugitive and call the police? Would his own performance betray him, his fears affecting his enactment so the bank people would know at a glance that he wasn't Clem—what was the name? It started with an N to go with the C of Clem so Cornie Nicora, alias Charles Nelson, could keep his own initials as people using assumed names always seemed to do—oh, yes, Nathan. Clem Nathan.

If he managed to pull it off, what would he do with the

box and its contents? Should he haul it to the hospital and sit beside Quick's bed with it until Quick recovered enough to proclaim Jeffreys' innocence and hail his surrender of Cornie's stash as proof of Jeffreys' virtue?

Or would the hospital people recognize him from his newspaper pictures and figure he'd come to complete the job of killing Quick that the newspaper stories said he botched in his hotel room? Wouldn't they hold him until the police came for prompt return to jail, a hasty trial and an instant conviction?

Was Quick even still alive? Could he possibly survive those two chest holes so he could one day testify that Jeffreys didn't inflict them? Had his death perhaps already precluded such testimony? Or was it about to do so?

Why were his eyelids soooo heavy, as TV hypnotists always said while willing their subjects to sleep? And wasn't it nice to be so warm and comfortable and ...

He woke when the coffee cup clattered to the floor.

It was black dark.

He felt around on the carpet, found the cup, picked it up, and set it back on his thigh. He tried to wake up, inventorying his senses. Was this overwhelming sense of foreboding an omen of something sinister about to happen? Or was he just a victim of the doubts and the fears that unsettle anybody thinking about his problems, especially an anybody whose problems included the probability of imminent capture and confinement as a multiple murderer?

Sure, he decided. *That's what it is.* Just a down-swing in mood. Actually, he was in pretty good shape for the shape he was in, except for the hunger. But now he had money. So why didn't he go get something to eat?

He rose, clutching the cup, and moved toward the kitchen, his eyes accommodating to the darkness so he could distinguish between objects in the room that were slightly less black than their background.

Through the kitchen archway, he flipped on the overhead fluorescent circle, rinsed his cup under the faucet, and dumped the coffee pan into the sink. He rinsed the coffee pan, set it and the cup on the drain board alongside the aluminum pan. It still displayed a few crumbs of yellow-green detergent particles.

With the kitchen light doused but his eyes remembering its brilliance, the living room seemed blacker. He felt his way across it. He turned into the bathroom, closed its door, and flipped on its light. He freshened up, dried his hands on the still-damp bath towel, switched the light off, opened the door, felt his way into the bedroom.

Pulling on the closet light with the string hanging from the overhead bulb inside the sliding doors, he found the black overcoat and fedora hat that Cornie was wearing the night he … that other night, and put them on. Both were a trifle too large. The coat was thick and heavy. It would feel good in the cold outside.

He walked to the bed. He drew the gun from beneath the pillow, opened the overcoat, shoved the little automatic into Cornie's blazer pocket. Then he pulled the closet-light string.

He felt his way back to the living room and through it. He listened at the door, heard nothing, cracked it open, and peered into the corridor. It was deserted. He squared his shoulders and pulled in his stomach, stepped out into the hall, shut the door quietly behind him, and strode silently toward the stairway door opposite the elevator.

The elevator whooshed to a stop just as he started to open the stairway door. He yanked it wider and dove through the doorway, forcing it shut against its hydraulic closer at the moment the cage hissed open. He caught a glimpse of a grey-haired man inside the elevator before the heavy door latched closed. Wasn't it the old guy he'd last seen in a bathrobe screeching that he'd called the cops? Did they make eye contact just now for a fraction of an instant before the stairway door went fully shut?

Jeffreys hurried down the stairs to the ground floor, listened at the door for a moment, heard only silence, opened it a crack and peered out. The security station was deserted. Nothing stirred. Squaring his shoulders, he stepped out and walked casually toward the exit, hoping his manner made it clear to any possible viewer that he was an innocent visitor about to leave this building in which he had every right to be.

He walked past the security guard station, through the foyer door and then the street door. The wind was cold in his face. He shivered, though not from the cold, and grinned at his own fears.

He turned right, walking briskly toward the restaurant— what, three blocks down? Or was it farther? He'd been driving the last time and the blocks passed faster then than when you were hiking—where he remembered stopping for coffee and apple pie before he began his vigil in front of the apartment building the evening he found Cornie.

It turned out to be five blocks.

He was the only customer. He hung Cornie's hat and coat on the rack inside the door, nodded to the white-aproned, chef-capped young man behind the counter and sat down on one of the stools running its length.

"Evenin'," the counterman said. He looked to be about twenty-five. He had long brownish hair crowding the nape of his neck. There was a thin gold ring in his left ear lobe. "Need a menu?"

"Evening," Jeffreys said, nodding. "Please."

"Coffee?" the counterman asked. He proffered a half-sheet of paper covered with smeared words in the purple ink of a cheap copy-making device.

"Thought you'd never ask," Jeffreys said.

The coffee in the thick mug was strong and hot.

"I think the steak sandwich special," Jeffreys said, between sips. "With the French fries, the green beans and Thousand Island."

"You got it," the counterman said, busying himself at the refrigerator and then the grill. "Cold out there?"

"Frigid. That time of the year, though, I guess."

"Right. Wish it was June."

"Shouldn't wish your life away."

"So how about we make it last June?" the counterman said, setting a bowl of chopped lettuce down in front of Jeffreys and dropping a tinfoil packet alongside it. The edges of the lettuce were brown.

"I'll drink to that," Jeffreys said, tearing the packet open and squeezing its pink-orange contents onto the lettuce. "This your home town?"

"Nah. Come from Buffalo."

"Buffalo? And you're complaining about the weather here?"

"Weather's why I blew Buffalo," the counterman said. A slice of browned bread popped up in the toaster. He painted it with an oily brush, dropped it onto a thick, oblong china plate, and flipped a sizzling chunk of meat over on the grill. "Too goddam much snow."

The brown-edged salad wasn't bad. The aroma of the sizzling round steak was reassuring.

"Get much snow here?" Jeffreys asked, setting down the empty coffee mug.

"Any snow's too much snow," the counterman said, sliding his spatula under the steak and flipping it onto the toast. He plucked a wire basket from a pot of bubbling oil, dumped French fries onto the plate and set the plate in front of Jeffreys. "More coffee?"

"Please."

He ate in silence. The former Buffalonian bustled about behind the counter.

"Dessert?" the counterman said, when Jeffreys' plate was empty. "Got some cherry pie looks pretty good."

"Why not?" Jeffreys said. "With maybe a scoop of vanilla?"

"No ice cream," the counterman said, sounding aggrieved. "I keep telling 'em we ought to have ice cream, but they don't listen."

"Plain pie's fine," Jeffreys said, amused by the young man's apparent earnestness.

The tab was $7.90. Jeffreys peeled a twenty from his stack of five, accepted the change, dropped the two ones on the glass in front of the cash register, pocketed the ten and the dime.

"Buy yourself a snow shovel," he said. "And thanks for the feed. It hit the spot."

"Thanks, Mister," the counterman said, hoisting his apron to slide the bills into his pants pocket. "I'm savin' up to get the hell outta here."

"Good luck," Jeffreys said, shrugging into Cornie's coat. "Where you going?"

"Prob'ly Arizona. I hear they've got a place name of Sun City where the people that live there wouldn't reco'nize a snow shovel if they seen one."

"You heard right," Jeffreys said, pulling on Cornie's fedora. "Only you wouldn't like it there. It's hot and it's full of old people."

"I like it hot, and a lot of them old people are my kind of folks. I hear they got the biggest bunch of radio hams around Sun City than anywheres else in the whole world."

"You a ham?" Jeffreys asked, surprised.

"Sure am."

"Shake hands with King Niner Alpha Zulu Golf," Jeffreys said, thrusting out his hand. "The name is Sam. Sam Jeffreys."

"Double-You Bee Two Easy Jig Xray," the counterman said. "Andy. Andy Horton. Whattaya work, Sam?"

"Not much, lately," Jeffreys said. "Twenty and fifteen when I'm home, and a little ten when it's open. Some sideband, but mostly CW. And I've got a two-meter rig in the car."

"Me, too," Andy said. "But I like HF better. Mostly forty and seventy-five. My old Swan's about wore out so's it drifts pretty bad on the high bands. I'm savin' up for one o' them Kenwood contest-grade rigs."

"Nice radios," Jeffreys acknowledged. "I'd like one myself. Well, good luck Andy. Maybe see you on the air."

"Seven-threes," the counterman said.

Jeffreys stepped out into the wind, hugging Cornie's coat closer around him. He'd been right about the coat. It did feel good.

He saw the colored lights flashing from two blocks away. Were they in front of Cornie's place? Did they mark an accident scene? Was it a fire, maybe?

It was neither, he discovered. It was a pair of squad cars parked outside the Garrison Arms apartments, the revolving reflectors spinning about their roof lights sending streaks of red and amber whirling into the darkness.

Jeffreys stopped a half-block away and craned his neck to look up toward Cornie's windows. His earlier sense of foreboding returned in a crescendo of dread that seemed to press physically against the food in his stomach.

Cornie's lights were on. They were shining through and around the living room curtains. Figures inside the room cast moving shadows onto them.

"Shit," Jeffreys said, visualizing the elderly, grey-haired man whose elevator door was opening as Jeffreys' stairway door was closing. "That old SOB makes a career out of calling the cops to Cornie's apartment."

Fighting nausea, he turned away from the flashing cruiser lights and headed blindly back in the direction he came. He bowed his head against the cold wind and quickened his pace.

He didn't know where he was going, but he figured he'd better hurry.

He made up his mind before he reached the restaurant.

It was still alight, thank goodness, and he pushed in.

The counterman was alone, sweeping the floor. He looked up when Jeffreys came through the door. He appeared surprised.

"Hi, Sam," he said. "Forget something?"

"Hi, Andy," Jeffreys said, plopping down on the first stool. "No, but I was wondering. You have a car?"

"Sure. I'm savin' up for a better one, though."

"What time do you close?"

"Midnight. Gettin' ready now. Why?"

"Could I hire you to taxi me to the bus depot for ten bucks?"

"Ten bucks?" Horton echoed, leaning on his broom. "Bet your ass." He grinned. "I'm savin' up."

"I know," Jeffreys said. He looked out the window, half expecting to see colored lights sweeping the sky, listened, half expecting to hear sirens. "I'd really appreciate the ride."

"No problem," Horton said, resuming his sweeping. He stopped again, said, "Want some coffee while you're waitin'?"

"No thanks," Jeffreys said. He stood up, peeled off Cornie's coat, draped it across the stool next to him. "I will borrow your restroom, though."

🛡

Horton's car wasn't much, Jeffreys saw, climbing into it. It was a '79 Chevrolet two-door with peeling paint, a dirty windshield and a decided list to the passenger's side. It started right up, though.

"You said the bus depot?"

"Right. Actually, the parking lot behind it. I left my car there."

"Gotcha," Horton said and pulled out into the street.

There was little traffic. Jeffreys could see the patrol-car lights still flashing their revolving shafts of red and yellow into the sky as his driver approached the Garrison Arms.

"Some kind of trouble in there again," Horton said, eyeing the squad cars as he drove past them. "Had a killin' a while back."

"That so?" Jeffreys said.

"Yup. An old geek took three in the head. Man name of … unh … Nelson."

"You knew him?"

"Sort of. He used to stop in the restaurant sometimes. Quiet guy, spiffy dresser, never had much to say and a real stingy tipper."

"Stingy, huh?" Jeffreys said, grinning into the darkness of the car's interior.

"Gimme a dime a couple times after eatin' the steak sandwich special like you had. How's about if we monitor two?"

"I'd like that," Jeffreys told him. "What's your radio?"

"An old Azden Two Thousand," Andy said, reaching down to punch its power-on button. Red numerals flashed under the middle of the dashboard, sequencing through preset segments of the two-meter amateur band. "I'm savin' up for a better one."

"I used one of these for years," Jeffreys said, watching the readout numbers. "It was a good little rig."

The flashing numerals stopped sequencing and a new voice came from under the dashboard. "Double-You Zed Two Fox Xray Fox, this is Alpha Xray Two Fox. You around, Ralphie?"

There was no response, and the numbers resumed sequencing.

"Nothing much doin', this time of night," Andy said. He reached down and punched the power button. The red readout disappeared. "How come you left your car at the bus depot?"

"It's a long story," Jeffreys said carefully. "There were some people looking for me that I didn't want to see."

"Uh huh," Horton said, staring through the windshield at

the nearly deserted street moving toward them in the yellow glow of the headlights. "If they know your car, maybe they found it and it ain't there anymore."

"Possible. My guess is they didn't, though."

"You figure they quit lookin'?"

"I hope so, but probably not."

"It doesn't matter any more if they find you?"

"It still matters."

"You still don't want to see 'em?"

"I still don't want to see 'em."

"They bill collectors?" Horton pressed. "Repo guys or whatever you call them car grabbers?"

"No," Jeffreys said, deciding to share a part of his problem with his friendly chauffeur. "These people aren't really after my car. They're after me."

"You owe 'em money?"

"No. There's money involved, but it's neither mine nor theirs."

"I don't dig that."

"I suppose not," Jeffreys said. "These are ... unh ... bad people. They want me dead. They ... think I have something they want and they're willing to kill me to get it."

"Geez," Horton said. "Kill you? You talkin' about gangsters?"

"Or whatever," Jeffreys said, smiling into the darkness again. "Mafiosi, wiseguys, mobsters, soldiers, hit men—some kind of bad guys."

"You a cop? Undercover or like that?"

"No. I'm a ... journalist. I'm a retired reporter chasing a story."

"Hey, neato. Do they know you when they see you?"

"Sure do."

"So if they're watchin' your car and waitin' for you to show up, you could be in big trouble?"

"I'm betting they're not," Jeffreys said, musing that the police might have located it by now, with their manpower, resources and tipsters, but probably not the Poo Boys. Unless, of course, their mob bosses back in Indiana had mob contacts here with local cops on the pad. "Anyway, it's late, it's cold, and the car's been there for some time. So I figure that even if they did find it and stake it out for a while, they've probably given up on it by now."

"There's the bus depot," Horton said, nodding at the lights looming ahead through the grimy windshield. "We want the back parkin' lot, right?"

"Right," Jeffreys said. "You might park on the street behind it. The car's part-way in from the far end about the middle of the lot."

"How's this look?" Horton said, pulling to the curb in a shadowy spot midway between two feeble streetlights.

"Perfect," Jeffreys said, plucking from his coat pocket the ten-dollar bill he'd placed there back at the restaurant. He handed it to Horton, said, "Thanks for the ride. I really appreciate it. Would you mind giving me a couple more minutes? I'd like to sit here and see if anything moves over there."

"No problem," Horton said, taking the bill. He shut off the ignition, leaving the keys in the lock. He stuck the money in his coat pocket. "I got an idea."

"What's that?"

"How about you give me your keys and I go find your car and drive it around the block?"

"Around the block?"

"Sure. You sit here and watch if anybody takes off tailin' me. If they don't, we'll swap cars when I get back here, and you're on your own."

"Oh. And if I do see somebody start up after you—"

"—You beat it. If I come by here and you're gone, I'll know somebody's tailin' me."

"And then?"

"And then I'll lose 'em, and we'll meet at the restaurant, and we'll swap cars back."

"You really want to do that?"

"Sure. If there is somebody stakin' out your car, they'll know I'm not you, right? They'd have no reason to do anythin' to me, right?"

"Makes sense," Jeffreys said. "But it could be dangerous. These are bad people. I can't ask you to do that."

"So don't ask," Horton said, his teeth shining white in the darkness. "I want to."

"Are you sure?" Jeffreys persisted, reminding himself that it would be cops staking out the car, if anybody, not the Poo Boys. And while cops may grab young men getting into other people's vehicles, they don't shoot at them.

"I'm sure. How'll I tell your car?"

"It's just about straight through there in the fifth tier," Jeffreys said, holding his hand in front of Horton's face to point toward the middle of the parking lot. "It's a white Caprice Classic with Indiana plates and a two-meter antenna on the trunk lid."

"Quarter-wave vertical like mine? Nineteen incher?"

"No. It's a five-eighths-wave whip right at four feet long."

"Gotcha," Horton said.

Jeffreys fished his key chain from his trouser pocket, held it up to the light filtering in.

Horton found it, took it, opened his door. The overhead light came on.

"Oh, wait a minute," Jeffreys said. He snaked his hand into his trousers pocket, felt for his money, peeled one of the twenties off the little stack. He handed it to Horton. "I almost forgot. My gas tank's low. If you do take off from here, better fill it up at the first station you come to."

"Gotcha," Horton said. "Catch you later, alligator." He

jumped out, closed the door. The car went dark again.

"After while, crocodile," Jeffreys muttered reflexively, and began scanning the darkness. Wriggling over into the driver's seat to have a better view through the side window, he couldn't pick anything out of the gloom until his eyes accommodated. When they did, Horton's dark figure was faintly visible from time to time moving among the cars across the street, now barely discernible, now vanished, now a vague blur of motion again.

Time dragged past, and Jeffreys' eyes ached from staring into nothingness.

Then, suddenly, a pinpoint of light flashed on in the middle of the lot, winked out again.

"My dome light," Jeffreys told himself exultantly. "He found the car and he's in it."

There was a huge plume of reddish-white light where the pinpoint had been. There was the shock wave of a prodigious explosion that shook the old Chevrolet Jeffreys sat in. There was a sea of flames rising from the middle of the parking lot to paint the surrounding cars red and yellow and orange in the flickering glare of their billowing blaze.

"My God," Jeffreys gasped. "I've killed another one!"

XV
THE PLAN

SLEEP CHEEP, the flashing neon letters proclaimed to the surrounding darkness from atop the roof.

He turned into the parking lot.

Climbing out of the car belonging to Andy Horton—the late Andy Horton, he reminded himself, the young man who, because he did Sam Jeffreys a favor, died before he could save up enough for a car or a radio or a visit to the old people of Sun City who wouldn't know a snow shovel if they saw one —he headed into the office.

Behind a smallish counter sat a smallish man atop a regulation-size bar stool. He wore a brown felt fedora hat, a wrinkled brown suit coat and a green polo shirt open at the collar. His eyes were closed. His elbows were on the counter, his chin resting on his palms.

"Yoo hoo," Jeffreys said. The sleeper didn't move. "YOO HOO."

The sleeper stirred, opened his eyes, looked into Jeffreys', vacantly at first and then with dawning comprehension.

"Yoo hoo to you, too," he said, his eyes now bright. "Need a room?"

"Sure do," Jeffreys said. "Sorry to bother you this time of the night."

"The mornin'," the man corrected, still holding his chin-on-hands, elbows-on-counter position. "It's mornin', goin' on fer two."

"True," Jeffreys said. "We both need some sleep, so how about if we get cracking here?"

"Why not," the man said. He roused to an erect sitting position, yawned, stretched, and climbed off the stool. Standing, he was shorter than he had been sitting. He shoved a paper form and a ball-point pen toward Jeffreys. "Need your Johnny Handcock plus a little personal poop."

Jeffreys started to write *Sam*, caught himself in time to make it *Salvatore*, and finished with *Johnston*. He added a random-number address on a made-up street in East St. Louis, Ill., identified his car as a Chevrolet, left the license-plate-number blank unfilled, and listed Illinois Bell Telephone as his employer.

"Two nights," he said, shoving the register toward the clerk.

"Nineteen ninety-nine a night," the clerk said. "Be thirty-nine ninety-eight. Checkout time's noon Monday." He looked at the signature. "Salvation Johnston?"

"Salvatore." Jeffreys dropped two twenties on the counter. "My mother was Italian."

"Grahtsee," the man said, filing the money beneath the counter top. He produced a key attached to a leather fob the size of a shoehorn, slid it and two pennies across the counter. "Room one-ninety-three. Around to yer right an' down a ways. Park anywheres you find a spot."

"Grahtsee. From what I saw out there, I've got the whole parking lot to choose from."

"We ain't too full," the man said, defensively. "It's the slow season, plus the weekend to boot."

"Goodnight," Jeffreys said. He started for the door, looked back. The man was atop the stool again, his eyes shut, his elbows on the counter, his chin in his hands. He didn't answer.

Back in the car, Jeffreys drove the mile or so to the all-night supermarket he'd found after first spotting the Sleep Cheep Motel. Pulling into its sparsely filled parking lot, he chose a space between two beat-up autos whose appearances suggested they belonged to the lower-paid help. He left Andy Horton's car there, mingling unobtrusively with its peers, locked it, and went into the store.

There were a dozen customers pushing carts through the aisles, mostly men wearing the tan or blue shirt-and-pants uniforms of factory shift workers, plus a handful of employees shelving canned goods, lounging, chatting with each other.

Jeffreys picked up a roll of Scotch tape, a toothbrush, toothpaste and a bag of disposable safety razors, then headed for the courtesy checkout counter. He found it under a cardboard banner reading 8 OR LESS ITEMS, wondering why every store manager in the English-speaking world confused less with fewer.

Back outside, he pulled a six-inch length of transparent tape off the roll and pasted it across the crack between the car hood and the body at the latch end. He unlocked the car, climbed in, and headed back to the motel, driving slowly.

He found room 193 without difficulty, reading in the dim illumination of the nearly empty parking lot's overhead lights the rising numbers on the successive doors as he drove nearly the full length of the building. Climbing out of the car with his purchases, he locked it.

The motel door opened inward. It was chilly inside. He surveyed the furnishings—a double bed, a nightstand topped by a lamp and a telephone, a four-drawer dresser across from the bed with a swivel-based TV set bolted atop it, a round table barely big enough for a game of single-deck solitaire, one chair, one wastebasket, one floor lamp.

Jeffreys found the heat control below the room's window at the left of the door. He pulled up the drapery to have a better look at it and turned it toward the setting marked *Warmer*.

He heard the blower fan respond, felt the air from it in his face.

There was a windowless bathroom beyond the bed, walled off from the rest of the room. Its doorless doorway was at right angles to the sleeping-sitting area. Inside it was a tub-shower, a toilet, a tiny washstand and a wall mirror.

"No way in or out except the parking-lot window and the front door, which opens inward in violation of every fire code everywhere," he told himself. He decided to some day write an exposé piece on fire-code violations in cheap motels, like, *How Greedy Innkeepers Bribe Greedy Fire Inspectors To Allow Wrong-Way Doors That Put Your Life at Risk!*" He chuckled and decided *Readers Digest* would love the title if not the content.

He went to the wrong-way door and locked its deadbolt. The room was warmer, now. He took off Cornie's coat and hat. He peeled down to his underwear, dropping his outer clothing into a heap on the floor, pulled back the bed cover, climbed between the sheets, and went instantly to sleep.

When he awakened, sunlight was peeping through the cracks between the window frame and the drapery.

He lay still for a moment, eyeing the splotches of brightness on the wall over the dresser beyond the foot of the bed, struggling to orient himself. Then memory came flooding back, and he shook his head in distress as the picture of an exploding car replayed itself across his mental screen.

"Four dead," he said aloud, as though to remind himself. "Four dead and one more shot up since I found Cornie. No, *because* I found Cornie."

He climbed out of bed and marched to the bathroom. He had a headache and his back hurt and he was hungry. He clambered into the shower.

He felt better when he emerged to dry himself on the single towel hanging over a hook above the toilet. But now he was ravenous.

He went naked into the sleeping-sitting room, turned on the television set, and punched the remote-control buttons until he found a newscast. He donned the clothes in the pile on the floor alongside the bed while he watched and listened. He hated it that he had no fresh underwear, socks or shirt.

The Sunday morning news anchor droned through dull rehashes of Saturday's international and national happenings, finally started in on the local news.

The story Jeffreys was waiting for was a long time coming. Then it was brief and sketchy.

"A car explosion in a bus-depot parking lot early today killed the out-of-state driver," the anchor reported. "Police called it a 'purposeful' bombing. The victim, burned beyond recognition, was tentatively identified through the car's license plate as an Indiana newspaper reporter wanted by local police for a double slaying in Bloomburgh. An investigation is underway and an autopsy is scheduled. The weather today is expected ..."

Jeffreys punched the remote controller's power-off button to silence the TV set. Retrieving the bag of disposable razors from Cornie's overcoat pocket, he went back into the bathroom to comb his still-wet hair with his fingers before the wall mirror, wishing he had thought to buy a pocket comb the night before. He soaped his face, shaved the whisker stubble from his chin and cheeks, rinsed, told himself he didn't look all that bad for a corpse and decided it was good the world thought him dead. He would be safer, less likely to be grabbed, jailed, even killed. It would end the police hunt and halt the Poo Boys' search.

No, hold it. It wouldn't, either, once some coroner's pathologist noticed that the burned bones belonged to a mid-twenties youth and not a late-thirties man. Or that the decedent's bridgework wasn't right. Or that the corpse had a partially melted gold ring in the remains of its left ear, while the police department's description of Samuel T. Jeffreys listed no such decoration. Or that the remains matched the description of one Andrew Horton, a mid-twenties counterman with a gold earring described in another police-department report filed with the Missing Persons Bureau.

He suddenly realized he couldn't let Geoff and Serena think him dead. Likewise Bart Van Til, Stanley Quick, Louis Lewis, Fifi Malloy, a lot of other people who needed to know he was still alive so they wouldn't mourn his passing or foreclose his mortgage or cancel his insurance. He'd have to call home, and so what if Quick was right about telephone taps?

Serena might already have been contacted by Bloomburgh authorities charged with notifying next of kin about deaths of relatives. She might even have shared it with Geoff. So he'd better hurry up and call her to assure them he was alive and relatively well, not lying on an autopsy table somewhere, a cinder without a face.

He dug his AT&T card out of his wallet. He sat down on the bed. Picking up the telephone handset on the nightstand, he dialed the outside operator, gave her his card number and his home phone number. He heard the ringing, the click of the connection, the familiar voice in his ear saying the familiar words, "This is the Jeffreys' residence."

"Good morning, Serena," he said. "Everything all right?"

"Oh, Sam," the voice said. It sounded surprised but not startled. "Why, yes. Shouldn't it be?"

"Sure. Is Geoff there?"

"You just missed him. There's a church breakfast for new freshmen this morning. He got all slicked up for it."

"I'll bet he did. Listen, Serena, there's a story going around that I ... was in a car accident last night. You'll probably be called about it. If and when you are, take my word for it, it isn't true."

"What isn't?" Serena demanded. "Was there a car accident?"

"Well, yes. But I wasn't in it. And obviously, I wasn't killed."

"Are you hurt?" Now she sounded anxious.

"No. I wasn't even involved. My car was demolished, but I wasn't in it. The man who was got burned beyond recognition. Because it was my car, the authorities figured it must be me."

"Oh, dear," Serena said. "Somebody you knew? Did he leave a family?"

"I knew him. He was a friend of mine, though I hadn't known him long. A very good friend, as it turned out. I'm not sure about a family, but I don't think there were kids, anyway."

"That's a blessing. And you're all right?"

"I'm fine, but I need you to do something for me. Dig my car title and my auto insurance policy out of the safe in the radio room."

"I'm not sure I can remember the combination."

"There's a copy of it under the pile of handkerchiefs in my top left bureau drawer."

"Of course. I knew that."

"Sure you did. Anyway, then call Bart Van Til and tell him my car was totaled in a ... in an accident. He'll need the policy number and the VIN number off the title so he can notify the insurance people and get replacement proceedings started. Tell him the incident's all documented in a police report on file in Bloomburgh. He'll know what to do."

"All right. When are you coming home?"

"Soon, I hope. How's Geoff doing?"

"Just fine. He loves high school. He's decided he's going to be valedictorian when his class graduates."

"That's what you call planning ahead."

"Right. Four years ahead. He'll make it, too."

"Sure, he will. Give him a hug for me."

"I will. Oh, Sam, that lady called yesterday. She said she'd be here Monday afternoon."

"What lady?"

"The lady publisher you told to pick up your files."

"Malloy? Fifi Malloy?"

"That's the name. She seemed pleasant."

"She is. She can be very pleasant," Jeffreys said. "Listen, Serena. I've changed my mind about those files. She's not to have them. *Nobody's* to have them. You understand?"

"Well, okay," Serena said. "Will you be seeing her to tell her that?"

"I'm not sure," Jeffreys said. "Whether I do or not, don't let her or anybody else even see my files. Don't let anybody you don't know in the house. Okay?"

"Okay."

"And remember, if and when you get a call saying I'm ... an accident victim, you know better. Right?"

"Right," Serena said. "Shall I tell the callers that?"

"No need," Jeffreys said. "They'll find out in due course. When you talk to Bart, though, you be sure to tell him the reports of my death are greatly exaggerated."

"Should I call him at home today or at his office tomorrow?"

"At home, please. And maybe you better do it right now, before he goes to church. You know how it is with those Dutch Reformed folks. Their services can run all day."

"Right."

"Guess that's it for now then. Love and kisses, Serena."

"Love and kisses," she said, and the connection went dead.

Hanging up the phone, Jeffreys pawed through the telephone directory from the nightstand drawer looking for Louis Lewis' home number. He found only an office listing. He dialed it.

The female voice on the recording device advised him the

office was closed now, but he could leave a message after the beep. It said nothing about an emergency number.

Jeffreys hung up, consulted the directory again, dialed the Holiday Inn and asked for room 412.

"Fifi Malloy," her voice said in his ear.

"Hi," he said. "Hope I didn't wake you."

"Jesus," the voice said. "You're alive?"

"And kicking. I need–"

"–The TV news said–"

"–The TV news was wrong," Jeffreys interrupted. "A guy was killed, but it wasn't me."

"Thank God," Malloy said. "Are you all right?"

"I'm fine. Only I need your help."

"You got it. Where the hell are you?"

"Have you got a car?"

"Sort of. A rental. One of those shitty little compacts."

"Whatever," he said. "Could you chauffeur me around town a little?"

"Sure. Where we going?"

"You'd be harboring a fugitive."

"Also a corpse. Big deal."

"You could get in trouble."

"I'm already in trouble, without the goddam book. Are you in the Holiday Inn here?"

"No," Jeffreys said. "Never mind where I am."

"How can I chauffeur you if I can't find you?"

"I'll meet you."

"Jesus," Malloy said. "You don't trust me?"

"How can I? You're planning to kidnap my files from my house."

The line was silent for a moment. Then Malloy said, "Your housekeeper sounds nice."

"My mother-in-law. She said the same thing about you. Don't bother driving six hundred miles to meet her, though.

She won't be giving you my things."

"I figured I'd organize the damn stuff for you so you could write faster if ever the hell you get around to writing."

"Decent of you, but forget it. Anyway, keep this afternoon open, please, and a piece of tomorrow. I'll call you. Meantime, you haven't heard from me, you don't know I'm alive, nothing." He hung up.

He went into the bathroom and brushed his teeth, feeling hunger pangs again. He remembered seeing an eatery down the block. He counted his money. There was a twenty-dollar bill plus fifty-seven cents in change in his pants pocket, a lone single in his wallet.

Jeffreys shrugged into Cornie's coat, put on Cornie's hat, and headed out to eat a breakfast to be paid for with Cornie's money.

The scrambled eggs at the Food-for-Thought Restaurant a half-mile down the road were delicate, the bacon was delightful, the jellied toast was delectable, the coffee was delicious. When he finished, he wished for a cigarette. Sighing, he dropped his last dollar on the table, laid the last twenty on the cashier's counter, pocketed the change, and headed for the motel.

On the way, during the five-minute walk back to his paid-for-until-Monday-noon lair, he worked out the remaining details of the admittedly risky scheme he'd been contemplating that, if it worked, could be the master plan for his survival.

"So that's it!" he said aloud, his breath steaming in the cold air. "If I live through it, I'll have something for the book. If I don't ..." He left the thought unfinished.

XVI
THE CHAUFFERING

It was a long, dull day despite the football games, the old movies and the other allegedly entertaining programs that succeeded each other on the television screen as the minutes and the hours succeeded each other in the real world.

Repeatedly he dozed, between channel-hopping sessions, sprawled out on the bed, his back cushioned by pillows pushed against the headboard, the remote-controller alongside him in easy reach.

He roused to eat in the early afternoon, strolling the half-mile down the road to the Food-for-Thought restaurant. The fried chicken was excellent, he found, and the fixings superb.

Back in the room, with his watch reading 3:45 P SU 19, he picked up the telephone and dialed the Holiday Inn again.

"Fifi Malloy," her voice said in his ear when the clerk rang her room.

"Hi," he said. "Ready for chauffeuring?"

"Thought you'd never ask. Where the hell are you?"

"I'm here," he said. "Go down to the desk, tell the clerk your name, that you're expecting a call, that you'll be waiting to take it on the house phone in the lobby, and that he shouldn't page you. I'll ring you there in five minutes." He hung up.

"Miss Fifi Malloy," he instructed the clerk, when his watch

told him it was time. "She should be waiting by the house phone."

"She is," the clerk said. "Hang on."

"Fifi Malloy," her voice said in his ear again. It sounded irritated. "Why all the damn cloak-and-dagger crap?"

"There's a restaurant called the Food-for-Thought in the twenty-four-hundred block of one-twenty-third Avenue West," Jeffreys said, ignoring the question. "Meet me there in half an hour. Don't ask the desk clerk for directions. If you need help finding it, stop at a gas station."

"What the hell–?" she was saying as he hung up.

Jeffreys went into the bathroom, returned, sat down on the bed, flipped on the TV set, flipped it off again, checked his watch, decided it was time to go if he walked slowly, and wished for a cigarette.

Donning Cornie's overcoat and hat, he started out, thought better of it, returned to the nightstand. He took Big Poo's gun from under the Gideon bible and the telephone directory in the drawer and slid it into Cornie's coat pocket.

Leaving the room, he locked the door behind him, stuck the key with its shoehorn-sized leather fob into another pocket and headed toward the restaurant, walking slowly.

A little white two-door Honda came whining down the street from behind him when he still was half a block away from his destination. He stepped behind a tree. The Honda swung into the restaurant parking lot. Its woman occupant clambered out. Jeffreys recognized the erect, raincoated figure trotting into the building. He stayed in the shadows across the street, watching for a follower.

After a minute, a blue Ford squealed into the lot and slid to a stop. Its interior light flashed on as both front doors swung open. Jeffreys held his breath. Two teenaged girls climbed out of the car, slammed the doors shut and giggled their way into the restaurant. Jeffreys breathed again. He waited

some more. After a while, he walked into the eatery to join
Fifi Malloy.

She was seated at the counter, wrapped in the trenchcoat, a
bright kerchief tied around her head, its tasseled edges leaking chestnut curls. She was sipping coffee. Her face was
flushed. Her figure was Edie's figure, he decided again, except for the sergeant-major shoulders.

"Hi," he said, sitting down on the stool beside her. "Thanks
for coming."

She swung around to face him, the coffee cup halfway to
her mouth. "You damn jerk," she said, her eyes flashing. They
were brown, he saw, not hazel like Edie's. "I don't–"

"–Hold it," Jeffreys told her, managing a smile. "Just coffee, please," he said to the waitress eyeing him quizzically
from down the counter a ways. He turned back to Malloy.
"Don't be upset."

"Why not?" she demanded. She pulled the kerchief off
her head, unbuttoned her coat. The sweater beneath it was
taut across her breasts. "I'm entitled. What the hell's all this
Alfred Hitchcock shit about, anyway?"

"It's necessary shit," Jeffreys said. "Drink up and let's get
out of here."

In the car, he said, "They're probably watching you."

"Who?" Malloy snapped, scowling at him from behind
the wheel. "What for?"

"Drive and I'll explain."

She started the engine, turned on the headlights, asked,
"Where to?"

"Anywhere. Just drive. And listen."

Malloy backed, turned into the street and headed south.
There was little traffic.

Jeffreys angled himself against the seat to peer through the
rear window, watching for followers. He saw none.

"I've had hoodlums tailing me since I left Indiana," he

said. "They trailed me to Cornie's and killed him. I only lost them after they shot up the FBI guys in my hotel room. They booby-bombed my car. I figure they're watching you, now, hoping you'll lead them back to me."

"Jesus," Malloy said. "That's crazy. How would anybody ... I mean why would anybody ... That's crazy. Isn't it?"

"Sure it is. The whole thing's crazy, but it's true." He saw a set of headlights behind them. "Hang a right at the next corner. See, after Cornie flipped ... uh ... turned snitch for the feds, a lot of people wanted him dead, including some of his former cronies with mob connections. Somehow they must have found out I was looking for him and put a tail on me. Old unconscious me, I never even knew I was being followed and after a few false starts I led them right to him."

"That's who killed him?"

"That's who killed him."

"Sankstone figured it was a contract hit," Malloy said, nodding. She steered into a right turn, straightened. "I can see why they'd want Nicora dead, but why in hell would they hang around to shoot FBI guys and blow up your damn car?" She turned her head to stare at him in the gloom of the Honda's interior, fixed her eyes again on the road ahead. There was a tremor in her voice. "And what would they want with me?"

"We figure they figure Cornie left a stash someplace, heavy money, incriminating records, maybe both. And they want it. We figure they figure I could lead them to that, too. They thought they were grabbing it when they shot Quick and Lukeman, only what they got was a cigar box with a brick in it. They thought they killed me when they booby-trapped my car. By now they know better, and they've got to be looking for me again. That's where you come in."

"Where? And why the hell me?"

"These guys do their homework. They know what's going on."

"So?" Malloy asked, after a pause. "Why me?"

"So they've almost certainly run across your tracks by now

and figured out there's a connection between us." He saw that the headlights were still behind them. "Hang a left when you can. The point is, if they haven't already got you staked out, they soon will have, along with Louis Lewis and my people at home and my Indiana lawyer and anybody else they think might know where I am."

"Jesus," Malloy said, making the turn. "And the cops want you, too. Maybe you should join the witness protection program yourself."

"No way," Jeffreys said. "I've got a life to get back to and a kid to take care of and a book to write. Anyway, there's another problem. The mob's got somebody on the pad inside the police department here. That's got to be how the bombers found my car."

"Jesus," Fifi said. "And you really think that crowd could be watching me?"

"Bet on it," Jeffreys said, still staring out the rear window. The headlights had gone straight when they made their last turn. "I need your help, but I don't need mob guys surprising me by trailing you to where I am, and I don't need you getting hurt."

"Me neither," Malloy said. "How do you mean, my help?"

"I think I've found the stash," Jeffreys said. "I've got a plan for using it to get out of this mess." He quit his rear-window vigil, swung around to face the front of the car, settled back into the seat, wishing there were more leg room. "That's why I need your help."

"Chauffeuring you?"

"Chauffeuring me. Checking me for a tail. Warning me if there is one. Mostly, yelling for help when the time comes."

"Yelling for help?"

"Right. Bringing in the cavalry, like Sankstone and his cops and the feds and the state police. All them cats."

Malloy drove in silence for a time. Then she giggled. "You know what?"

"What?"

"This kind of shit would read pretty well in the damn book."

"Not would," Jeffreys said. "Will. If I live to write it, that is. You'll help?"

"Damn right. Wouldn't miss it. When and where?"

"Tomorrow morning. How's eight o'clock, at the Food-for-Thought? We can breakfast before we head out."

"It's a date," Malloy said. "Hey, wait a minute. What if I'm followed?"

"Be sure you're not."

"How would I know?"

Jeffreys grinned. "You're asking the guy who was tailed from Indiana to Cleveland to Louisville to New Orleans to Bloomburgh without knowing it."

"How about if I don't go back to the Holiday Inn so they can't find me to follow me?"

"That'll work," Jeffreys said, glimpsing a momentary mental picture of Fifi Malloy sharing his room at the Sleep Cheep Motel, then instantly erasing it. "But I couldn't ask you to camp out someplace."

"Where're you staying? Or is it still a secret?"

"In a flea bag near the restaurant where we met tonight. It's called the Sleep Cheep motel. You wouldn't like it."

"I'd like it a damn sight better than being tailed by mobsters," Malloy said. "Find me a drug store for a toothbrush and some mouthwash, and steer me to the Sleep Cheep."

"My room's small," Jeffreys said, forcing himself to protest. "You wouldn't—"

"—Not your damn room," Malloy said. "A room of my own. With a key of my own."

"I knew that," Jeffreys said, trying to ignore the flash of disappointment he felt. "I just meant my room is small, so they probably all are."

"No problem," Malloy said. "I'm a small-room person.

You know where there's an all-night drug store?"

"I know where there's an all-night supermarket with a toothpaste-and-aspirin department," Jeffreys said. "Listen, Fifi, I don't have any money for another room and I—we—can't use my plastic because—"

"—Because you're a damn fugitive," Malloy interrupted. "Good Christ, Sam, do you think I'm a damn idiot? Anyway, I haven't let a man pay my room rent since ... never mind when. Besides, a girl can't afford to be seen with a damn fugitive. Just steer me to that all-night supermarket and quit your damn whining."

He did.

While she was wandering through the store, Jeffreys bought himself a pocket comb.

Back in the Honda, he said, "Home, James," and half-turned in the seat to watch for headlights through the rear window. He saw none. They drove in silence for a time.

He broke the quiet to direct Fifi Malloy to the Sleep Cheep Motel, into the parking lot, and around to 193. Its brass numbers glinted dully in the Honda's headlights as she stopped alongside the dark bulk of Horton's Chevrolet listing heavily to the passenger side.

"You're one-ninety-three?" she asked. Her forehead was furrowed and she sounded anxious. "Suppose you've got company?"

"I hope not," Jeffreys said. "Not yet, anyway. I'm not ready for them."

"Why the hell else would anybody park his damn clunker in front of your damn room when the rest of the damn lot's empty?"

"Oh," Jeffreys said. "No. That's my clunker. Or at least I'm using it. See, it belonged to ... this friend of mine that ... got blown up in my car."

"Jesus," Malloy said, digesting that. Then she said, "Hey, if you've got a car, why the hell am I chauffeuring you?"

"You call that a car?" Jeffreys countered. "A heap like that draws attention. Anyway, like I told you, I need more than just chauffeuring. I need you to check me for a tail, to warn me if there is one and to yell for help when I need it."

"I suppose. Okay. I'll go get myself a room and a night's sleep and I'll see you here eightish for breakfast. Right?"

"Right," he said. He climbed self-consciously out of the Honda, unsure whether to offer Fifi Malloy a grateful handshake or an appreciative peck on the cheek. A hug and a buss on the lips would be unthinkable, wouldn't it?

He left the dilemma unresolved by mumbling an embarrassed, "See you in the morning," and scuttling to his door as she drove off towards the motel office.

Jeffreys walked into his room, shut and bolted the door. Tossing the key onto the nightstand, he put the gun from Cornie's coat pocket under the telephone directory in its drawer. He hung the coat, his trousers and shirt on one of the theft-proof hangers attached to the clothes bar screwed to the wall alongside the bathroom doorway, then stretched them and palmed them to minimize their wrinkles.

He undressed, feeling more alone and lonely than any time since Edie's passing. He took his underwear and socks into the bathroom and washed them out in the tiny sink, using the minuscule bar of soap provided by the management. He wrung them as dry as he could. Carrying them to the window, he draped them across the grillwork housing the heater blower.

He crawled naked into bed, and fell instantly asleep to dream of Edie. She was swathed in a figure-hugging trenchcoat, her hazel eyes now brown and her shoulders thrust back like a sergeant-major's to pull her coat taut across her breasts. She kept beckoning him from the doorway of another room.

XVII
THE STASH

It was day when he woke. There was enough pale light sneaking into the room around and beneath the window draperies to let him see his watch. It read 6:38 *A MO* 20.

Jeffreys groaned, rolled over, closed his eyes and tried to go back to sleep. Failing, he sat up, groaned again and went into the bathroom to shower. He soaped his face and scraped it free of whiskers with the razor he had used the day before. He ran the new pocket comb through his wet hair.

He found his shorts and one sock dry, but the T-shirt damp and the other sock moist. He put them on anyway, pretending they weren't cold and clammy. He donned the rest of his clothes and went into the bathroom to examine himself in the wall mirror.

Jeffreys decided the person in the wrinkled, open-collared shirt staring back at him could pass for ... uh ... Clem Nathan, wasn't it? Yes, Clem Nathan. But only if Clem Nathan were an unnoticed and unremembered middle-class working man among a horde of others who rented safety deposit boxes at the Midwest Industrial Bank in which to store worthless valuables like insurance policies and mortgages and army discharge papers and cemetery-lot deeds. If Clem Nathan happened instead to be a noticed and remembered high-visibility client

who employed the bank's facilities to guard valuable valuables, then Sam Jeffreys was in big trouble.

Ah, well, he told himself. So what else was new?

Sighing, he sat down on the bed, punched the 0 button on
the telephone, and asked for Fifi Malloy.

"Who?" the grumpy female voice at the other end of the
line rasped.

"Fifi Malloy," he repeated. "I don't know her room number."

"Oh," the voice said. "A guest, huh? Hang on. I'm lookin'.
Ahhh, she's in seventy-seven. I'm ringin'."

The telephone buzzed repeatedly in his ear. Why didn't
she answer? Was she a sound sleeper? Was she showering?
Had the mob found her? Was she ... An auto horn blared outside his door. He hung up.

He donned Cornie's coat and hat. The auto horn beeped
again.

It was Fifi in the Honda, peering at him through the driver's
window as he emerged into the sunlight. She smiled and the
skin around her eyes crinkled as Edie's used to.

"Morning," he said, smiling back and walking around
behind the car to clamber in on the passenger side.

"About time you showed up," she said pleasantly. "Do you
always keep your damn dates waiting?"

"Always," he said. "I like 'em eager. Hungry?"

"A little. The Food-for-Thought?"

"Sure," he said. "Not starved, though, I hope."

"Pardon?" Malloy said, looking puzzled.

"I hope you're not starved. I've got something like eleven
dollars to my name."

"Ah," Malloy said, grinning. She drove out of the lot and
down the street. "I'm a cheap date. Especially at breakfast. It's
rye toast and tea, remember?"

"With peanut butter. How could I forget?"

"Eleven dollars," she said. "You need a loan?"

"No thanks. I'm expecting to come into money."

Jeffreys ordered coffee and a Danish, sitting across from Fifi Malloy at the tiny table for two, trying to keep his eyes on her face. She'd shrugged out of her raincoat and tossed it over the back of her chair. Her sergeant-major posture stretched her sweater tightly across her chest. She looked fresh and pink and clean, and she smelled of mouthwash and toothpaste and cologne. She was Edie with her hair done differently and wearing a too-tight bra ...

"So," she said, derailing his train of thought. She knifed a dab of peanut butter onto a fragment of rye toast, "What's our mission this morning?"

"We're robbing a bank," Jeffreys said, chewing a bite of apple-cinnamon Danish.

"Get serious," Malloy said testily. "If I'm going to help you do whatever the hell you're doing I've got a right to know what the hell it is."

"I'm serious, too," Jeffreys said, amused by her intensity. He lowered his voice to a whisper. "We're robbing a bank. Figuratively, anyway. We're hitting a bank where Cornie had a lockbox and we're helping ourselves to whatever's in it."

"Money?" she whispered back. "Millions of ill-gotten dollars stolen from taxpayers and widows and orphans and coveted by the mob?"

"Maybe. Or maybe records, ledgers, diaries, materials to write a book from, also coveted by the mob."

"Jesus," Malloy said. "How do we get in the damn box?"

"We've got a key," Jeffreys said. "But I misspoke. I said *we* were hitting a bank. I should have said I am."

"What about me?"

"You're the outside man. You're going to chauffeur me and guard my flank."

"Hot damn," Malloy whispered, spreading peanut butter

on a piece of rye toast. "I always wanted to be wheel man—make that wheel person—on a bank job. Wouldn't mom be proud?"

"It isn't every daughter can drive a getaway car," he agreed, grinning. "Or handle peanut butter for breakfast, either. Yuck."

Their check came to $4.60. Jeffreys left a dollar on the table, pocketed the change the cashier gave him, and followed Malloy out of the restaurant.

"This better be a good heist," he said, climbing into the Honda alongside Fifi Malloy. "I've got four bucks and pennies to my name."

The Midwest Industrial Bank was where the telephone directory said it would be. Jeffreys felt better when he saw it was in an old and fading section of town, one paint-peeling, brick-faced, frame building surrounded by a horde of other paint-peeling, brick-faced, frame buildings. His—Cornie's—wrinkled shirt collar and suit surely wouldn't be too out of place here.

"Let's go around the block again," he said, as they drove past the bank. "I saw a couple parking places back there near the corner. Pull in one, let me out, and I'll walk from there. You watch for anybody tailing me."

"How'll I know?" Malloy demanded.

Jeffreys shrugged. "Look for anything suspicious, like people walking too slow or too fast. Checking reflections in shop windows. The same car driving past repeatedly. Whatever."

"Can do," Malloy said. "I hope." She pulled into a parking space a half-block from the bank. "Okay if I keep the damn engine running and the heater on?"

"Sure," Jeffreys said. "Good wheel men always do. Just lock your doors." He grinned at her, wrapped to her chin in the figure-shrouding trenchcoat, hoping his apprehensions didn't show. "Back in a flash with the cache," he said, and climbed out of the car.

He shoved one of his remaining dimes into the meter at the curb and started walking. The wind blew cold in his face. He stared into each store window he passed, watching for reflections of others doing the same. He saw nothing suspicious. He sneaked a look at his watch. It was 9:17. He slowed his pace. It must be 9:30 or later when he entered, his master plan provided. It had to be well past opening time so the bank's daily commerce would be fully underway, its employees into their day's activities, enough other customers on hand to divert attention from him.

His watch read 9:33 when he reached the particular paint-peeling, brick-faced, frame building that was his target among the other paint-peeling, brick-faced, frame buildings. Taking a deep breath, he threw his shoulders back and entered.

The interior of the Midwest Industrial Bank was larger than he had judged it from outside. There was a row of cashier cages to his right, three of them with customers bellied up to them. There were a half-dozen standup desks to his left, two of them in use by people endorsing checks or filling out deposit slips. There was a line of smallish offices along the left wall, presumably the sanctora of loan officers, trust officers, vice presidents, whatever other office-dwellers ran old and fading banks. There was a huge vault door near the right rear corner, beyond the cashier cages.

Jeffreys headed toward it.

There was a woman behind the waist-high counter. She was heavyset, middle-aged, frowzy. Her greying hair was pulled into a bun. She wore a beige linen jacket over a high-necked, greenish blouse and a beige linen skirt. Jeffreys, able to see only the bulging waistband of the skirt above the counter, decided absently that it would be ankle-length, stopping just above low-heeled, sensible shoes. He forced his walk to a saunter, thrust his chest out and his shoulders back.

"Good morning," he said, reaching the counter. He pulled the tiny envelope from his coat pocket, unsnapped its flap, withdrew the key, laid it on the counter top, pocketed the envelope. "I need to get into my box, please."

"Of course," the clerk said, eyeing the key. She picked it up, read the number, flipped back the battered lid of a large mahogany card file atop the counter and began riffling through its contents. Withdrawing a card, she glanced at it, asked, "Name, please?"

"Nathan," he said. "Clem Nathan."

She nodded, slid the key across the counter to Jeffreys, stuck the card into a device he recognized as a date-stamper, pressed its handle, took the card out, inspected it again, handed it to him. She said, "Sign, please."

He eyed the card as he laid it on the counter. Across its top was typed 914 and *Clem Nathan, 3537-51st Ave., City. No telephone.* Beneath that, on a line by itself, was the handwritten legend, *Clem Nathan,* probably the sample signature against which other sign-ins would be compared, Jeffreys decided. Further down, four lines marched across the card. Each started with a date in stamp-pad black ink and ended with *Clem Nathan* scrawled in black ball-point ink. The top date, he saw, was June 4, the bottom one Sept. 14.

So the nine grand in Cornie's detergent box was the remains of whatever he'd picked up here just over a month ago. The signatures, each characterized by cramped, erect, rounded letters, were similar but not identical. He felt a surge of confidence that he could pull it off.

With the ball-point pen the clerk proffered, he carefully scrawled *Clem Nathan* across the card to the right of the newly stamped date, doing his best to emulate the style of the signatures above it. Then he handed the card and the pen to the clerk and tried to force a carefree smile.

"Started your Christmas shopping yet?" he asked.

"Hardly," the lady said, eyeing the card. "It's still a month to Thanksgiving."

"True," Jeffreys said, managing to retain the smile. "But why wait until the last minute?"

The clerk sniffed, laid the card on the counter atop a thin stack of similar cards, opened a drawer, and withdrew a handful of keys on a leather thong. "Follow me, please," she said.

Jeffreys did, noting absently that the beige linen skirt was ankle-length, stopping just above flat-heeled, sensible shoes. He caught up with the clerk at the barred vault door. She passed two aisles of deposit boxes stretching floor to ceiling, turned into the third aisle, walked part-way down the line, stopped, and held out her hand. Jeffreys put Cornie's key into it. She inserted it in a keyhole at eye level, sorted through her ringed keys, pushed one of them into a second keyhole alongside the first, turned both, swung the little door open.

"Help yourself," she said, stepping aside and pointing at the box front revealed within.

Jeffreys did, finding the wire bail, using it as a handle to slide the box out, shoving it under his left arm and helping support it there with his right hand. It was larger than the last box he had held, nearly a foot wide by six inches high, though not as heavy. *No brick*, he thought.

"You wish a privacy room?"

"Please."

"Of course." She shut and locked the door, withdrew the keys, handed one to Jeffreys, said, "Follow me, please," and set off the way they came. She unlocked and opened the vault door, waved him through it, latched it behind them, led him past her counter to the first of a series of curtained doorways he hadn't noticed when he came in, and pulled aside the curtain.

He stepped into a tiny, dark cubicle, stood there for a moment, confused. He heard a switch click behind him, and an overhead light sprang on. He heard the swish of a curtain closing and looked around. He was in a room three feet by five feet, separated from the rest of the world only by the curtain. There was a foot-deep shelf attached to the wall in front of him. There was a thin stack of blank paper atop it, and the stub of an eraserless pencil.

Jeffreys felt the rising tingle of excitement in his belly as he set the steel box on the shelf. He lifted its hinged cover and peered inside. Two brown paper sacks were crammed into the interior. He pulled one out, taking care not to tear it. It was an everyday Kraft-paper grocery bag. It rustled when he squeezed it, as though filled with dead leaves.

He unfolded its end and peered inside.

It was stuffed with stacks of currency.

His heart pounding, he pulled a handful from the pile and stared at the bills in disbelief. They were thousand-dollar notes. He was holding seven grand in his one hand, a whole bag full of big bills in the other.

Jeffreys put the notes back in the sack and set it down. He took the other bag from the box, opened its folded end and gawked at its contents. It, too, was full of currency. He withdrew a handful of bills. They also were thousands.

His pulse racing and his mind numb, he checked the emptied box. There was a smallish green cardboard envelope Scotch-taped to its bottom, its flap secured by a metal snap. He peeled it free of the tape, opened it, and dumped its contents into his hand. It was another key, he saw with rising excitement. Another safe deposit box key. The number 712 and MOSLER were stamped into it. He examined the envelope. Faintly handwritten across it, embossed into the paper by the pressure of a ball-point pen, he read in tiny letters, Clarence Nichols and Fltchr Ntl.

Willing himself to calm down and concentrate on what he was doing, Jeffreys replaced the key in its envelope, pocketed it and stared at the little stacks of bills he had dropped onto the shelf. He took a bill off the top.

"Another loan, Cornie," he muttered under his breath, folding it and shoving it into his trouser pocket.

He put the remainder back in the bag, replaced the sacks in the steel box, and closed its hinged lid. Then he stood there quietly for a moment, forcing his breathing to slow before shoving the box under his arm, pulling aside the curtain, and stepping back into the real world, his chest thrust out and his shoulders back.

Jeffreys' mind was a blur as he went through the motions of following the lady in the ankle-length linen skirt and the low-heeled, sensible shoes through the barred door again, past the tiers of lockboxes and into the third aisle, surrendering his key, replacing the box in its cubbyhole, watching the door closed and locked, accepting the key, pocketing it, marching out.

"Thanks, Ma'am," he said, when they were back outside the vault. "Don't wait too long to start that Christmas shopping," and he headed for the door.

He remembered as he was passing the bank of cashier cages that he was insolvent except for four dollars and change plus the thousand-dollar note. Did he dare risk longer exposure here by trying to break the big bill? Would that be tempting fate?

Probably, he decided. *But the plan needs some funding.*

He forced himself to stop at the last cage, chest out and shoulders back, working at controlling his breathing. He fished the thousand-dollar bill from his pocket and thrust it through the cage opening.

"Give me nine hundreds, please, and five twenties," he told the girl behind the bars, hoping his voice was strong and confident.

Evidently it was, because she nodded, smiled, and began counting.

XVIII
THE READYING

Fifi Malloy saw him coming and reached across to unlock the Honda's passenger-side door so he could clamber in.

"Well?" she demanded.

"Piece of cake," he said, feeling the warmed air wash across his face as he settled into the seat and pulled the door closed to block the chill that followed him into the car. "We hit the jackpot."

"Money? Records?"

"Money. Mucho cash plus another key."

"How mucho cash?"

"I didn't count it," Jeffreys said, grinning at her. Her trenchcoat was open, revealing the tautness of the sweater across her breasts and the skirt across her lap. "Two sacks full of big bills. Looked like they were all thousands."

"Jesus," Malloy said. "So where the hell are they?"

"I left them there. In the box. All but one."

"One what?" Malloy demanded.

"One bill. I broke it into hundreds and twenties so we've got eating money and room-rent money again."

"Jesus God," Malloy said, shaking her head and staring at him. "You found a damn mill and you took a damn thou?"

"Plus a key."

"You're something else, you know that? So what's the key for?"

"Another lock box in another bank. That's at least three Cornie had in Bloomburgh."

"What bank? And what the hell's in it?"

"Beats me," Jeffreys said. "I'm hoping for book-writing materials, like ledgers, records, diaries."

"Or dirty pictures, or paid-off mortgages, or maybe somebody's old damn love letters," Malloy said. "Let's go find out. Where's the bank? How do we get there?"

"We don't, yet. We save that for later. Right now, we get my master plan started."

"What master plan?"

"The one that jails the bad guys and unfugitives me so I can visit banks and other public places without getting shot at or blown up or locked in."

"Care to brief me on how this super plan is supposed to work?" Malloy asked, sounding irritated again. "Or is that another damn secret?"

"I'm happy to share it with my getaway driver," Jeffreys said. "I plan to set a trap for the bad guys, lure them into it, snap it shut on them, and turn them over to the cops, thus getting myself off the hook. Then I finish the book, deliver it to you, do what minor rewrites and insignificant revisions your editorship has to require in order to remain a bona fide member of the editors' union, and we all live happily ever after."

Malloy stared at him in silence for a time. Then she said, "What kind of a damn trap are you planning to set?"

"An ambush trap," he said.

"For where?

"For in my motel room."

Malloy shook her head as though in disbelief. Her face reddened. "You're planning to ambush two goddam mob guys? Professional killers with goddam guns? In your goddam motel room?"

"That's my plan," Jeffreys said, wondering why this lady who reminded him so much of Edie sprinkled her conversation so liberally with damns and hells. "You know what, Fifi? Profanity doesn't become you."

Malloy sat silent for a moment, her face still flushed. Then she said, "So where to?"

"To a hardware store for ambush supplies," Jeffreys said. "I remember seeing one a couple blocks back." He gestured behind them. "Thataway, please, James."

"Yessir," Malloy said. She drove out of the parking spot, waited for a break in traffic, swung into a U-turn, and headed back the way they had come.

"That wasn't smart," Jeffreys said, looking around for a cop car. He didn't see any. "You can't afford to be stopped, you know."

"I suppose," Malloy said. "Harboring a fugitive and all that crap."

"For you. Worse for me. Fugitiving and murdering and all that crap."

"I'll keep it in mind," Malloy said, pulling in to the curb. "Here's your damn ... your hardware store."

It was a huge, well-stocked establishment.

"I need a box of twenty-two caliber cartridges, hollow-point, long rifle," he told the busty girl in the short skirt and low-cut blouse who met him inside the door. She looked out of place here, he thought, a teenage female who belonged behind the cosmetics counter of a dime store or in the brassiere department of a ladies' boutique, not in the macho-male world of the hardware business. "You know what I'm talking about?"

"Sure do," the girl said, grinning at him. "We got a special going on Copperlubes. They okay?"

"Just fine," Jeffreys said, grinning back. "I also need the biggest package of BB-shot you carry, and the biggest, shallowest cookie sheet."

"How about one-seventy-seven pellets instead of BBs. They're a whole lot more accurate."

"BBs," Jeffreys said. "They're not for shooting."

The girl's brow furrowed, then cleared. She shrugged. "We've got packs of five-thousand. How many packs you need?"

"One'll be enough. How about the cookie sheet?"

"You want a non-stick surface?"

"Definitely not."

"Stainless steel or aluminum?"

"How about plain old tin-plate, shiny and shallow."

"Shallow?"

"With low sides," Jeffreys said, searching for words to make his needs clear. "The rim around the cookie sheet that keeps the dough or the batter or whatever from running off the edges can't be higher than a half-inch."

"You can look at what we've got," she said. She started toward the rear of the store. "I think the shallowest are probably the disposables."

"Disposables?"

"Them," she said, pointing at a display case of heavy foil throw-away cookie sheets, two to a package, sealed in cellophane. The label said they were 12 inches by 18 inches.

"Ideal," Jeffreys said, noting that the rim around each sheet was only a quarter-inch high. "That gives me door clearance." He picked up one of the packages, stuck it under his arm.

"I'll get your cartridges and your BBs," the girl said, and strode off. She was back in a minute carrying a brown paper bag. "Somethin' else?"

"Fifty feet of two-conductor electric zipcord, a pair of needlenose pliers and a baseball bat," Jeffreys said.

"Hardball or softball?"

"Hardball. I need a skinny handle and a thick barrel."

"No problem," the girl said. "The bats are in the basement this time of year. Want to go downstairs and look 'em over?"

"No need. You know what I want."

The girl eyed him up and down, said, "Like thirty inches and thirty ounces?"

"Like perfect." Jeffreys said.

"Meet you at the cash register in five, and then we'll get your zipcord and pliers," she said, handing him the bag. It was heavy. She trotted off.

Ten minutes later, Jeffreys was tossing his purchases onto the rear seat of the Honda and climbing into the front.

"A bat?" Fifi Malloy said, craning her neck to stare at the packages. "A baseball bat? That's your damn ... your armory? That's your arsenal for trapping ambushed gangsters carrying guns?"

"For starters," Jeffreys said.

"What other high-tech armaments did you stock up on? A slingshot and an ice pick, maybe, or a pocket knife?"

"No slingshot, no ice pick, and I've already got a pocket knife," Jeffreys said. "I bought some BB-shot and some twenty-two cartridges, though, and pliers and wire. Oh, and a couple of cookie sheets."

"You're weird, you know that?" Malloy said. "You need a keeper. Where now?"

"That Sears store across the street," Jeffreys said, grinning. "You need anything?"

"Getaway drivers don't shop while they're on duty."

The Sears store was a one-floor affair, well-enough stocked for his needs. He bought three pairs of shorts, size 36; three T-shirts, crew neck, size 42; three pairs of socks, black, calf-length, size 10 1/2; three white dress shirts, 15 1/2 neck, 32 sleeves. Then he picked out a yellow necktie, a pair of light brown slacks, 36 waist, 33 inseam, and a dark brown sport coat, 40 regular. He paid for the lot in cash, using two of

Cornie's hundred-dollar bills, and pocketed the change without counting it.

Back in the car, he said, "Home, James," and tossed his
packages onto the back seat with the others.

Fifi Malloy didn't grin. She just put the Honda in gear and
took off, heading back towards the Sleep Cheep Motel.

Around to the right," he said when they got there. "One-
nine-three."

"I knew that," Malloy said, pulling up alongside Andy
Horton's leaning Chevrolet and cutting the engine. "I dropped
you off here last night and picked you up here this morning.
Remember?"

"Keep it in mind," Jeffreys said, reaching back for his packages. "Memorize that number. One-niner-three. Burn it into
your brain so you can recite it in your sleep."

"Why?" Malloy asked.

"So you'll know where to send the troops when I need
them," he said.

Leaning over into the back seat to pick up his bundles, he
dropped a couple of them, said, "Damn," and tried to retrieve them from the floor with both arms already full.

"Clumsy," Malloy said, reaching over to pick up the fallen
packages. "You need help. Boy, do you need help."

"True," Jeffreys said, clambering backwards out of the car
with his load. He pulled the leather-fobbed key from Cornie's
coat pocket, stuck it in the lock and turned it. Inside, he tossed
his cargo onto the unmade bed.

Malloy, right behind him, dropped her parcels there too.

"No maid service?" she asked.

Jeffreys shrugged. "Not yet, anyway. Maybe later this afternoon."

"I've been in some dumps," Malloy said, "but none
dumpier than this one."

Jeffreys walked to the door, closed it, snapped on the floor lamp. "Welcome to my dump," he said, gesturing towards the room's one chair. "Mi dumpa es su dumpa."

Fifi Malloy's face softened. She sat down, shaking her head. He saw a smile start to curl her lips, then fade again. "What'd you mean about memorizing your room number so I could call in the troops? You sounded serious."

"Earnest is the word," Jeffreys said. He took off Cornie's coat and hat, tossed them onto the bed atop his purchases and sat down alongside them. "Solemn, even. My plan has you sending the cops here in a hurry when the time comes. You'll need to remember the number because I'll want them to come straight here, not stop off half a block away knocking on strange doors and asking if anybody's seen the late Sam Jeffreys."

Malloy thought about that for a moment. She shrugged out of her coat, threw it behind her across the top of the chair. She said, "Where'll I be sending the cops from? I mean, where will I be? And how'll I know when to send them?"

"You'll be at the Holiday Inn," Jeffreys told her, trying not to notice the tautness of her sweater, the shapeliness of her thighs straining against her skirt. "I'll call you, and then you'll sound the alarm, through every Middlesex village and farm for the constabulary to be up and to arm."

"Tell it to me straight, Paul Revere. You'll call me and then I'll call the cops?"

"Right."

"Why not call them yourself? Eliminate the middleman?"

"Because I'll have time for one quick phone call, if I'm lucky, but I want all the cops sent here. That means calls to the city police, to Sergeant Sankstone personally, to the sheriff's police, to the state police. You'll have all their numbers ready, and you'll start summoning them the instant I ask you to."

"And while they're on the way, you'll be clubbing and pelleting two mobster-type gunmen with your baseball bat and your BB's, right?"

"I'll have a couple other things going for me," Jeffreys said, uncomfortably aware that her appraisal was essentially accurate. "Like a twenty-two pistol."

"Oh, that's good. An amateur shooting it out with two professionals. For a minute there I thought you were maybe overmatched. So how're you going to lure them here?"

"With Cornie's stash. When they learn we found it and where it is, they'll come after it."

"And how do they learn that?"

"From me," Jeffreys said. "I tell them. You hungry?"

"Starved," Malloy said. "How do you tell them? Where do you tell them?"

"I leave them messages," Jeffreys said. "How about if we eat? You can chauffeur me to the Food-for-Thought one more time, and then head back to the Holiday Inn."

"Won't they be watching for me there?"

"I hope so. More than that, I hope they're listening in on your phone calls."

Malloy's brow crinkled. She stared at Jeffreys. Her eyes, Jeffreys saw, were definitely brown, not hazel.

"I'll explain over sandwiches," he said, getting up. He held out a hand and pulled her to her feet. Her palm was moist in his clasp. Impulsively, he pulled her to him, held her for an instant, chest to breasts, stomach to stomach, thighs to thighs. She was warm and soft and yielding. He kissed her lightly on the lips, let go of her, stepped back, tried to read her expression. He couldn't.

She stood there eyeing him, her face blank. After a moment, she said, "Damn, Sam."

"Damn Sam, indeed," Jeffreys said. The room was suddenly very warm. He thought of a dozen things to say, discarded them all. He snatched Cornie's hat and coat off the bed, strode to the door, and stopped with his hand on the knob. "There's no door on the bathroom, so I'll wait outside if you want to freshen up."

The cold, fresh air felt good. He walked to Andy Horton's car, ran a hand across the crack between the hood and the body near the latch end. The tape was intact.

Fifi Malloy came out, wearing her trenchcoat. She walked to the Honda without a word, unlocked the driver-side door, and climbed in. Jeffreys waited for her to unlock the passenger-side door. Then he clambered silently in alongside her.

The Food-for-Thought was moderately busy. The tiny table they'd shared at breakfast was occupied. Jeffreys steered Malloy to the counter. She scanned a menu plucked from between a napkin dispenser and a sugar shaker and ordered a cheeseburger. Jeffreys told the young counterman in the white apron and chef's cap he'd like a steak sandwich with French fries, green beans and a tossed salad with Thousand Island dressing, trying not to think of Andy Horton. While they waited for their food, he thought of Andy Horton.

Halfway through her cheeseburger, Fifi Malloy found her voice.

"My room?" she asked.

"Pardon?" Jeffreys said.

"Or the lobby, like last time?"

"I don't ... oh, where I'll be calling you?"

"Right."

"I think your room. I don't want you waiting in the lobby for maybe hours and hours."

"Me neither."

"So I'll call your room."

"When?"

"That's a problem," Jeffreys said. "I don't know when. Hopefully early evening, maybe late evening or midnight or not until early morning." He shrugged. "Maybe not at all."

"Tell me again how you hope to lure the mob guys into your snare."

"It's a trap," he corrected. "An ambush. By making them think I'm sitting on Cornie's stash."

"Tell me again how the hell you do that?" Malloy demanded, chewing her final bite of cheeseburger.

"By telephone," Jeffreys said, hoping he sounded more confident than he felt.

"You know their phone number?"

"I know some numbers I think they've got bugged."

"Jesus," Malloy said. "They're line-tappers, too? These're nice people you're fooling around with. You springing for dessert?"

"Cornie is," Jeffreys said, trying not to think of Andy Horton. "I'm going to have a big chunk of cherry pie with vanilla ice cream. You too?"

"Damn right," Fifi Malloy said. "Thought you'd never ask. You need help making those phone calls?"

"Absolutely not," Jeffreys said. "I don't want it known I've got a confederate."

"I never thought of myself as a damn confederate. Why don't you want it known?"

"I don't want them bringing in reinforcements. Two-to-one is odds enough for them."

"Makes sense," Malloy said, forking pie into her mouth. A splotch of cherry juice stained her chin.

"Right. I'm going to take some grub with me so I don't have to leave my room, once I'm ready for invaders. You want something to go?"

"No, thanks. Another meal today and I'll start spreading out."

Jeffreys shook his head, making a point of looking her up and down. "Honey," he whispered, "you've got a long ways to go."

"Thank you, Sam," Fifi Malloy whispered back. "That's the nicest thing you've ever said to me."

Jeffreys asked the counterman for a ham and cheese on

white, a pint of milk and a large container of black coffee, all to go. Then he donned Cornie's coat, surrendered some of Cornie's money to the white-garbed counterman-cum-cashier, and tried not to think of Andy Horton.

Back at the Sleep Cheep Motel, Fifi Malloy parked alongside the listing Chevrolet in front of 193 and waited for Jeffreys to disembark. He leaned over to peck her on the cheek, caught her on the lips instead, and wondered whether he'd missed or she'd moved.

"I've got work to do and calls to make," he said quietly, opening the car door. "When I'm ready for the ambushing, I'll call you to say so. After that, we wait. When they come, if they come, I give you a call and you turn out the militia. Got it?"

"Got it," Fifi Malloy said. Her eyes were into his. They were definitely brown, not hazel at all. "Be careful, Sam."

"Bet on it," he said, picking his sack of restaurant goodies off the seat. He climbed out of the Honda and bent over to peer in at her through the open door. "Listen, Fifi, one of my calls'll be to my mother-in-law. I'll tell her if anything happens to me to give you my Cornie files."

"I don't want your damn Cornie files."

"They'd be helpful for maybe salvaging the book–"

"–Shove the goddamn book," Fifi Malloy interrupted. Her voice was hard. "Shut the goddamn door."

He did. She squealed the Honda's wheels backing away, squealed them again speeding out of the parking lot.

He watched her disappear beyond the motel office. Then he sighed, shifted his bag of goodies to the other hand, reached the leather-fobbed key from Cornie's overcoat pocket, and headed for his door.

"Edie never talked like that," he told himself.

XIX
THE SETTING

Jeffreys found that the bed had been made during his absence. The packages he'd left strewn amidst the bedding were now neatly stacked atop the spread.

Shrugging out of Cornie's coat, he hung it on one of the theft-proof hangers attached to the clothes bar alongside the bathroom doorway. He put Cornie's hat on the shelf, and spent the next ten minutes unpackaging and stowing his Sears clothing purchases. Then he put the rest of his parcels on the dresser, filled the wastebasket with their wrappings, and visited the bathroom.

With his needs attended to, he dug the two lockbox keys from his pocket and read aloud the legends on their envelopes.

"Clem Nathan, box number nine-fourteen, Midwest Industrial," he recited. "I can remember that. Clarence Nichols, box seven-twelve, Fletcher National. I better remember that, too."

He emptied the envelopes into his hand, took Andy's car keys from his pocket, unhooked the ends of their ball-link chain, strung the lockbox keys onto it, hooked the ends together again, and pocketed them. Then he flushed the envelopes down the toilet.

Back in the sitting-sleeping room, he went to the nightstand. On a piece of dog-eared stationery and a shop-worn envelope from the bottom of the drawer, he addressed the envelope to Bartel Van Til at his Highland law office and wrote a note:

> Dear Bart:
>
> I'm expecting company in the form of the lovely folks who did Cornie and three other people. If I don't survive their visit, see that Geoff and Serena are taken care of, please, Geoff to be my sole heir, Serena executor and whatever.
>
> Also, do what needs to be done with this information, if I don't survive to take care of it myself: Cornie Nicora AKA Charles Stevens had two more aliases, Clem Nathan and Clarence Nichols. There is a stash under each name in two Bloomburgh banks, Midwest Industrial and Fletcher National, boxes 914 and 712 respectively. Box 914 is full of money. The other I haven't seen yet, though I'm hoping to.
>
> Regards,
> Sam

Sealing the note in the envelope, Jeffreys shrugged into Cornie's overcoat, put on his hat, and headed for the motel office.

There was a fat female clerk astride the stool behind the smallish counter. She wore a sullen look. Her bristly, carrot-colored hair pointed in all directions. Her huge, drooping breasts bulged the front of her high-necked cotton print dress. She was filing her nails.

"Hi," she said. "Checkin' out?"

"Nope. I'll be staying another night." He laid two twenties

on the counter. "Right now I'll be making a bunch of phone calls. I'm in one-ninety-three."

She dropped the nail file, snatched up the money, and grinned, sending the bristle ends of her carrot hair waving like weeds in a windstorm.

"Room's nineteen ninety-nine," she said. "What's the rest for?"

"Phone calls and a stamp."

"Oh," she said, her grin fading. "Thought it was a humongous tip." She held one of the bills toward him. "I can't take yer phone money 'til after so's the computer can figure yer charges."

"I'll be making them in the next half hour," Jeffreys said. "Just a few locals, plus some credit-card long-distance. You check the computer, take out what I owe, and keep the rest."

"AwRIGHT!" she said. "Thank ya. Did ya say somethin' about a stamp?"

"Right," he said, handing her the envelope addressed to Van Til. "Could you stamp this and mail it for me?" He slid a dollar bill across the counter.

"Sure," she said. "Mailman'll be here in a while. I'll see he takes it."

"Appreciate it," Jeffreys said, and headed back to his room.

He sat down on the bed, picked up the telephone from the nightstand. The first call went on the credit card. It was to Bartel Van Til.

"Mr. Jeffreys?" Cile asked. "I thought I recognized your voice. I'm sorry, but Mr. Van Til's not here. He's in court again. Can I take a message?"

"Please," Jeffreys said. "You tell him I found Cornie's stash."

"You found what?"

"Cornie's Stash. I spell: C-O-R-N-I-E-apostrophe-S S-T-A-S-H. He'll know what it means. You tell him it's huge, a real bundle, more than anybody thought. You tell him I found

Cornie's—same spelling—account books, too. They're fascinating, full of names and dates and dollar amounts. You tell him I'm in the Sleep Cheep Motel, two E's in Cheep, in Bloomburgh, room one-ninety-three. I'll be here until tomorrow, Tuesday, and after that I'll be in court and maybe in jail myself. Did you get all that?"

"Did you say you could be in jail?"

"In jail. Thank you, Cile."

The next call, also on the credit card, was to Serena. It rang four times without an answer. On the fifth ring, his own voice came back to him. "This is the Jeffreys residence. We can't come to the phone right now. If you'll leave your name and number when you hear the beep, we'll get back to you as soon as we can."

He waited for the tone, said, "Serena, this is Sam. I'm still in the Sleep Cheep Motel in Bloomburgh, room one-ninety-three. I have to go to court tomorrow. It's just a formality, now, but I still have to go. Meanwhile, I've got great news. I've found boxes full of the money the man I've been chasing stole and hid away, plus his record books that tell who helped him steal it. I'll be turning it all over to court authorities tomorrow, and then I'll be coming home."

Hanging up, he dug the telephone directory out of the nightstand drawer, and started in on the local calls.

The first one went to Louis Lewis.

"Whom shall I tell Mr. Lewis is calling?" a female voice said in his ear.

"Sam Jeffreys," he said. "I'm a client."

There was a gasp, an instant of silence, then, "Oh, yes, Mr. Jeffreys, I know you're a client," the female voice said. "Just a moment, please."

There was a click and Lewis' voice was in his ear.

"Jeffreys?" it said, sounding incredulous. "Is this you?"

"Who else? Listen, what time is my arraignment tomorrow?"

"I ... we thought you were dead!"

"You thought wrong."

"Obviously. But who—"

"—Wasn't me. What time's my arraignment?"

"Two o'clock, but ... I've filed a motion for continuance."

"Why did you do that?"

"The ... unh ... people who posted your bond asked me to. They ... weren't ready to produce proof of your death, and they didn't want to forfeit their bail money."

"You're working for me, not them!"

"You seemed to forget that when you let them bail you out without my knowledge."

"Touché," Jeffreys said. "Okay, so we're even. When's the motion to be heard?"

"Two o'clock."

"No problem, then. Instead of arguing the motion, you can withdraw it, note my appearance in court, and enter my plea of not guilty."

"I can't do that the day after I filed for continuance," Louis Lewis said. "It would make the earlier motion appear frivolous and Judge Bigler's a real bear about dilatory pleadings. Anyway, what we've got to do right now is surrender you."

"Forget that," Jeffreys said. "I'm not surrendering."

"You have to. You've no choice. You're a wanted man, a fugitive. I shouldn't even be talking to you. Harboring is a very serious offense. Obstructing is even more serious. I'm an officer of the court, and it's my duty to—"

"—You're also my attorney protected by lawyer-client confidentiality," Jeffreys said. "Listen to me, goddamn it! I'll meet you on the front steps of the courthouse at a quarter of two tomorrow, and you will escort me before the judge to enter my plea of not guilty. Are we clear on that?"

There was silence for a moment. Then Lewis asked, "Are you in town?"

"Sure. I'm in room one-ninety-three of the Sleep Cheep Motel."

"I withdraw the question. You didn't tell me where you are. I don't want to know."

"Listen to me, goddam it," Jeffreys said. "I have Cornie Nicora's money stash, his diaries, and his account books. When I turn them over to the authorities tomorrow, it'll prove I'm a victim of the killings, not the culprit."

"What money stash, diaries, and account books?" Lewis demanded.

Jeffreys ignored the question, asked, "Do you know an investigator named ... uh ..." he cudgeled his memory, grop-ing for the buzzwords he had assigned them as a retrieval trick, remembered *Sherlock Holmes* ... "Holmes, Shirley Holmes?"

"I know of her. What money stash, diaries, and account books?"

"You ever use her?"

"My associates have. When she was free-lance. She's tied to another firm, now. How much money?"

"Landgrebe's firm? Christopher Landgrebe's?"

"That's the one. Why? What's she got to do with all this?"

"I'm not sure," Jeffreys said. "But I think she can spread some gospel I want spread. What I need is her phone num-ber. Can you give it to me?"

"My secretary could look it up for you," Louis Lewis said. "Tell me what money and diaries and account books you're talking about."

"Cornie Nicora's. We'll talk about them tomorrow. Right now, I need Shirley Holmes' number."

"Very well," Lewis said. "Hang on."

The phone went dead, came alive again with a female voice asking if he were ready.

"Ready," he said. She recited a number. He wrote it down, hung up, dialed it. The phone buzzed, clicked and another female voice came on the line.

"Landgrebe Associates," it said.

"Miss Holmes? Shirley Holmes?"

"Who's calling, please?"

"Sam Jeffreys. Are you Miss Holmes?"

"One moment, please."

There was a click and yet another female voice sounded in his ear.

"Mr. Jeffreys?"

"Miss Holmes?" he said. "I'm gratified you recognize my name."

"Mrs. Holmes," the voice corrected calmly. "Your name was in all the papers."

"And in all the court documents and arrest records and warden's files you checked out a few days ago so your clients could keep track of my whereabouts."

There was a silence. Then the quiet voice said, "It's your quarter, Mr. Jeffreys."

"True. I'm calling to ask you who those clients are."

"Our client list is confidential."

"I'm not interested in your client list. I just want to know the name or names of the person or persons who hired your firm to check on me."

"If there were such a person or persons, it would be confidential, too, wouldn't it?"

"I suppose," Jeffreys said, enjoying the exchange. "I'm asking anyway."

"Don't bother, Mr. Jeffreys. Was there something else?"

"Yes. If you change your mind, give me a ring at ..." he looked at the number on the base of the phone ... "five-five-five, three-four-oh-two, extension one-niner-three."

"I shan't change my mind."

"Jot it down anyway, just in case," Jeffreys persisted. "See, your client would be interested to know that I have with me here what he's been looking for, and I might be willing to consider ... uh ... an offer for its purchase. I'm at five-five-five, three-four-oh-two, extension one-niner-three. And if you should decide to drop by in person with your client's name and where they can be reached, I might ... uh ... express my appreciation. I'm in room one-ninety-three of the Sleep Cheep Motel out on one-hundred-twenty-third Avenue West. Did you get that? Room one-ninety-three of the Sleep Cheep Motel on one-hundred-twenty-third Avenue West."

"Goodbye, Mr. Jeffreys," the quiet voice said. The line went dead.

Jeffreys hung up, referred to the directory, flipped its pages, dialed again.

"Bethany Hospital," a female voice answered.

"Public relations."

"One moment, puleeze."

There was a click, a sudden surge of canned music, an orchestra playing a quiet version of *Smoke Gets in Your Eyes,* another click, and a male voice.

"Public Relations, Zuckerman," it said.

"This is Sam Jefferson at the Detroit Free Press," Jeffreys said. "Can you give me the condition on Stanley Quick? He's the FBI guy brought in last Friday with gunshot wounds to the chest."

"Still serious but stable unless there's been an update in the last few hours. You want to hold while I check that?"

"Yes, please."

There was a click, the return of the canned music, the orchestra still working on the muted version of *Smoke Gets in Your Eyes.* Jeffreys hummed along with it for a few bars. Then it clicked off.

"Jefferson?" the male voice said. "There has been an update. The new condition report is good. Anything else you need?"

"Yes. His room number."

"I can't give out that information," Zuckerman said. "It's flagged. You know how it is with VIPs and cops. Sorry."

"I was hoping to talk to him."

"Sorry."

"No problem," Jeffreys said. "Thanks anyway."

He hung up, climbed off the bed, walked to the chair and sank down in it to take mental inventory.

So Quick was alive and likely to make it. Great. Meanwhile, he told himself, Jeffreys' whereabouts and his possession of Cornie's stash should by now be known to the Poo Boys, if Van Til's office line was tapped as Quick figured, or if either his home line or Louis Lewis' office phone had a bug on it, or if Shirley Holmes passed it along to the Landgrebe client or clients for whom she had done the snoop-and-scoop job on him when he was in jail. Besides all that, there was still Fifi Malloy's Holiday-Inn phone that might well be tapped, too. So what else could he do to ensure a visit here from the Poos?

"Nothing," he told himself, shifting gears. "Nothing at all except get ready for visitors."

Unwrapping the heavy aluminum-foil cookie sheets from their cellophane packaging, he laid them side by side on the floor in front of the door. Pushed together, they made a metallic threshold two feet long by eighteen inches wide—plenty big enough, he decided. He unlocked the door and swung it open to be sure its bottom cleared the trays. It did. He nodded in satisfaction, closed it again, and flipped the dead bolt into its socket.

Fetching the roll of zipcord from the bed, he snipped four inches off of it with the cutting blades of the needlenose pliers, zipped apart the conductors of the short piece to make two pieces, removed their insulation, and tightened the twisted bare copper strands into separate cables. He sat down on the

floor and bent over the cookie sheets. Using the nose end of
the pliers, he punched two holes in each end of each sheet
where it touched the other. Lacing one of the copper cables
through each pair of holes, he twisted the free ends together,
connecting the foil trays electrically.

"How's that for a wired welcome mat?" he asked himself,
grinning at the thought.

He slit the BB package open, poured the lead shot into the
cookie sheets, dividing its contents between them. The stream
of pellets hitting the trays sounded like a low-pitched drum
roll. He grinned again, decided that it was a symbolic drum
roll of sorts, the opening of the overture preceding the performance.

Getting up, he uncoiled the zipcord as he walked, leaving
one end and some slack near the door, snaking the roll under
the bed, taking a turn around one of the bed legs at the foot
end to anchor it there, running the wire across the floor to
the dresser, then up the dresser to the television set atop it.

He turned on the floor lamp and swung its shade and bulb
up to shine on the TV set. He swiveled the TV around, pulled
its power cord from the wall socket, and began unscrewing
its back fasteners with the screwdriver blade on his pocket
knife. Removing the back, he laid it on the bed. It was diffi-
cult to see much inside the cabinet housing the dusty works
of the television set.

He readjusted the lamp to shine into the interior and found
the terminal he was looking for. He scraped it shiny with his
knife. He pulled the end of the zipcord apart to split the first
six inches into separate cables, removed an inch of insulation
from one, wrapped its bare copper end around the terminal
he had burnished and, with the pliers, twisted the wire about
itself to anchor it there. He stripped an inch of insulation
from the other conductor, loosened a machine screw in a
metal brace fastening the loudspeaker to the chassis, wrapped

the bare end of the wire around the screw head, and tightened it again. He tied the zipcord in place with a turn around the metal brace so there'd be no strain on the inside connections and led it out of the cabinet. Then he replaced the back, being careful to snap the power cord interlock plug all the way into its socket, and turned home the retaining screws.

He put the power plug into the wall outlet, swiveled the TV set around so the screen faced the corner of the room to the left of the door. Adjusting the floor lamp to shine on the door, he dressed the zipcord unobtrusively down the back of the dresser and along the floor to disappear under the bed.

Back at the door, he split three feet of the free end of the zipcord apart to separate its two conductors, removed six inches of insulation from one and an inch from the other. The short bare end he sewed through two pliers-punched holes in the door-hinge end of the cookie-sheet pad, twisting it around itself to anchor it there. The six-inch end of bare wire he coiled twice around the metal door knob, then twisted it also around itself.

Wishing for a cigarette, Jeffreys got up, walked to the nightstand, retrieved Big Poo's pistol from under the telephone directory and sat down on the bed with it. He removed the clip and thumbed the cartridges out of it. There were three. Counting the one he had earlier removed from the chamber and the two fired into Stanley Quick, that meant Big Poo carried only six bullets in a seven-cartridge magazine.

Jeffreys nodded. The man *was* a professional, or at least an expert. An auto-loading pistol was most prone to jamming when the feed spring in its magazine clip suffered metal fatigue from being too tightly compressed over time, as when a seven-shot clip was routinely loaded with seven cartridges. Compressing the feed spring less by loading only five bullets into a seven-bullet magazine avoided such over-compression, making the weapon more reliable and less likely to jam. Loading a sixth shot into its firing chamber, then, provided double-compensation: It added another shot to its firepower, and it readied the pre-cocked weapon for instant use at the release of its safety catch and the touch of its trigger.

Jeffreys dumped Big Poo's cartridges into the wastebasket. Opening the box he had bought at the hardware store, he loaded five bullets into the clip. He shoved the clip into the weapon's handle, pulled back the slide and released it, levering a cartridge into the firing chamber. Then he set the safety catch, unlatched the clip, removed it, thumbed a sixth bullet into it and slid it into the grip again.

He put the pistol in his right-hand jacket pocket and a handful of extra cartridges in his left-hand jacket pocket.

He unwrapped the baseball bat. Its heft and balance were right, he decided.

Sitting down on the bed, he picked up the telephone and dialed the Holiday Inn.

"Fifi Malloy, please," he told the answering clerk. "Room four-twelve."

"Fifi Malloy," her voice said in his ear, after a few seconds.

"It's me, Sam Jeffreys," he said. "Guess what? I found Cornie Nicora's stash and it's dynamite."

Malloy started to say something, stopped, said, "Oh?"

"I've got it here with me. A ton of money and a box of ledgers and diaries and journals full of names and dates and stuff."

"Ah ... what're you going to do with it?"

"I'm going to turn it over to the feds tomorrow."

"I see. Uh ... where are you now?"

"The Sleep Cheep Motel out on one-hundred-twenty-third Avenue West," he said, hoping somebody besides Fifi was listening. "I'm in room one-ninety-three. That's one-twenty-third Avenue West, room one-ninety-three."

"Ah ... how are you feeling?" Fifi Malloy asked.

"I'm okay," Jeffreys told her.

"Me, too."

"So I'll see you tomorrow, Fifi."

"I hope so," she said. Now her voice sounded gruff, he thought. "I certainly hope so."

Jeffreys hung up, moved the phone from the nightstand onto the bed as close to the corner of the room as its short cord would allow, rose, took a deep breath, threw out his chest, thrust back his shoulders and walked towards the door. He picked the remote control off the top of the TV set and the paper bag of restaurant goodies from the table, taking them with him. At the door, he slid the dead bolt out of its socket.

He sat down in the corner toward which the door would swing when it opened, stretching his legs comfortably in front of him, and leaned back against the outside wall of the room.

He laid the bat on the floor to his right, its handle touching his thigh.

He took the gun from his pocket and placed it atop his right leg.

He set the TV controller on his left thigh.

Opening the paper sack from the restaurant, he ceremoniously laid its contents out on the floor in a little semi-circle to his left, first the coffee, then the sandwich, then the milk. He crumpled the bag into a ball, tossed it toward the bed, watched it hit and bounce away.

He picked up the Styrofoam coffee container, pulled off its plastic lid and took a swig. The coffee was tepid, room temperature, bitter. He set it down. Picking up the sandwich, he peeled the waxed paper back and took a bite. It, too, was tepid, but tasty.

He looked at his watch. It read 3:35 P MO 20.

"Please, God, let them have gotten my message," he said.

Taking another swallow of coffee and another bite of sandwich, Jeffreys began his vigil.

XX
THE SPRINGING

The first time Jeffreys had to leave his secure corner to visit the bathroom, he cursed the coffee for compromising his master plan.

That was at 6:12, according to his wristwatch. It had been dark for a while, the coming of night betrayed by the fading of the daylight sneaking around the drapes at the window behind his bastion. He told himself then that if he were there in the john relieving himself when the Poos came, they could be picking at the door lock before he knew it. If that happened, and if they managed to spring the latch before he got back to his control center, his trap and his bat would be useless, his survival then dependent solely upon his automatic pistol and his amateur skills pitted against two such pistols, both in the hands of professionals.

He was gratified at returning to his stronghold behind the door without incident on that occasion.

The second time he had to rouse from the floor, his watch read 9:57. He told himself then he should have stuck to milk with his sandwich. This time, he pocketed the TV remote control, just in case.

Seems like cold coffee goes through me faster than hot coffee, he mused as he headed for the bathroom again. *Seems like cold coffee expands even more than hot coffee after I swallow it.*

A moment later, they came.

He was just about to push the toilet's flush handle in the semi-darkness when he heard the snick of a lock unlatching.

"They've got a key," he told himself. "A goddam key!"

So they wouldn't be fiddling around with lock picks, as he'd expected, scraping about in the lock mechanism to alert him to their presence and giving him time to prepare his act. But neither would they be forcing the door, kicking it open to dive inside as when they'd surprised him and Quick by breaking into the Holiday Inn room to grab the phony package, kill Lukeman, and shoot Quick.

On balance, maybe this is better, Jeffreys thought. *But where'd they get the goddam key?*

He pulled the TV remote control from his jacket pocket, thankful he'd brought it and the gun to the bathroom with him instead of leaving them in his bastion with the baseball bat. Cautiously, he stuck his head around the corner of the bathroom to peer at the door bathed in the pool of light cast by the floor lamp. It was inching open. There was the silvery glint of a nickel-plated pistol reflecting the lamplight back through the door crack. He saw hairy fingers wrapped around the gun handle.

Jeffreys dropped to his knees, his left thumb ready to push the power-on button of the TV controller clutched in his left hand. He slid the gun from his coat pocket with his right hand, his right thumb flicking off the safety catch. He fixed his eyes on the widening crack between the door and its frame.

The door swung farther open. The lamp shone on the crouching figure of a huge man in a rumpled dark suit poised in the doorway. The brim of his felt hat shadowed his eyes. His right hand clutched the door knob. His left hand swept the gun back and forth across the room.

Big Poo, Jeffreys told himself, sickeningly aware that he should at that moment be breaking the wrist of the intruder's gun hand and knocking the weapon across the room with one swing of his bat. But that's if he were in the corner behind the door where he was supposed to be instead of crouching in the bathroom twenty feet away. So much for the master plan. But the bat was only one weapon. How about the others? Could he still salvage a portion of the plan? *Damn right,* he told himself. *Got to!*

But where was Little Poo? Was he right behind his partner, his gun also ready, waiting to spring into the room the moment Big Poo cleared the doorway? Or was he covering Big Poo's entry from somewhere outside, behind Andy Horton's car maybe, crouched out there in the semi-darkness where he could see his target without being one?

Could the power-on sensor in the TV set pick up the remote controller's command signal from this angle, with its screen facing away? Or would that part of his preparations, too, be nullified by his trip to the john?

The door eased wider open. Big Poo stepped in. His gun hand was extended. His pistol was scanning the room. His left foot came down onto the BB-topped cookie sheet. It skidded as it settled into the roller bearings.

Jeffreys heard the sharp intake of breath. He saw the right hand clutch the door knob more tightly, the left hand fly toward the ceiling in an involuntary balance-restoring reflex, the gun muzzle pointing suddenly skyward.

Jeffreys leaped out of the bathroom. He pointed the remote controller at the TV set and thumbed the power-on button.

The figure in the doorway convulsed and a blast of music blared from the TV set's loudspeaker.

Big Poo dove head-first into the room, slammed to the floor on his face, and lay there twitching.

Jeffreys thumbed the remote-controller button again. The music died and the room went silent except for the gasping of the man on the floor.

Big Poo lay well inside the room, his head and shoulders between the bed and the dresser. His left leg was stretched straight out behind him, his right bent at the knee. His left arm was extended beyond his head, palm down, his right arm folded under his body. His hat was a yard in front of his head, inches beyond his extended hand, brim up, partially covering his gun. He was breathing jerkily, in short, sharp, shallow gasps.

Jeffreys lunged toward him. He grabbed the gun from under the hat, and dove back into the bathroom, expecting a shot from Little Poo. There was none. After a moment, he peered around the corner again.

From the semi-darkness outside, beyond the pool of brighter light cast through the open doorway by the floor lamp, he heard a hoarse stage whisper.

"You awright, Al?" it said. "You okay?"

Jeffreys remembered that Big Poo's name was Alex. Alex Pucci, wasn't it? He strained to see the whisperer, couldn't.

On the floor, Big Poo groaned, gasped, groaned again.

Holding the two guns at the ready, Jeffreys leaped out of the bathroom, jumped over the prostrate form, dove for the door. Reaching it without drawing a shot from outside, he slammed it shut and turned the dead bolt into its socket.

Behind him, the body on the floor stopped gasping. It took a deep breath and stirred. Jeffreys pocketed the guns. Picking up the baseball bat, he strode to the prostrate man and stood over him.

"Gently, gently," he cautioned himself under his breath, and rapped Big Poo on the back of the head with the bat. Alex Pucci jerked, gasped, went quiet again, his breathing shallow and fast. He smelled of cough drops.

Jeffreys jumped onto the bed. He grabbed the telephone handset and held it to his ear. There was no dial tone. He hit the hang-up button several times. Hearing nothing, he slammed the receiver back in its cradle.

Great, he thought. *So now what?* He looked around the shadowy room for inspiration, telling himself his master plan should have included purchase of handcuffs or at least a length of rope. His eye landed on the nightstand lamp. He pulled the line cord from the wall outlet, hefted it in his hands, nodded.

His pocket knife cut through the power cord at the lamp base and lopped off the wall plug. He got down on his knees straddling Big Poo's body. The cough-drop odor surrounded him like an invisible cloud. He pulled the unconscious man's right arm from underneath him, folded it and his left arm behind the small of his back. He crossed Big Poo's wrists and wrapped them repeatedly with the lamp cord. He criss-crossed the wire at each wrap and finished with a square knot pulled tight.

He went to the door, listened, heard nothing. He switched off the floor lamp, plunging the room into blackness, listened some more. Still he heard nothing.

Checking his pockets for the two guns and the TV controller, he squatted down on the floor to the right of the door. He hung onto the door knob with his left hand to keep his balance as his left shoe tried to roll around on the BB-bearings in their cookie-sheet races. He twisted the knob gently, feeling the wire wrapped around it. He pulled. The door didn't yield. Then he remembered the dead bolt, released it, tried again. This time the door came free. Cracking it open, he peered out into the night, the sudden breeze cold in his face.

The feeble light from the overhead lamps made the parking lot comparatively bright in contrast to the blackness of the darkened room. Jeffreys waited for a movement, a sound, ready to pull in his head and slam the door. There was no movement, no noise except the faint whisper of traffic from the highway off to his left and the jerky rasping breathing of Big Poo behind him.

Where the hell is Little Poo? he asked himself. Was he inside another room, like one-ninety-one or one-ninety-five, maybe listening at the partition, ready to lean out his door and fire at a head sticking out of one-ninety-three? Or was he hiding behind Andy Horton's car in the parking lot? *Does he have me in his sights right now? Is he just waiting for a clearer shot?*

Jeffreys' skin crawled. He wanted to duck back inside, double lock the booby-trapped door and wait for daylight. That reminded him of the key Big Poo used to sneak in on him. He cracked the door wider open, peered up at the outside lock from his squatting position. There was a key extending from it. It dangled a leather fob the size of a shoe horn.

Jeffreys recoiled into the room, shaking his head. He closed the door to a crack, listened. He heard no sound, no movement from outside or from the rooms flanking his.

He pulled the gun from his right-hand jacket pocket. He thumbed off the safety lock. He hauled the door open, jumped through the doorway and pulled the portal shut behind him. Ducking low, he ran for the shelter of Andy's car, the gun in front of him, ready to fire at first glimpse of Little Poo skulking in the shadows. He saw no one. He crouched behind the car, shivering in the cold wind, his head pivoting to scan the area and the windows of 191 and 195.

Nothing moved. There was another car parked several doors away. No lights showed from any of the rooms. The highway traffic sounded louder now. Otherwise, there was silence. A muted groan came from inside 193. Then all was quiet again.

Jeffreys squatted on his heels in the shadow of Andy's car for minutes, watching, listening, wondering. *Where the hell was Little Poo?*

He stood up, took a deep breath, and thrust his shoulders

back. Then he began walking rapidly toward the motel office and its telephone. He felt his neck hair standing erect. He expected to see a muzzle flash, hear a cartridge explode, feel a bullet penetrate.

Nothing happened.

He reached the office, seeing no movement, hearing no sound. Turning the door knob, he pushed into the smallish room, blinking his eyes against its relatively brilliant lighting.

He recoiled at what he saw.

The little man in the wrinkled brown suit and green polo shirt was sitting on the high stool, his torso sprawled forward onto the counter. His head lay on his arms in a pool of drying blood. His eyes were open, staring vacantly at the wall. His mouth was agape, still leaking bloody drool. There were two holes in his forehead. Red streaks ran from them onto the counter top. A shapeless brown hat was on the floor behind the stool.

"Five," Jeffreys said aloud. "That makes five, goddam it!"

Averting his eyes, he stepped to the counter, reached across it for the telephone standing inches away from the corpse's right arm resting on the counter top and held the handset to his ear.

It was dead.

"Ah, boy," Jeffreys said under his breath. "So now what?"

Then he remembered Andy's car and Andy's two-meter radio and wondered whether he could reach them alive.

It's the only shot you've got, he counseled himself. No pun intended.

Jeffreys' skin crawled and his neck hair came to attention as he suddenly realized he was an easy target for a sniper sighting on him here in the brightly-lit office from the comparatively dark parking lot outside. Scanning the room and spying a wall switch just inside the door, he snapped it down. The room blackened. He stood in the darkness for a minute to let his eyes accommodate. Then he stepped outside.

Walking as silently as he could, wishing the nearly empty lot had more cars in it to hide behind, he made a looping detour toward his room and the old Chevrolet listing to the passenger side parked in front of it. He came up behind the car and crouched in its shadows for minutes. The cold penetrated his blazer and raised goose bumps on his body. The car in front of 199 was gone. He hadn't heard it leave. He opened the driver's-side door of Andy's car, panicking at the sudden illumination cast over him by the dome light. He dove inside, pulled the door shut and lay across the front seat staring at the darkness, listening to his heart pound, hearing nothing else.

After a while, he raised his head to peer at 193 through the grimy windshield. The door was shut. A crack of light leaked from one edge of the drapery covering its window. The lock was empty. The key dangling its shoehorn-sized leather fob wasn't there. That and the light leaking from the window crack must mean Little Poo had let himself into 193 while Jeffreys was visiting the office.

But then what? Little Poo untied Big Poo? Were they gone, fled into the night, maybe in the car from in front of 199? Was the trap empty, the birds flown, his chance to capture them and clear himself vanished as well?

Risking the gleam of the dome light a second time, Jeffreys slunk out of Andy's car, shut its door, and crouched in the shadows until his eyes adapted to the parking lot's semi-gloom. When they did, he stepped noiselessly to the door of 193 and tried the knob. It was locked. He drew his key from his pocket, the one the brown-suited, polo-shirted clerk—the late lamented brown-suited, polo-shirted clerk—had given him, when? Was it only yesterday?

Jeffreys fitted the key into the lock as silently as he could, turned it, tried the knob again. The door didn't budge.

"Hot dog!" he exulted. So the dead bolt was seated from

inside! So the Poo Boys were still in there! So if he could keep them there until he could get the cops here, the master plan might still be functional.

Or is this their trap for me? he suddenly wondered, feeling panic again. Did Little Poo emerge from an adjacent room, enter 193, rouse Big Poo, untie him, confer with him? Did they work out their own master plan? Did they split up, with one of the Poos now inside and one outside? Was the inside man, secure behind that double-locked door, systematically searching the room for Cornie's stash and record books? Was he going through the underwear and socks, the pockets of the Sears jacket and trousers, rummaging around under the bed, peering into the toilet tank? Meanwhile, was the outside man watching from another window, stalking from the shadows? *Is he right now sighting on me from somewhere? Is he at this instant squeezing the trigger of a gun aimed at my head?*

"Nah," he whispered. "Couldn't be."

He stepped quickly away from the door, strode to the shadows of Andy's car, and sat down on the cold ground behind it. He stared into the blackness and strained to hear the silence for a full minute before he moved again.

When he did, it was to fish Andy's keys from his pocket, find the smallest one, feel it into the trunk lock, turn it, lift the lid, slowly, quietly, hoping an interior light wouldn't flash on before the lid got high enough for him to reach inside. It didn't.

Holding the lid partially open with his left hand, Jeffreys probed about the trunk interior with his right. Maybe there'd be a rope, a tow cable, a chain. There wasn't. But there was something with a rubbery feel. *Hot dog,* he exulted. *Jumper cables. Thick, strong, heavy, battery jumper cables.*

He hauled them out of the trunk, pressed the lid shut, squatted on his heels, and uncoiled them carefully in the murky light of the parking lot's overheads. There were two, each fitted at the end with a heavy spring clamp.

He brought one end of each cable together, tied a looping square knot, and yanked on them. The knot tightened, held.

"Hey, hey," he told himself.

Dragging the cable behind him, Jeffreys stepped to the door of 193, looking and listening. He turned his key to lock it, looped the cable twice around the knob and then through itself to form a half hitch. He looped it through itself again to complete a double knot and pulled it tight.

Feeling almost euphoric, he went quietly back to Andy's car, picked the free end of the cable up from the macadam surface of the parking lot, and felt for a place to tie it around Andy's front bumper. There was no place. He dropped to his knees, groped around underneath the car, found a steel brace fastening the bumper to the chassis near its driver's-side end. He pushed the cable under the bumper, over the top of the brace and pulled the cable around it. He took up its slack behind him and hauled it taut against the door knob. Then he wrapped his end of the cable twice more around the brace and tied it off in another double half-hitch.

"Gotcha," he said, breathing heavily as he backed out from under the car. He eyed the knot-spliced cable. It hung taut from the door to the car, the bulky connecting knot and two end clamps suspended a foot off the ground part-way between.

"That should keep you guys inside while I yell for help," he whispered to himself. "Or one of you guys, anyway."

XXI
THE CONFRONTING

Sam Jeffreys crouched in the shadows alongside the driver's door of Andy Horton's car, the pistol in his hand, looking, listening, shivering in the cold wind. He saw nothing except the crack of light leaking from beside the window drapery in room 193. He heard only the traffic whispering along the distant highway.

After a bit, he worked the car door handle with his left hand and opened the door a fraction of an inch. Squatting on the ground alongside the car, he bent his back and his neck so the door would clear his head. He fumbled inside the door frame for the light-switch plunger, found it, pressed it.

For a long minute he held his position, squatting on his haunches, his left hand clamped against the switch plunger, his right grasping the gun, listening, looking. He saw nothing, heard only the whisper of the distant traffic and now the rustle of the rising wind blowing colder on his face. Keeping the plunger depressed with his left thumb, he swung the door wider, struggled to his feet, clambered into the car, swung his gun butt against the dome light, heard glass break, felt shards showering his face.

Cautiously, he released his hold on the switch, letting it slide slowly out, impelled by its spring. The car stayed dark.

Jeffreys sighed in relief, swung his legs into the car and closed the door quietly.

It was a bit warmer here out of the wind. Reaching down into the darkness, he felt around beneath the dashboard for the two-meter transceiver. It was angled up from the floor, his fingers told him, straddling the carpeted transmission hump. He closed his eyes and tried to visualize the front panel of the Azden Model PCS 2000 that rode with him for so many years. The left-hand knob turned on the radio when pushed in, he recalled, and adjusted the audio volume. The knob to its right doubled as the squelch adjustment and power switch, boosting the transmitter output from five watts to twenty-five watts when pushed in, and varying the receiver squelch level with its rotation.

He turned the right-hand control counter-clockwise, pressed it in. Then he did the same with the left-hand knob. At once, light-emitting diodes began flashing red numbers across the readout screen. He turned the volume up slowly until he could just hear background hiss. He adjusted the squelch control until the hiss dropped out. The red numbers continued to sequence as the radio scanned its preset channels. Abruptly, they stopped counting and locked onto a signal. They read 6.910. A low voice came from the speaker. "Double-U X Two Y listening nine one," it said. "Anybody around?"

Jeffreys felt for the microphone in the darkness, found it hanging from a clip along the right side of the transceiver. He lifted it off, felt for the thumb-button switch that activated the transmit-receive circuitry, intending to push it in and power up the transmitter.

He was too late.

Another voice sounded from the speaker. "Double-U X Two Y, this is Double-U Two Bee Zed Zed," it was saying. How you doin', Jimbo? Haven't heard you on in a while."

The first voice returned instantly, before Jeffreys could thumb his transmitter on. He sat fuming in the dark, watching the crack of light from the window of 193, waiting for his next chance.

"Doing okay," the speaker was saying. "How about you, Spud. Anything new and different?"

Jeffreys held the mike to his mouth, pressed the thumb button, said "Mayday, mayday," released the switch.

"... is something new and different," Jimbo was saying. "Got me this new toy, a ten-meter FM H-T. It's a blast. Haven't figured out all the bells and whistles yet, but it's fun workin' the world through a repeater with a hand-held."

"Mayday," Jeffreys said softly into his microphone, squeezing the push-to-talk button with his thumb and staring at the crack of light from 193. Nothing moved there. "Mayday, mayday."

"I been wantin' ta give ten FM a try," Spud's voice was saying from the speaker when Jeffreys let go of the button and his receiver came to life. "Only them hand-helds are too pricey for me. You hit the Lotto or something?"

"Mayday," Jeffreys said, squeezing the button. "Mayday."

"You doubled with somebody," Jimbo's voice said. "Think we got a breaker out there. Who's the breaker? Go ahead breaker."

"I'm the breaker," Jeffreys said into the mike, squeezing. "With emergency traffic. I've been trying to break you guys with 'maydays', but you kept hot-switching me. This is Kilo Niner Alpha Zulu Golf, slash two. Name's Sam, and I'm in big trouble. You copy? Over."

There was a garbled cacophony of sound in the speaker as he released the mike button. It lasted half a minute.

"Dandy," Jeffreys said into the mike, when the noise died. "Now I've got a pileup. Listen, guys, I need help, not a crowd jamming the channel. Jimbo, I think your call was WX Two Y,

wasn't it? Whatever, please take over as control station. The
rest of you callers please listen. WX Two Y only. You copy? Over."

"Roger, roger," the speaker said. "Copy you fine business.
What's your emergency traffic and where's it go? Over over."

"I need cops," Jeffreys said, watching the door of 193.
Nothing was moving. "Lots of cops. Locals and sheriff's and
state. Get me a bunch of squad cars here in a hurry, but quietly, without sirens. I'm in the parking lot of the Sleep Cheep
Motel in Bloomburgh on one-twenty-third Avenue West. I'm
outside room one-niner-three. I say again, the Sleep Cheep
Motel, one-twenty-third Avenue West, outside room one-
niner-three. You got that? Over over."

"Got it," said the voice from the speaker. "Uh ... is this
some kind of a test? Or a practice exercise? Over."

"No, goddam it," Jeffreys said into the microphone,
squeezing the thumb button. "This is the real mayday McCoy.
Get me cops here in a hurry, and no sirens. I've got a corpse
in the motel office with bullets in the head. I've got two professional hit men gunning for me. And I've got no place to
hide. Does that sound like a practice exercise? Over over."

"QSL," the speaker said. "This is Double-U X Two Y, act-
ing net control with emergency traffic on one-forty-six-nine-
one. Spud, you land-line the Bloomburgh police, and then
the county cops. Larry, I heard you in there, too. You pass the
traffic to the State Police post. I'm sure you guys copied Sam,
but I repeat his traffic and QTH in case: He needs squad cars,
lots of squad cars, without sirens, at the Sleep Cheep Motel,
one-two-three Avenue West, Bloomburgh. The officers are to
contact Sam, Kilo Niner Alpha Zulu Golf, in the parking lot
outside of room one-niner-three. You confirm Spud? Come
now."

"QSL," said Spud's voice. "I'm doing it."

"Confirm Larry?"

"QSL," said a new voice. "I'm gone."

"QSL, guys," said Jimbo's voice. "Sam, what's your last name?"

"Jeffreys. Samuel T. Jeffreys. Jimbo, once Spud gets those patrol cars started out here, could you have him call the local PD dispatcher again with a priority to a Sergeant Sankstone in homicide? That's Sergeant Joe Sankstone. I spell, S-A-N-K-S-T-O-N-E, Sankstone. Have him repeat my traffic to Sankstone, including my name. Okay? Over over."

"Will do, Sam," Jimbo's voice said. "Spud's checked out for the moment land-lining your emergency traffic. I'll give him the follow-up when he checks back in. Meanwhile, you have any more needs? Go."

"No more," Jeffreys said. "Except I need to cut out of here. I'm a sitting duck where I am. Thanks for the help. Over."

"Pleasure," Jimbo said. "How about we keep this repeater open in case you need something else? Go."

"Appreciate it," Jeffreys said. "I'm clear."

He punched in the left-hand knob on the radio set. The red numbers disappeared and the speaker went silent. He sat there awhile, resting his elbows on the wheel, the gun in his hand, listening, looking.

The crack of light along the drapery in Room 193 suddenly widened, filled half the window for a moment, narrowed again to a sliver, widened once more and winked out.

Did one of the Poos pull the drapery aside to peek into the night? Had the peeker spotted him? Turned off the lamp to see better in the semi-light of the parking lot overheads? Was one of the Poos, maybe both of them, right now peering out of the window, aiming a gun, tightening a forefinger to send .22 caliber slugs through the window, the windshield and into his head?

Jeffreys ducked down behind the dashboard to put steel between himself and the window of 193, panicking. Should he shoot into the room? No. It would be folly to fire blindly through a windshield and a window at presumed targets he couldn't see. Okay, then wouldn't the Poo Boys have precisely the same problem? Of course they would.

"So what are they likely to do?" he asked himself under his breath, hunkered down on the seat.

He answered himself. "They'll likely sit tight until the patrol cars get here, and then come running out, heading for their own car, firing at anything that moves,"

Wait, he mused. They couldn't know the patrols were on the way, so that couldn't be right. Anyway, they couldn't come running out through a locked and tied-shut door. The car, though. The goddam car. Why didn't he think about their goddam car before? They didn't walk here. So maybe he was half right a while ago. Maybe after Little Poo cut Big Poo loose, one stayed inside to hunt for Cornie's stash while the other high-tailed it for their car. If so, where was it? And where was the high-tailer? They wouldn't have left their vehicle so far away it would take the outside man long to reach it and fetch it. Was it their car parked outside 199 a while ago? Did the outside man move it off someplace where he could watch 193 and anybody or anything that approached it?

Probably, he decided. Probably their master plan called for the outside man to sit tight in the getaway car until the inside man signaled him that he either found Cornie's stash or gave up on it. Then those two flashes of light weren't from opening the drapery to peek out—it was a signal for the outside man to come pick up the inside man.

"Oh boy," Jeffreys told himself aloud. "The outside man's on his way here right now. The inside man's about to discover the door's tied closed. And here I sit between them!"

He peered out of Andy Horton's Chevrolet's rear window. He saw nothing. But didn't he hear an engine? Yes, he did. Where was it?

Suddenly headlights were bouncing toward him from the

far corner of the parking lot behind him and a half-block to his right. He ducked his head to avoid being silhouetted in their glare. He hit the door handle, flung the door open, jumped out, shut it. He crouched alongside the car, peeking through its windows at the approaching lights.

There was the sound of exploding glass behind him. He swung his head in time to see a baseball bat emerging from the window of 193. It was clutched in the left hand of a monstrous man in a wrinkled suit who was diving through the window frame. His right hand appeared empty in the dim light of the overheads.

Big Poo, Jeffreys realized. *He's got my bat! But I've got his gun!*

Jeffreys stepped out from the shadow of the car into the gloomy light of the overheads, steadying the gun with both hands.

"Freeze," he heard himself shout. "Drop the bat and freeze!"

Big Poo reared back on his heels, the bat still upraised. He swiveled his head to stare in disbelief at Jeffreys a dozen feet away from him. His face distorted and he roared an animal scream. He leaped toward Jeffreys, the bat swinging, the roar rising in pitch and intensity.

Big Poo rammed into the jumper cable, tripped, pitched forward onto the macadam surface of the parking lot. He landed hard. He clambered to his feet again, screaming. He dove toward Jeffreys, swinging the bat as he came, roaring his fury.

Jeffreys held low and fired twice at the charging figure. He side-stepped, fired twice more as Big Poo went by. He whirled to shoot again, but decided he didn't need to.

Big Poo had stumbled and fallen. He lay face down in a crumpled heap. Still screaming, he was beating the macadam of the parking lot feebly with the baseball bat clutched in his right hand.

The headlights were closing from behind, twin shafts of light waving up and down as the approaching vehicle bounced along the uneven surface of the parking lot. They reflected off the shattered glass in the window of room 193 and Andy Horton's Chevrolet. They bathed Big Poo's prostrate figure in growing yellow brilliance.

There was the screech of brakes. The car skidded to a stop. Its door burst open. Little Poo flew out, gun in hand. He ran to Big Poo, whose scream had dwindled to a whimper. He bent over him, crouched there, rested his gun hand on Big Poo's back as though to comfort him.

Jeffreys, still in the shadow of Andy Horton's car behind the Poo Boys, raised his pistol to point at them in their pool of light.

"Freeze," he shouted, thinking about the two cartridges left in the gun and wishing there were more. He remembered the second gun in his left-hand jacket pocket. He reached for it, brought it also to bear. "Move and you're meat."

Red and yellow splotches of color began splashing across the doors and windows of the Sleep Cheep motel building and grounds. They were faint at first, then flashing ever more brightly. The sound of wheels grew louder. There came the screech of brakes and of sliding tires, the slamming of car doors. There were voices yelling "Police" and "Drop the gun," and "Sergeant, get on your radio and get us an ambulance here."

Jeffreys stepped out of the shadows of Andy's car. He bent over to lay the two pistols carefully on the macadam. He straightened up again and raised his hands high over his head.

Grinning happily, he told himself he was ready for a warm and secure jail cell, for a cup of hot coffee and a cigarette, for friendly voices and familiar faces, for questions and answers, for explanations, and, most of all, for a bathroom.

XXII
THE DEBRIEFING

Again the police were professional, efficient, and fair, Jeffreys told himself sleepily, sitting on the hard cot and nursing a cup of tepid coffee in the familiar one-man holding cell he'd drawn again in the Bloomburgh jail.

This time there'd been swarms of them, local and state cops, all responding to his *mayday* as relayed via the local ham community.

Blue-uniformed policemen had disarmed Little Poo, picked up the pistols Jeffreys surrendered, cuffed Little Poo and Jeffreys, each with his arms behind his back, and pushed them separately into the rear seats of different patrol cars.

Brown-uniformed officers patted Big Poo's prostrate form for weapons and wounds, walked alongside his gurney carrying the plastic pouches the Emergency Medical Service people had piped into his arms to replace the blood he was losing, and watched his ambulance siren off into the night.

Plainclothes investigators inspected the vehicle Little Poo bailed out of when he spotted Big Poo lying face down on the pavement, then transferred their attention to Andy Horton's listing Chevrolet.

An unmarked car came screaming into the parking lot as the ambulance was speeding away. It screeched to a stop and disgorged a bare-headed man in a thigh-length car coat. His hair was tousled, as though from finger-combing. His neck-tie was awry, as though from nervous yanking.

"Hi, Sergeant," Jeffreys shouted, grinning through the car window. "About time you showed up."

Sankstone opened the car door, climbed into the front seat, slammed the door shut again. Running his fingers through his hair, he twisted around to eye Jeffreys. "Alive and kicking," he said, as though to himself. He shook his head as though in wonderment. "Not even marked up."

"Cold, though," Jeffreys said, "and hungry, and needing a bathroom."

"They say you had two guns. Where'd you get 'em?"

"From Big Poo."

"Who?"

"Alex Pucci. The character who shot Quick and Cornie. The goon they were hauling away in the ambulance you just passed."

"He gave them to you?"

"Sort of. I took them away from him. One of them here in my room a little bit ago and the other a couple days back at the Holiday Inn. He was lying on the floor both times, though, let it be noted."

"You've got more balls than brains," Sankstone said, shaking his head again. "You're not only the stupidest man I ever met, but also the luckiest."

"Thank you," Jeffreys said. "I think you're nice, too. "

"Do you know who those two guys are?"

"Sure. The Poo Boys. Big Poo and Little Poo. Alexander Pucci and Sylvester Poodle. So?"

"So they're real hard-assed *hoodlums*. Quick says they're *mob*."

"How is Quick?"

"Better. He's going to make it. He says to blame you for it."

"Me?"

"You. He says the clown that put the slugs in his chest was about to give him one in the head when you tackled him."

"He was?" Jeffreys said, thinking about that. "I guess he could've been. I remember seeing him fire twice at Quick. I remember being pissed off about it and diving at him from the bed. That was kind of foolhardy, wasn't it."

"Yes it was. Stupid."

"It worked, though. We both wound up on the floor and I had his gun and he left without it. That's better than if he hung around to kill Quick and me."

"You left, too," Sankstone said. "Why?"

"Seemed like the thing to do. I guess I panicked. You'd already charged me with killing Cornie and ... that janitor guy. Now I've got people in the hall staring in at me. I'm holding a smoking gun. I'm surrounded by two more bodies. The hotel dick comes pounding in. He looks at me like I'm an assassin about to add him to my dead list and starts promising to perjure himself at my trial if I'll refrain from killing him, too. So I ran, hoping I could catch up with the shooters."

"I guess I can understand that," Sankstone said grudgingly.

"Good. How about understanding me out of these hand cuffs and pointing me at the john," Jeffreys said. "I'm getting desperate."

"I suppose," Sankstone said.

It took a while.

First the sergeant announced to a cadre of fellow cops that he'd be personally responsible for Jeffreys. Then he helped him out of the car and removed the cuffs.

Jeffreys rubbed his wrists to restore the circulation to his numb hands and shrugged his shoulders to reduce their cramping. He tried to ignore the pain in his lower abdomen. He stood around shivering in the chill as he and Sankstone watched a police photographer snap strobe-lighted pictures of the jumper cables lashing 193's doorknob to Andy Horton's bumper brace.

Later, with the cables removed and the door open, he had to wait some more while the photographer shot pictures of the room's interior. The place was a mess. The shock-wire still connected the inside door knob to the television set, Jeffreys noted, but now the TV cabinet was smashed open and the works exposed, as though by a searcher looking for something hidden inside. The aluminum-foil cookie sheets, still tied together and still wired to the shock-cable, were crumpled and trampled, their cargoes of BB-shot leaking out to roll away in twos and threes through low spots in the foil levee where the rims were crushed and flattened.

The room's furniture and furnishings were destroyed. The chair was backless and upside down. The dresser drawers were on the floor, their bottom panels split apart. The nightstand was kindling, its half-opened drawer splintered, the Gideon bible and the telephone directory ripped to scrap paper and strewn across the floor. The bed clothes were torn and ragged, piled in a heap atop the dresser. The mattress had been slashed, its stuffing poking through its cover in a dozen places.

The theft-proof hangers hung empty alongside the bathroom doorway, Jeffreys saw. Cornie's coat and hat were part of a tangled heap on the floor beneath them. Protruding from under the coat was an arm of the sport jacket and a leg of the slacks he had bought at Sears—when—a lifetime ago?

Edging anxiously into the bathroom, Jeffreys flipped on the light switch and looked around in disgust. The toilet-tank cover lay on the floor in three pieces. Interspersed with its fragments were shards of the mirror that had been fastened to the wall.

Really hurting now, he beckoned Sankstone inside, pointed at the mess.

"Whatever they were looking for, they sure wanted it bad," Sankstone said.

"Speaking of which," Jeffreys said. "What I want real bad is a minute in here alone. No. Make that five minutes."

Sankstone grinned and stood guard outside the doorless john.

Jeffreys emerged, feeling better. He pulled the remote control from his jacket pocket and tossed it into the shattered TV cabinet.

"Guess I won't need this any more," he said.

Sankstone looked mystified.

"You had to be there," Jeffreys explained. He shrugged into Cornie's overcoat and hat, gathered up his Sears purchases, and hauled them to Sankstone's car.

There was a light on in the Sleep Cheep office and shadows moving around inside when they drove by it.

"Coroner's people?" Jeffreys asked.

"And my people," Sankstone said from behind the wheel.

"Wouldn't you think the Poo Boys'd just biff that poor bastard in the noggin' after they took his keys and cut the phone lines?"

Sankstone shook his head soberly.

"Hard-assed hoodlums don't think like we do," he said. "They don't leave witnesses or loose ends."

"I wish you hadn't said that," Jeffreys said. "It scares me."

"It ought to," Sankstone said. "When you mess with The Mob, Mister, you've got a right to be scared. They never quit."

There followed an hour-long question-and-answer session around the scarred table in the interrogation room. Sankstone logged Jeffreys in as an apprehended fugitive and read him his rights after Jeffreys agreed to questioning without his lawyer present.

Lieutenant Dudley showed up, looking sleepy. He didn't have much to say.

Probably the obligatory third-party witness, Jeffreys decided, as Dudley sat down across the table and peered at him with glazed-over eyes.

Sankstone did the quizzing, operated the recorder, and promised him an unedited copy of the tape without being asked.

His preliminary question was a shocker.

"You know a kid named Horton?" the sergeant asked, scrawling the date and time and place across the label of an audio cassette he was preparing for insertion in the tape recorder.

"Horton?" Jeffreys echoed, wondering how Sankstone had gotten onto it so quickly.

"Horton," Sankstone repeated. "Andrew G. Age twenty-six. A short-order cook. We think it was his body we found in your car. We think he was stealing it when it blew."

"No," Jeffreys said, rattled. "I mean yes. I mean yes, it was Andy Horton, but no, he wasn't stealing my car. Actually, he was doing me a favor."

"Hell of a favor," Sankstone said, eyeing him intently. "That bomb was meant for you."

"I know. How did you identify ... ahhh ... the remains?"

"Routine. Investigators checking out missing-persons reports found one filed by Horton's employer that mentioned a gold earring in the left ear. They matched that with the coroner's report listing a partially melted blob of gold in what remained of the corpse's left ear. That led to the tentative ID. We're hoping to clinch it through dental charts."

"Don't bother," Jeffreys said, feeling sick. "I can confirm it. Andy Horton, for sure. I saw the explosion from half a block away."

"It was a biggie," Sankstone said conversationally, slipping the cassette into the recorder and latching the door. "Hell of a bomb. One of those potent plastics. It was wired to your engine's starter solenoid. Whoever planted it knew his business. The blast blew everything away, so there's not much chance to trace wires, detonator parts, or anything else."

"Know who planted it?"

"No idea."

"You said the bomb was meant for me and I agree it probably was. But who knew it was my car? And who found it there?"

"Now that's a funny thing," Sankstone said. Jeffreys saw him exchange glances with Lt. Dudley. "We asked ourselves that, too. A patrolman noticed the Indiana plate Saturday morning and reported it. You were wanted at the time, remember?"

"I remember."

"The duty officer ordered a stakeout on the car so if you came for it they'd grab you, but then somebody canceled it Saturday night for lack of weekend manpower."

"Too bad," Jeffreys said. "If the stakeout hadn't been canceled, your people could've grabbed a couple of killers in the act of bomb planting. Who in your department told the Poo Boys where they could find my car? The same somebody who scrubbed the stakeout?"

Sankstone shrugged. "We're looking into it."

"Dandy," Jeffreys said, feeling cold again. "You keep telling me the Poo Boys are mob, and now you're saying the mob's got some of your people on the pad."

"I'm not saying that," Sankstone said. "You are." He ran his fingers through his hair, flipped a switch on the tape recorder, yanked his necktie further awry, and began talking. "This is Tuesday, October twenty one, at oh-one-twelve hours," he said. The tape had begun moving with his first word, Jeffreys saw. "I'm in the Bloomburgh PD interrogation room with Lt. Wayne Dudley and Samuel T. Jeffreys, age thirty-eight, of Crown Point, Indiana. Mr. Jeffreys is the subject of this interrogation."

He stopped. So did the tape. He yanked at his necktie again, and fixed his eyes on Jeffreys'.

"What'd you find in the coffee can?" he asked.

"In the coffee can?" Jeffreys echoed, startled.

"In the coffee can."

"I found coffee. It was stale, but it tasted pretty good anyway."

"How about the Cascade box?"

"Cascade? You mean the dishwasher detergent?"

"Right. What'd you find in the box?"

"Money," Jeffreys said. "A whole wad of it."

"How much?"

"About nine thousand dollars."

"About?"

"Nine thousand even."

"There was eighty-nine hundred when we found it. You kept a hundred and put the rest back?"

"Right. I borrowed the hundred for eating money. I intend to repay it ... to Cornie's daughter or maybe his wife."

"How'd you know where to look for it?"

"I didn't. See, Cornie told me he never ate in. That should mean he never had dishes to wash. So when I saw dishwasher detergent, it made me wonder why, and when I dumped the box to see if it *was* dishwasher detergent, there was the money."

"Makes sense," Sankstone conceded. "What was in the coffee can?"

"Coffee," Jeffreys said calmly. "Stale coffee. Didn't you find the pan I brewed it in?"

"Sure," Sankstone said. "And also the pan you emptied the whole can into before you dumped the Cascade box."

"What makes you think that?" Jeffreys asked.

"The lab people checking the pan found detergent flakes on top of coffee dust. What were you looking for?"

Jeffreys shrugged, said, "Coffee. I wanted a cup. Then when I discovered a can of coffee and no coffee maker, it made me wonder. So I dumped the can to see if something else was in it. Later, when I noticed the dishwasher detergent, I dumped it, too, and that led to the money. How'd you get onto it?"

"We found your pans on the counter, so we dug around." Sankstone hit the recorder's pause button. The tape stopped. "I'm embarrassed we didn't check out the coffee can and the detergent box the first time we tossed the place." He sighed, shrugged, tapped the recorder button. "Why'd you leave the apartment?"

"I was hungry. Now I had eating money, so I hunted up a restaurant. When I came back, there were police cars parked in front and people walking past the windows upstairs. I bummed a ride back to my car with Andy Horton ... and ... after that I holed up at the Sleep Cheep motel."

"How did the hoodlums find you there?"

"I sent them invitations."

That drew a scowl from Sankstone and a stirring from Lt. Dudley. He looked suddenly interested, Jeffreys saw.

"Invitations?" Sankstone said.

"Invitations. I put the word out that I had Cornie's money stash plus his account books in room one-ninety-three of the Sleep Cheep."

"Bluffing," Sankstone said, nodding. "Put the word out how?"

"By telephone calls—to my lawyer and my housekeeper in Indiana and to a couple of law firms in Bloomburgh."

Dudley stirred again, looked mystified.

Sankstone nodded. "You figured your lines were bugged back home. Why the local law firms, though? Did you think your own counsel here would leak your location to mobsters?"

"Not unless his line was tapped, which I thought it might be."

"Anyway, it worked," Sankstone said. "They did show up."

"Didn't they, though," Jeffreys said.

Later, after the interrogation, with all the questions and

answers safely stored as strings of magnetic pulses on plastic ribbon and Lt. Dudley gone yawning back to his bed, Sankstone posed one more question, this time without a tape recorder.

"Doesn't it bother you they'll keep showing up?" the sergeant wanted to know, as a jail guard stood by waiting to return Jeffreys to his cell. "Different guys with different faces, all carrying guns and all under orders to get from you what you claim to have?"

"Damn right," Jeffreys said, rising from his chair to follow the guard.

"Doesn't it bother you they'll keep on coming?"

"Of course it does" Jeffreys said, thinking how much of an understatement that was. "Big time! Do me a favor, will you?"

"Depends," Sankstone said. "What?"

"Call Fifi Malloy at the Holiday Inn Downtown and tell her I'm okay."

"At two in the morning?"

"At two in the morning. Please."

"Will do," Sankstone said.

"Appreciate it," Jeffreys said, and followed the guard out of the interrogation room for the familiar walk back to his cell. He was thinking about different guys with different faces, carrying guns.

Now, finishing the coffee on the hard cot, he heard Sankstone's voice on his mental tape. It was asking, *Doesn't it bother you they'll keep on coming?*

And he heard his own voice, answering again, *Damn right. Big time!*

XXIII
THE YEARBOOKS

Fifi Malloy drove the rented Honda through the light mid-morning traffic towards the street number the telephone directory said was assigned to the Fletcher National Bank.

Jeffreys scanned the cars behind them, hopeful that, with the Poo Boys in the lockup, there'd be no followers for a while.

He'd enjoyed yesterday afternoon and evening once they left the courtroom, he reflected. Hand-delivering to the court clerk and to the jail warden certified copies of Judge Bigler's order dismissing the charges against him was particularly gratifying. So was using his own name and AMEX card to check back into the Holiday Inn Downtown, carrying his reclaimed suitcase and wearing his own Sears clothing under Cornie's topcoat and hat.

There'd been a pleasant late-afternoon exchange of farewells with Louis Lewis over Manhattans in the Holiday Inn lounge. Then came an enjoyable dinner with Fifi, followed by an evening-capping telephone conversation with Serena during which he promised to be home Friday in time for a spaghetti-and-apple-pie supper.

Now, after a comfortable if solitary night in his new room a floor above Fifi's, and a morning tryst with an otherwise acceptable lady who swore too much and breakfasted on peanut-buttered rye toast, here he was, alive and free, with one more shot at maybe salvaging something from his two-year chase after Cornie Nicora.

They passed the bank. Malloy parked.

"Wish me luck," Jeffreys said, climbing out.

He paused outside the bank, hoping his apprehension didn't show. He took a deep breath, and pushed inside.

The safe-deposit-vault sign was in the middle of the building. The brunette beneath it was pretty, middle-aged, wedding-banded. Her dress was cut low enough to suggest, but not to display. The name plate on her desk read *Blanche*.

She looked up and smiled. "Help you, Sir?"

"I need to get into my box," Jeffreys said. "Seven-twelve. The name is Nichols, Clarence Nichols."

"Certainly, Sir." Blanche slid a printed form across the desk to him and pointed at the pen in its holder on the desktop.

He looked at the form. It was a one-shot sign-in slip with no sample signature to emulate. He shrugged resignedly, filled in the blanks, wrote *Clarence Nichols* in his best imitation of Cornie's cramped, tiny-lettered handwriting, and gave Blanche the form.

She held it alongside an index card plucked from a box in her desk drawer. Replacing the card, she laid the form on her desktop.

"This way, please," she said. Jeffreys followed.

She led him down a hallway, turned into a steel-walled room. "Should be on the left," she said, pointing to one of the tiers of boxes lining the walls. "Yes, there's seven-twelve. Your key, please?"

She fitted it and one of her own into the twin locks. She swung the door aside, and slid the box partway out.

"There you go, Sir. Will you want a privacy booth?"

"Please," Jeffreys said, removing the box. He was disappointed at its small size and light weight.

Blanche led him back into the hallway, and turned into another corridor lined with wooden doors. The first two were closed. She waved him into the third. "Call me when you're ready."

Jeffreys shut the door behind him. He set the box down on a table. Taking a deep breath, he swung back the cover.

There were only books in the box, he saw. They were the cheap, black, cardboard-covered books with red-tape spines sold by drugstores as ledgers, diaries, journals, account books. These had the word *CASH* on their covers in gold-leaf-emulating letters.

He picked up the top one and riffled through it. Its ledger-lined pages were filled with entries in Cornie's cramped handwriting. He read one.

Jeffreys thumbed backward through the pages for a numerical entry signifying a year. He found a page with only a number: 1985.

He riffled through pages the other way, came to another single-number entry: 1986.

"Hot damn," he said under his breath. "Cornie was Sheriff then. These are what he meant by 'yearbooks,' not high-school annuals! So some cat named Whitsell bought protection for the Topside Tap through September. He was probably running electronic slots. Wonder what happened then."

He flipped more pages, found what he was looking for.

Jeffreys dumped the rest of the books on the table and paged hastily through each. There were diary-like listings of places, people, events. Some of the names he recognized as Cornie's cronies, public officials, political hacks. Some of the entries were detailed narratives; others were sketchy notes. Some recorded dollar amounts of presumed payoffs, kickbacks, campaign contributions; others reported apparent payouts, expenditures, campaign costs. The earliest date he found was 1979, scribbled across the first page of one of the books. The latest was 1992, jotted just past the halfway mark in another.

Fourteen years of Cornie's notations and records and reports, Jeffreys exulted. Enough to hang half the politicians in Lake County, or anyway those involved recently enough so the statute of limitations hadn't yet run.

He divided the books among Cornie's overcoat pockets. Then he closed the lockbox and left the privacy booth.

Blanche was at her desk. "Ready, Mr. Nichols?" She led him back to 712, accepted his key, opened the little door, watched him replace the box, closed the door of its receptacle, and handed him his key.

The wind was colder outside and the sidewalk was more crowded as he headed toward Fifi and her rental car. He was elated at his find, but concerned about carrying it. The lumps in his pockets seemed suddenly huge and protruding. Any successors to the Poo Boys assigned to tail him could surely see the bulges from a block away. Still, nobody was running toward him. No one in the throng of pedestrians or the auto traffic seemed to be eyeing him.

Fifi shoved the door open as he reached the rented Honda. "Well?" she asked.

"Bingo," he said, getting into the car.

"Really? Stuff for the book?"

"Stuff for the book. Diaries, ledgers, names, dates, amounts."

"Jes ... wow. Where are they?"

"In my pockets," Jeffreys peered through the back window, scanning the sidewalk traffic for a suspicious face. He saw none.

"Are we talking payoffs, bribes, and shit ... stuff like that?"

"And stuff like that. Let's hit the road."

She did, nosing the Honda out into traffic.

He turned in his seat to watch for followers. The street

behind was choked with autos. Was one of them the vehicle of mobsters assigned to find him, to track him to the stash, to make off with it and to—how had Bart put it?—leave no loose ends?

Probably not, he decided. Not for a day or two yet, anyway. Or did they work faster than he thought? He wished he still had Big Poo's guns.

XXIV
THE COPYING

"Can you find the car-rental place?" Jeffreys asked.

"Sure," Fifi said. "I got this heap there. Why?"

"We're taking it back."

"What the hell ... what for?"

"To rent another one."

"What's the matter with this one?"

"Nothing, only I want a different one."

"You figure the mob knows this one?"

"Possible. Anyway, it's on your tab and I don't want my chauffeur paying for my car."

"So how come you're so damn ... uh ... so sensitive, all of a sudden?"

"What's with the interrupted swearing?" Jeffreys asked, ignoring her question. "Trying to quit?"

"You said you didn't like it."

"I said it didn't become you."

"Same damn ... same thing."

"Hey," Jeffreys said. "It's to please me, isn't it?"

"Don't be so damn conceited." She looked flustered.

"I'm flattered."

"Don't be that, either. What happens now?"

"Couple things," Jeffreys said. "First, a different car. Then lunch. After that we find a copy machine."

"What for?"

"For copying the books. I'm nervous about carrying the originals around." The lumps in Cornie's overcoat pockets were feeling like hot bricks.

"Makes sense."

"I wish we could take them to one of those copy shops."

"Why can't we?"

"We don't want to leave a trail."

"Aha," Fifi said, nodding.

The car-rental agency loomed ahead. DEALS ONWHEELS the sign read. Fifi parked.

"Hold it a minute," Jeffreys said, staring out the back window. He saw only what appeared to be the normal flow of traffic. "Okay. Let's head on in."

"Aye, aye, Sir Hitchcock," Fifi Malloy said. "I hope we can get some of this cloak-and-dagger shit ... uh ... stuff into the book."

They climbed out and went into the rental office. Jeffreys waited while Fifi surrendered her keys and signed reams of forms.

Yes, they did have a Caprice Classic, the pimply faced, mustached clerk in jeans and turtle-neck sweater told him, when Fifi was finished. What kind of a credit card would he be using? VISA'd be fine. It was company policy to photostat his operator's license, okay? Okay.

While the clerk was filling out forms, Jeffreys picked up a battered leather attache case he'd spotted earlier. "Yours?"

The clerk looked up from his papers. "The brief case? Yeah. My ma wanted me to be a lawyer. I use it for carryin' my lunch in."

I'll give you fifty bucks for it," Jeffreys said.

"Can I keep my lunch?"

"Whatever's in it." Jeffreys produced two twenties and a ten.

The clerk opened the attache case, dumped its contents onto a desk, snapped it shut, handed it back. He counted the money at a glance, pocketed it, and went back to his papers.

Jeffreys hefted the empty case. He decided he'd overpaid.

"Where to?" Fifi asked, sitting behind the wheel of the white Caprice with the engine running. "Hey, this thing is smooth."

"The kid in the car-rental place said there's a good restaurant about a mile down the road," Jeffreys said. He was tugging Cornie's yearbooks from Cornie's overcoat pockets and stacking them inside the attache case. Closing it, he tossed it onto the rear seat. "You hungry?"

"Damn right. I mean, yes. How about you?"

"Starved. The kid said Hennesseys has a non-rowdy crowd, the best food in town, and a really rotten ambience."

"My kind of joint," Fifi said. "Let's head."

"Head," Sam told her.

♣

The car-rental guy was right about Hennesseys, he decided, washing the last bite of filet mignon down with the last swallow of coffee. The lounge was acceptable, the pianist low-key, the drinks unwatered. The dining room was clean and well-lighted and the food was great, though the eating-area ambience was indeed rotten, featuring slow service provided by sullen young men with tousled manes sprouting from the backs of their necks slouching around in faded blue jeans. "This's the best damn pie ... I mean, wow!" Fifi said, chewing. "Just like mother couldn't make."

"Mine could," Jeffreys said. "And did. So does my mother-in-law. No better than this, though."

"Listen, Sam." Fifi's face was solemn. "About the profanity. I am trying to quit, only I forget, I've been doing it so long."

"Don't worry about it. I'm flattered you're trying."

"Swearing's a sort of veneer a working girl learns to put on with her job clothes. It's her defense in a man's world, a kind of protective armor. You figure if you cuss enough the guys'll accept you as one of the boys."

"I know," Jeffreys said. "I worked around it for years. Women in the newspaper business depend on profanity to prove they're cool and to demonstrate their competence. Most do, anyway."

"Really?"

"Really. A typical newsroom female can't say 'hello' to a male colleague without throwing in two 'fuckin's', three 'shits', and a couple of 'assholes'. Seems to work, too. The ones that swear the best seem to climb the corporate ladder the fastest."

"I'll be damned," Fifi said. "Ah, sorry."

"It doesn't usually bother me," Jeffreys said, suddenly recognizing his own feelings. "I don't even notice your kind of mild swearing among other females, and I couldn't complain if I did, because I cuss up a storm myself sometimes. I just don't like to hear a *lady* swear. I mean a real *lady*."

Fifi sat silent for a time, alternately forking apple pie and cheddar cheese into her mouth, her eyes on her plate. Then she looked up and smiled at him. "Thank you, Sam," she said.

The check was pennies under $40. He dropped a five and a one on the table, put two twenties into the leather folder their sullen waiter had left beside him with the tab, and followed Fifi to the coat rack. There was a pay phone across from it.

"Thank you for calling the Holiday Inn Downtown," the female voice said in his ear.

"This is Sam Jeffreys, room five-twenty. Do I have any messages?"

"Messages? No, Sir. No messages."

"I had a call, though?"

"Yes, Sir. Several calls, but no messages."

"The same caller each time?"

"I believe so, yes, Sir."

"He leave his name?"

"No, Sir."

"Or *her* name?"

"His."

"Umm. Any calls for Mrs. Malloy, room four-twelve?"

"Yes, Sir. One call, no message."

"Same voice?" Jeffreys demanded.

"I'd say so, Sir," the operator said.

"Thanks. If anybody asks, I've gone to Jamaica."

"What was that all about?" Fifi wanted to know. She was wearing her trenchcoat and holding Cornie's overcoat and hat.

"Trailers," Jeffreys said. "The new team's here. They've got us staked out at the Holiday Inn."

"Us? They've got *us* staked out?"

"Right. You, too. They've been calling our rooms."

"Great," Fifi said. "So what do we do?"

"We stay away from there. For now, anyway."

"Oh my God," Fifi said. "Not that el dumpo again tonight."

"No," Jeffreys said, grinning. "Not the Sleep Cheep. How about the Astor? It's a couple miles beyond the Holiday."

"I remember passing it," Fifi Malloy said. "The Astor, hunh?" She eyed him speculatively. "Like the place she had to go and lose it at? Listen, Sam, how do I know there really are trailers waiting for us at the Holiday Inn?"

"You don't," Jeffreys said, grinning. He took Cornie's coat from her, shrugged into it, took the hat, put it on. "Maybe I lied."

They found the Astor without difficulty. Fifi parked and locked the Caprice, and Jeffreys steered her into the hotel lobby by her elbow, carrying the decrepit attache case.

"Evening," he told the clerk at the registration desk. "The

airline people'll be bringing our luggage later, if they ever get their baggage foulup straightened out. Meanwhile, Miss De Lila and I need separate rooms, please. Adjacent, but not connecting." He drew what was left of Cornie's thousand dollars from his pocket, eyed the clerk expectantly, said, "Just the one night."

"Certainly, Sir," the clerk said, pushing two registration cards across the counter. "One-twelve each, with tax. Two-twenty-four."

Jeffreys peeled three hundreds off the roll. He wrote *Bessie De Lila, Cincinnati*, on one card, *George Samson, Cleveland*, on the other, aware that Fifi was reading over his shoulder.

The clerk barely glanced at them. He counted change onto the counter. He plucked two magnetic keycards from an array behind him. "I'll send your luggage up as soon as it arrives, Sir. "The dining room doesn't open until six, but our coffee shop is serving."

"We ate on the plane," Jeffreys said. "We'll need a copy machine in my room. Press releases, you know."

"I'll have one sent up, Sir. Will you need an operator?"

"No, thanks," Jeffreys said, taking Fifi's arm and pointing her toward the bank of elevators off to the left. "I'd rather do it myself."

He consulted the keycards, punched 3 into the control panel of the self-service elevator, and waited for Fifi to disembark when the door opened again.

"Samson and De Lila?" Fifi giggled, stepping out. "Whatever happened to Smith and Jones?"

"To the right, the sign says," he said, ignoring the comment. "We're three-fourteen and three-sixteen. You have a preference?"

"Three-sixteen. Three-fourteen's probably actually three-thirteen. Most hotels skip the thirteens, you know."

"You've got something against thirteens?"

"Why tempt fate?"

"I suppose," he said, stopping in front of three-sixteen and pushing the keycard into the door slot. The lock clicked, the door opened, a light came on. He followed Fifi inside.

"This is a regular Taj Mahal," Fifi said, looking around and nodding her approval, "compared to the Sleep Cheep."

"I bet the bathroom even has a door," he said.

Fifi sat on the bed, bounced up and down. "Oooh. Comfy."

"Need anything?"

"Other than a change of clothes, no. I've got a toothbrush in my purse. You sure we have trailers at the Holiday Inn?"

"Yup. How about we freshen up before the copier comes?"

"Sounds good."

Inside three-fourteen, he put his keycard on the dresser, slid the attache case under the bed, hung Cornie's coat on a hanger that was removable — *stealable, even*, he told himself, *therefore, by Sleep-Cheep standards, at least, classy* — tossed Cornie's hat onto the shelf atop the hanger area, shrugged out of his Sears jacket, and hung it alongside the coat.

He went into the bathroom to freshen up. It had a door.

He was relaxing atop the bed when the knock came.

"It's open," he yelled.

It was a bellman pushing a cart carrying a copy machine.

"Over there by the desk, please," Jeffreys told him, getting up. "I hope there's plenty of paper."

"It's full, Sir," the bellman said, stopping his cart near the desk. "And I brought an extra box."

"Great," Jefreys said. He helped the bellman lift the heavy contraption off the cart and onto the floor, fished a five from his pocket, held it out.

The bellman pocketed it, plugged the machine's line cord into an outlet on the wall behind the desk, and left.

Jeffreys examined the copier. It was a familiar type. He punched the button labeled *letter-size* and lifted the fabric screen-cover curtain. He retrieved Cornie's yearbooks from the attache case, and laid them on the desk top. Picking one up, he opened it to its first page, placed it face down on the screen, dropped the curtain over it, and pushed the copy button.

The machine came to life with a whirring sound. A bright light flashed on, streaked from left to right, extinguished. The whirring ceased. A sheet of paper emerged. It was a facsimile of the inside cover and page one of the yearbook. The words and numbers were clear and readable.

"Hot damn," Jeffreys said aloud. "And away we go."

Putting the open attache case alongside the machine as a receptacle for completed copies, Jeffreys settled into the routine of reproducing successive pages of Cornie's yearbooks. After a while, he was startled by the sound of the door opening behind him.

"Hi," Fifi said, striding in. She was wearing a wide grin. She was the image of Edie, except for the shoulders and the posture and the brown eyes that weren't hazel.

"I thought that door was locked," he said. "Lock it will you?"

She did, asking, "Are you about through?"

"Lord, no," he said. "I'll be a while."

"It goes slow, huh? Maybe we can speed it up a little. Let's see what a fast female can do."

"With what?" Jeffreys asked.

"With the damn ... with the copier."

"You know how to run one of these?"

"Do I know how to run one of these? Move your ... move over and watch a professional copy cat do her thing."

He did, sitting down on the bed and watching Fifi make copies. She made copies not only with ease, competence and precision, he decided, but also with elegance, grace and style.

He stretched out, dozed for a time, wakened, dozed again, wakened. "Want me to spell you?" he asked drowsily.

"Your timing is superb," Fifi said. "Two pages to go."

"I knew that."

"There," she said brightly. "The deed is did."

"You're good," Jeffreys said, rising and accepting the year-books from her. He went to the wardrobe, took a paper laundry bag off its shelf, placed the books inside it, and secured it with its tie string. He carried the package to the bed. He slid it underneath the head end. Returning to the desk, he took a page from the top of the pile in the attache case, a second from halfway down, a third from near the bottom. "Copy these, please, and then we can quit."

"We?" Fifi said. She made the copies and handed him the six pages.

Placing three in the attache case, he snapped it shut and shoved it under the bed. Then he put the other three pages together, folded them into thirds, took them to where his suit jacket hung on a stealable hanger, and slid them into a pocket."

"Hungry?" he asked.

"Not really," Fifi said. "But ask me if Id enjoy a leisurely drink and a modest meal."

"Consider yourself asked."

"Damn right ... uh ... you betcha."

"Thewn how about we get our butts the hell downstairs so the bartender can start making us manhattans."

"Why not?" Fifi said, smiling at him. "Only you know what, Sam? Profanity really doesn't become you."

Jeffreys thought about that for a moment. Then he said, "Touche," and joined Fifi in giggling.

XXV
THE REFUSING

He took her to the door of three-sixteen. He said, "How about we get comfortable first, and then watch a little TV before we...."

"Hit our separate sacks?" she cut him off, grinning. "I'm for it. Your room or mine? For TV-watching, that is?"

"Yours," Jeffreys said, heading for his room. "It seems less unseemly for Samson to call on De Lila than the other way around."

In three-fourteen, he found paper bathrobes in transparent wrappers alongside his bathroom sink, and paper slippers. Taking off his clothes, he donned a bathrobe and stepped into a pair of slippers. The robe, off-white, soft, opaque, reminded him of a paper towel.

Putting the keycard into the bathrobe pocket, he surveyed himself in the mirror. He looked old and tired and gawky, he decided. He headed out, hoping there was nobody in the hall.

Fifi Malloy opened the door the instant he knocked.

"Hi," she said brightly, clad in a reasonable facsimile of his paper-towel bathrobe. Her version was a bit large for her, Jeffreys decided. Its draping folds secured around her waist by its paper sash effectively camouflaged her curves. "Come on in."

"You, too, huh?" he said, ogling the robe and trying not to. "Me too." She shut the door. "Like it?"

"Love it." She looked shorter in the heel-less paper slippers, smaller, more delicate, fragile, defenseless. Smiling up at him, she was a replica of Edie at home, stripped of the cold toughness she'd put on with her go-to-work clothes and then shed again at day's end to reassume the softness, the sensitivity and the warmth only he was allowed to see. Would he have exposed Edie to the mob?

"You look serious," Edie's successor was saying. "Something bugging you?"

"Yes," Jeffreys said, making up his mind. "Listen, Fifi. First thing in the morning, we're putting you on an airplane."

Her smile faded. She stared at him. "Where'm I going?"

"Home. New York. Away from here."

"What the hell are you talking about?" she flared, her eyes into his. "We've got work to do, a book to write."

"I've got work to do and a book to write," Jeffreys corrected, trying to stare her down. She looked like Edie in work-mode with her face going red like that. "I ... don't want you with me while I do it. It could be hazardous to your health."

"Just a damn minute," Fifi Malloy said. She glared at him with Edie's work-mode fire in her eyes. "It's not your choice. You owe me a goddamn book and I'm sticking close until I get it."

"You'll get it on my terms," Jeffreys said. "Until it's written, I don't want you near me. You're ... a distraction."

"A distraction?" Fifi echoed. "Was I a distraction chauffeuring you around this dismal goddamn town looking for banks and hardware stores?" Her voice grew more shrill. "When I sat agonizing in my goddamn room waiting for your telephone SOS so I could send the cops to cover your ass and not hearing from you and figuring you were dead? When I was told your goddamn car blew up with you in it and...?"

"Whoa," Jeffreys said gently. Now she was Edie in at-home mode again, her feelings hurt, her heart stepped on. "Hold it. What I meant was, my concern for your safety is a distraction. I'm too worried about you to think straight."

"Ha!"

"Fact. I've appreciated your help and I've enjoyed your company and I love being with you and I only want you out of here because I'm afraid for you."

Fifi went silent. Then she said, "That makes sense." Her tone was less strident. "I'm afraid for me, too. I'm afraid for both of us. I've been scared to death ever since Sankstone told me you were messing with the mafia. So what's that got to do with anything?"

"Everything. I can't risk mobsters hurting you."

"It's not your choice. And they don't know where we are."

"They'll find us," Jeffreys said. "They want Cornie's stashes, they think we're their way to them, and they'll find us."

"I suppose," Fifi said.

"And if they get tired of tailing us, they'll kill us."

"Jesus," Fifi said. She shuddered.

"That's why I want you out of here. First thing tomorrow, before the new team locates us. I want you back in New York, behind your desk, swearing at writers over the telephone."

"I'm staying," she said, sounding like Edie used to sound.

"You can't," Jeffreys said, knowing he'd lost. The realization made him angrier. "You've got to go. You wait for me in New York, and I promise you a publishable expose of the crimes and the cronies of Cornie Nicora as recorded in his journals and his account books."

"No dice. I'm hanging around."

"Goddamn it, Fifi," Jeffreys heard himself bellowing. "Can't you understand? You'll get yourself killed."

"I hope not," Fifi Malloy said softly. "I'd hate that."

He threw up his hands. It was amazing. This woman even

had Edie's trait of quiet, absolute obstinacy; not just Edie's eyes, only browner, and not just Edie's hair, only curlier, and not just Edie's figure, only erecter, but even Edie's unshakable mulishness.

"Good night," he said, struggling to keep his voice low. He strode to the door. "I'm going to bed."

In three-fourteen, with his door chain secured, he stamped to the window, pulled aside the curtains, and stared down into the street, remembering Edie and how it had been, thinking of Fifi and how it might be, wishing for a different set of circumstances, for a cigarette, for a drink.

He'd been staring out the window for an eternity when the knock came. Or did it? It was almost inaudible. His imagination? He went to the door, his paper slippers whispering across the carpet.

"Does it seem unseemly for De Lila to call on Samson?" Fifi Malloy askied in a small voice, looking up at him from the hallway.

"Come on in," he said, trying not to ogle the off-white paper bathrobe. Its sash had loosened and some of the folds draping Fifi's shoulders had fallen away so they no longer camouflaged her curves. He shut the door behind her. She stood just inside the doorway, her head tilted up and her eyes into his. "I was serious, Fifi," he said. "I'm scared for you."

"So was I," she said. "I'm scared for both of us."

"Listen," he said. "All I had in mind was to send you home where you'll be safe while I do what needs to be done here so I can head back to Indiana to write the damn book. Then, after it's published, then we can get together."

"No," Fifi said softly, her eyes in his.

"It won't be dangerous, then," he said, trying to ignore his peripheral-vision picture of the off-white paper bathrobe slipping lower on her shoulders to no longer fully cover her curves. " Once the book's out, everybody knows what I know and there's no point in taking me down to shut me up, or you for being with me."

"No," Fifi said, her eyes in his.

"Please," he said, surprised at the plaintiveness of his own voice. "Don't be so ready to die for a damn book."

"It's not the damn book I'm ready to die for."

"Listen to me," Jeffreys said. "Here's what I'm trying to say. I've already lost a lover, and I couldn't handle it again."

"I have, too," Fifi said, her eyes in his and her robe slipping lower. "And I couldn't, either." She stepped towards him.

Jeffreys' arms went around her. He pulled her to him. She pressed against him, breasts to chest, stomach to stomach, thighs to thighs. She was warm and soft and yielding through the thicknesses of their paper robes. His lips found hers.

After a minute, Fifi Malloy pulled away from him, drew her mouth from his, looked up into his eyes.

"Am I really a distraction?" she whispered.

Sam Jeffreys nodded. He loosened the paper belt that held the robe around his waist, let it fall open, reached out to undo Fifi's sash, swept apart the paper folds that camouflaged her curves, ogled unabashed the flesh revealed, and pulled her to him once again.

A while later, with Fifi asleep, he got up, climbed into the paper bathrobe and stalked to the window to stare out of it some more.

It was time, he told himself, to concoct another plan.

XXVI
THE HANDSHAKE

"No trailers," Fifi Malloy reported, as Sam Jeffreys climbed into the passenger side of the Caprice. "You were in there a long time."

"Really? I was just putting the books back in the lockbox and asking for directions."

"Directions?"

"To a packaging shop and to Bethany Hospital."

"What's a packaging shop? And why the hospital?"

"I'll show you one. Straight ahead three blocks. They wrap stuff and ship it. The hospital to see Quick."

"What are we wrapping and shipping?" Fifi demanded, pulling out into the sparse traffic.

"The attache case."

"We're mailing it somewhere?"

"Not mailing. UPSing. It beats carrying the copies around."

"UPSing where?"

To a friend back home. With a note saying to sit on it until I pick it up."

"Makes sense. Three blocks you said?"

On the left. *Package Lickers,* it's called."

"I hate cutesy names. Why've you got to see Quick?"

To get the mob off our back, if my plan works."

"Jesus," Fifi said. "I mean, wow. What plan?"

The one I came up with last night."

"Last night? When last night?"

"When you convinced me I couldn't make you leave."

"I'd have sworn you had other things on your mind about then. What's the plan?"

"Tell you later, if Quick plays. If he doesn't, it won't work."

Fifi turned into the curb. "I watch for trailers?"

"Right." Jeffreys reached into the back seat for the attache case. "This sucker's heavy. It'll cost a fortune to ship."

"No trailers," Fifi said, when Jeffreys climbed empty-handed back into the car. "Get it done?"

"Got it done," Jeffreys said. "Straight on ahead to the second stoplight, turn right, and it's three blocks to the hospital."

When they turned into the visitor parking area, Jeffreys watched for followers. There were none.

"Cross your fingers," he said, clambering out of the Caprice. "Maybe pray a little."

The lady at the reception desk was polite. Yes, there was a Stanley Quick on the register. It was flagged, though, meaning Mr. Quick's room number couldn't be given out. Yes, he could have visitors. They had to be met, however, and accompanied by an interceptor from the nurse station on the fourth floor.

Jeffreys rode the elevator, found the nurse station. The lady behind the counter was busily writing something.

"Hi," he said. "I'd like to see Stanley Quick, please."

The nurse's finger found a bell-push on the counter. She resumed writing.

"Thanks." Jeffreys waited, wondering whether for a uniformed cop, a plainclothes bodyguard, a marine. It turned out to be another nurse.

"You're here for Agent Quick?" she asked. Her voice was gruff but not unfriendly. She was a big woman, tall, wide, breasty, her body straining the seams of her starched white uniform.

"Yes, Ma'am," he smiled. "Name's Jeffreys. Sam Jeffreys."

"This way," the nurse said, unsmiling.

Sam followed her to a closed door marked 474. She knocked softly. It opened. A man stood in the doorway. He wore a string necktie and a western-style, square-cut suit of brown gabardine.

"Says his name's Jeffreys," the nurse told him.

"Thanks, Irma," the man said. He searched Jeffreys with his eyes. A familiar voice from beyond him said, "He's okay." The man said, "Come on in."

Irma left and Jeffreys went in.

It was a large room, illuminated only by the daylight penetrating the curtained window in the far wall. The bed was empty. Quick sat in an easy chair on its far side facing Jeffreys in the semidarkness.

"Hi," Quick said. "You'll pardon me if I don't rise?"

Jeffreys advanced on him with his hand out. "You had me worried." He clasped Quick's outstretched hand. Quick's grasp was firm.

"You weren't alone," Quick said. He was wearing a flannel bathrobe. "You had *me* worried when I heard about your car bombing. This's Dan Kinowski, my gin-rummy partner."

"*Marshal* Kinowski?" Jeffreys asked, shaking hands.

"Right," Kinowski said. "Is it that obvious?"

"Not obvious at all," Jeffreys said. "I just figured the man body-guarding an FBI guy on loan to the Marshal Service had to be either an FBI guy or a marshal, and you don't look FBI."

"Like you don't look mobster-slayer," Quick said from his chair. "Congratulations on bagging the Poo Boys. But what a damn-fool thing to do."

"Thanks a lot," Jeffreys said, stung. "I remember you personally approving me as a decoy."

"Not as a loner," Quick said. "It was stupid to tackle those hoodlums without backup, is all I meant,"

"Where was I going to get backup?" Jeffreys shed Cornie's overcoat and hat, tossed them onto the bed, sat down on it.

"My people could've helped," Quick said. "And Sankstone."

"Anyway, it worked out," Jeffreys said, anxious to get on with the business that brought him. "How're you doing?"

Quick shrugged. "I'm healing. I'll be here another day or so, they tell me. Then I go home for a while, and then back to work."

"Still on loan to the Marshal Service?"

"No. I didn't protect my witness, so I go back to the bureau."

"Can we talk? Just us girls?"

"Oh. Sure." Quick looked at Kinowski. "Kinnie...."

"How about I go find us some coffee?" Kinowski cut in.

"Sounds good," Quick said. "And take your time."

Jeffreys slid the three folded papers from his jacket pocket when the door closed behind the marshal. He held them out to Quick. "Where's the light switch?"

"Over there by the door," Quick said, unfolding the pages.

Jeffreys flipped the switch. An overhead light came on.

"I found Cornie's stashes," Jeffreys said, sitting down on the bed. "He had separate hidey-holes for his money and for his records."

"I heard about the money stash," Quick said, thumbing through the papers. "Nine thousand, wasn't it?"

"Not that. The *real* stash. Two paper sacks stuffed with thousand-dollar bills, all old, untraceable. A ton of moolah."

"Aha. I'm impressed. But what the hell are these?"

"Sample copies of a random pages from Cornie's journals. 'Yearbooks,' he called 'em. The other stash."

"How many?"

"Five. A hundred and forty-four pages each, most of 'em written on. Fourteen years of names, dates, times, places, amounts, payoffs, kickbacks, payouts. All in Cornie's handwriting."

"Thank you, Lord," Quick said softly, riffing through the papers. "Where are they?"

"In bank boxes," Jeffreys said. "The books one place, the money another."

"I see." Quick's eyes found Jeffreys eyes. "*Where?*"

"My secret for the moment," Jeffreys said, staring back. "I tell you where they are after you agree to my proposal."

Quick's face went grim, though his eyes didn't waver. He sighed. "Proposal? Like you keep the money and we get the books?"

"Not what I had in mind," Jeffreys said. "I thought you knew me better than that."

"I thought so too. So what's your proposal?"

"I give you the keys, the lockbox numbers and the bank locations. You get me off the hook with the mob."

"How would I do that?"

"By having your people grab the stashes and go public with them," Jeffreys said, his eyes boring back. "First they leak it to the media and the wire services here, and then they hold a full-blown news conference in my bailiwick."

"Announcing what?" Quick looked confused.

"Confirming that the Department of Justice has taken custody of Cornelius Nicora's stashed bankroll and records," Jeffreys said, holding up a finger as he remembered Bart Van Til doing. He raised another finger. "That those records include ledgers listing names, dates, and amounts of Cornie's financial transactions with a horde of named public officials, contractors, union leaders, mobsters and assorted crooks." He stuck up a third finger. "That the U.S. Attorney for Indiana's Northern District will immediately begin using those records to seek indictments and to pursue prosecutions."

"Aha," Quick said. "You want...."

"What I *don't* want," Jeffreys interrupted, "is for anybody but you to know who found those records, who made copies of them, and who plans to disclose their contents in a fascinating, beautifully written, best-selling book that probably'll be retitled *Godfather Twelve* or some such when it's turned into a high-budget, immensely-profitable movie."

"I see," Quick said. "You want us to cover your tracks. You want my people identified as the finders and possessors of Nicora's stashes so his mob buddies won't be interested in you, anymore."

"You got it. I want your people identified as the exclusive owners of the goodies, the sole holders of both stashes."

"I'm sure my people will be willing to convey that impression."

"Impression's not good enough," Jeffreys said. "I need your people to be absolutely convincing, so they have to *believe* it."

"Whoa," Quick said. "Are you saying my people aren't to know you've got copies of Nicora's books?"

"That's exactly what I'm saying."

"Forget it! My people *have* to know."

"Sorry," Jeffreys said. "Nobody but you. That's the deal."

"I can't agree to it." Quick shook his head. "Bureau regulations specifically prohibit field agents from withholding relevant information from their superiors. They simply can't do it."

"This time they must," Jeffreys said. "*You* must. It's vital. Innocent lives depend on it. Like mine."

Quick held up a hand. "There's another way. I'll label knowledge of the copies restricted, classified, a need-to-know matter. Then only my immediate superiors will be in on it."

"No!" Jeffreys shook his head. "Nobody but you until everything I have is published." He shook his head again. "Either I get your word that absolutely nobody's told about the copies, or there's no deal."

"Suppose I notify the local PD that you've found Nicora's stashes," Quick said. "Sankstone could grab you, hold you, retrieve the keys on you or hidden among your things, and chase down whatever bank boxes they fit."

"I'd be dead before Sankstone could find me." Jeffreys kept his eyes locked into Quick's. "We both know the mob's got people inside Sankstone's department. We both know what'd happen if you passed along that word. They'd kill me, search my body, toss my room, go through my belongings. They'd find the keys. They'd trace them to their respective banks. They'd wind up with the money and the books, I'd be dead, and you'd have what the little boy shot at."

Quick looked glum. He nodded. "Probably."

"Not probably," Jeffreys said, maintaining eye contact. "Undoubtedly. Then you could spend your declining years consoling yourself that you didn't keep a secret from your brass. You'd be a pastured federal cop who flunked the only truly important assignment of his entire career, remembering that you helped the mob protect itself from the law and kill off some decent people in the process."

Quick blinked. He dropped his eyes again to the papers in his lap. He sighed. "Okay," he said. "I'll buy it."

"Tomorrow you'll give your people the keys, they'll pick up the stashes, and they'll leak their finds to the media?"

"Yes."

"And then your people'll go to my bailiwick and announce a federal grand jury investigation based on the yearbook entries? That they'll probe, indict and prosecute? With *nobody* knowing about the copies?"

"Copies?" Quick echoed. "What copies?"

"We've got a deal," Jeffreys said, feeling the elation begin to bubble deep inside him. He fished the keys from his pocket, detached two from the chain, held them out to Quick. "This is for lockbox nine-fourteen at Midwest Industrial Bank. It's full of money. Cornie rented it under the name `Clem Nathan.' There's a sample signature on the sign-in form for your people to forge."

"We won't be signing for it," Quick said, accepting the key and eyeing Jeffreys thoughtfully. "We'll go in with an order." He nodded at the key. "Is this what you found in the coffee can?"

"They kept you briefed, didn't they? Yes, that's what I found in the coffee can."

"Two lockbox keys?"

"One. The other was with the money." He held it out. "The second stash, the biggie. Cornie's yearbooks. Lockbox seven-twelve, Fletcher National Bank, under the name 'Clarence Nichols'."

Quick looked thoughtful. He eyed the keys. "I could have my people clean out whatever's in the banks before you got out of the parking lot."

"You could, but you won't," Jeffreys said, trying to hide his sudden panic. "You're an honorable man, and you've made a deal."

Quick grinned. "You sure are a trusting soul." His grin faded. "I'll give them to my boss tomorrow. He'll want to know where I got them, who set the rules, and why we should follow them. What'll I tell him?"

Jeffreys shrugged. "Your problem. Work it out."

Quick nodded. "I will.".

"From the heart," Jeffreys said, "it's been an honor knowing you and working with you."

"Likewise," Quick said. He picked the sheaf of papers off his lap. "I keep these?"

"No," Jeffreys said, retrieving them and stuffing them into his jacket pocket. "I burn 'em. There are no copies, remember?"

"I remember," Quick said.

"Get yourself well."

"I will."

"We'll be subpoenaed as witnesses when the Poo Boys go to trial," Jeffreys said. "Let's do drinks and an evening on the town."

"I'll look forward to it," Quick said.

"Tell the marshal goodbye."

"I will."

Jeffreys shrugged into Cornie's overcoat and hat. He stood in front of Quick, looking down at him. He thrust out his right hand.

"So long, Friend," he said.

"Hold it," Quick said. Grasping the arms of his chair, he eased himself slowly to his feet. Then, standing upright, he said, "Ready, Friend," and extended his hand. His grasp was firm, as always. Now it was warm.

Jeffreys let go, turned on his heel, and walked to the door, the warmth of the handshake spreading over him.

⚜

"No trailers," Fifi said, when he climbed into its passenger side. "How'd it go?"

"It went," he said, grinning at her. "We're home free."

"What's that mean?"

"It means we're about to get the mob off our back."

"Jesus," said Fifi. "That is, wow."

"And it means we check back into the Holiday Inn."

"Won't the trailers find us there?" Fifi started the engine.

"Sure." Jeffreys said, grinning. "It won't matter. That's part of the plan."

"Must be a hell of a ... a real dandy plan." She pulled the Caprice out of the lot, into the stream of traffic. "Tell me more."

"Why not? First, we freshen up. Then, drinks and dinner."

"I like it so far. But what about the damn ... the trailers?"

"They'll watch us enjoy ourselves, and they'll spend the night staking out our room. Notice I said room? Singular?"

"I noticed. Is that a necessary part of the plan?"

"Vital," he said, not sure whether she was teasing or rejecting, pleased or offended. "Essential. Crucial, even."

"Do I have any say in this matter?"

"Veto power. The trailers'll follow us to Indiana tomorrow."

"You said `us'? We're going to Indiana tomorrow?"

"Oh yeah. We've got a date at my house for a spaghetti-and-apple-pie dinner."

"This is still part of the plan?"

"Definitely. While you're getting acquainted with Geoff and Serena, the trailers'll still be around for a little while."

"I thought you said... "

"In a day or two or three, depending on how fast the word gets out, the trailers'll leave us. For good."

"Why?" Fifi demanded.

"Because their bosses won't be interested in us anymore. They'll be busy conferring with each other, with public officials, with fellow crooks and assorted hangers-on who did business with Cornie Nicora over the years. They'll be finger-pointing, fighting, panicking, fleeing. Some'll even be looking to join the witness protection program like Cornie did."

"Jesus," Fifi said, pulling into the Holiday Inn parking lot. "I mean, wow. That's a hell of a ... that's a dandy plan."

"There's more. It's kind of personal. Want to hear it?"

"Naturally." She shut off the ignition and sat looking at him.

"Okay," he said, acknowledging to himself that brown eyes could be just as deep and as warm and as loving as hazel. "Here's the scenario. With the mafia off his back, Sam Jeffreys has got a book to write and a lady to love. So, under the plan, he does, and he and Fifi Malloy, AKA Mrs. Sam Jeffreys, live happily ever after. What do you think?"

"Jesus," Fifi said. "I mean, Gee, Sam. I think it's a hell of a ... that's a damn neat ... I like it."